TRAVESTY

HAYDEN BRADFORD

Travesty
First published as *I Taught God to Gamble* 2013 by Hayden Bradford

This edition published 2014

Copyright © Hayden Bradford 2014
Cover image composite of Shutterstock images
Cover art by Chameleon Print Design

EAN13: 9781742984384

For Jackie, Brianna and Liam
none are greater

DISCLAIMER

This book is fiction. It came from the place all fiction comes from – the imagination. In the case of this story, the imagination used was mine.

Any resemblance of any character in this story to any person, living or dead, nearly living or nearly dead, partly living or partly dead, is purely coincidental. Likewise, the events described in this book never happened.

ABOUT THE AUTHOR

I was born in Townsville, North Queensland, Australia. Due my father's employment, I spent most of my childhood as a Post Office nomad, and therefore I grew up in different places within Australia. We also lived in Port Moresby, Papua New Guinea for a few years. I will be forever grateful for those experiences. Today, I live in Melbourne, Australia with my wife and our two children.

If I had a resume, it would read that I'm an ex-stockman, ex-military man, and ex-corporate man. Too, I'm grateful for those experiences. I have a Bachelor's Degree, a couple of Graduate Diplomas, and a Master's Degree. I'm not sure why, as what I *learned* in academia land has been of little use to me. My real lessons have been learned outside of educational institutions. These lessons have come from *life* herself. In the main, I've found her to be unforgiving, intolerant, unrelenting, uncompromising, and mostly never fair. I've had no better teacher.

I've learnt that *my* life came to me with no certainties or guarantees. I can only play the cards I'm dealt. Sometimes I play well, sometimes I play badly, and sometimes 'shit happens'. When it does, I have to *carry on*. No regrets. I know of no other way to live.

All in all, my life is good; not as good as some, but better than others. I'm doing OK.

A NOTE TO THE READER

This story was originally published in 2013 in a book titled *I Taught God to Gamble*. I used the pen name *Joshua Hosea*. In 2014 I decided to republish the story as I had more laughs to add, and republishing gave me the opportunity to further polish the story. I also changed the title of the book and this time I've published the book under my real name.

The book is fiction. It came from the place all good stories come from – the imagination. In the case of this story, the imagination used was mine.

Any resemblance of any character in this story to any person, living or dead, nearly living or nearly dead, partly living or partly dead, is purely coincidental. Likewise, the events described in this book, they never happened. Although, I'd like to think there is a bit of the Profit T in all of us. He's a fun guy.

ACKNOWLEDGEMENTS

I am told by those far more qualified than me in the art of writing, that every writer requires help. I required much help. I greatly appreciate the assistance that came my way from the following people.

My wife Jackie was instrumental in me finishing this book. Jackie not only provided me the support and encouragement I needed when I became frustrated with my brain not working at times, and hence frustrated with this project, but she also laboured through a manuscript, or two, three, four, maybe ten. She, and she alone, has travelled the journey with me. She knows it well, better than me, better than anyone. As I don't have enough words to adequately describe my love for her, I'll simply say, 'Somewhere, somehow, somebody's God was smiling on me when we met.'

Our two children Brianna and Liam continually provide me with the excuse I need for my childish escapes from adulthood. With them I can create mayhem; without them I am a lesser man. My children also give me the ability to view the world through their eyes, the eyes of kids. I enjoy their world; it's less complicated than mine. In their world there is no killing, no suffering, no pain – only happiness, fun, and simplicity. I like their world better than mine. To my children, many thanks indeed.

My publishers at Dennis Jones & Associates (www.dennisjones. com.au), thank you for your kind advice. I've learned more from you guys than from any of the big publishing houses. The big publishing houses don't seem to like us new authors. It must have been something we said.

Luke Harris at Working Type Studio www.workingtype.com.au, thank you for the book cover and manuscript layout. Great work, mate.

My editor Ormé Harris – thank you, thank you and thank you. You are simply the best.

There are many others I must also thank for helping me with this book. Some I know, some I don't. Thanks to my wonderful friends and family who have stayed with me after my diagnosis. Too, thanks for leaving a touch of kindness, a smile, for having a chat on the phone, sharing a meal, a cold beer, a laugh, a hospital visit. I very much appreciate your efforts and your friendship. From you and from those I don't know, I may have stolen a few words, a lingering phase, a gesture or an attitude, a description, a colour, a mannerism and then mixed them together with other stolen bits and pieces, and turned it all into a character, an event, a happening, a something.

To Dr Praba Ratnarajah, Dr David Smith, and Dr Tom Eimany, thank you for giving me back my life. I also thank the other medical specialists and hospital staff who gave me their time, knowledge, skill, and expertise. I know it's all in a day's work for you people, but for me – it was a big deal.

Finally, I must thank my imagination. An imagination shaped in my childhood while I was taking the quizzical journey from there to teenager, to adult. An imagination which still takes me to places I've never been, to see things I've never seen, to do things I've never done, and to meet people I've never met. My imagination is fun, my imagination is good, and fun is good. There should be more good fun.

1

At birth, Mother called me *Travesty*. Travesty, a name meaning *disaster*. I could have given me a name which stood for something like great warrior, defender of the faith, or beautiful boy. She could have named me after somebody famous, but no, she called me Travesty. To Mother, I was a disaster. This was the world I entered. But, I should *not* have entered. Between you and me and the gatepost, I wasn't meant to arrive. I was an accident. A disastrous accident, a travesty.

Mother had her favourite people. Mind you, she changed them regularly. Her favourites were as changeable as the wind. I never reached the lofty heights of favouritism with Mother; I never reached any level of anything with her. I had set myself a *low* standard and failed to achieve it. I was the 'black lamb' of the family. Eventually, I grew up to become the 'black sheep' of the same family. I wear the title proudly, my badge of honour.

Twelve months after my birth, in Mother's beloved Baptist church, I was *christened* Travesty. In hindsight, I'm glad I was christened in a Baptist church by a *minister*. Knowing what I know now, it may have been a risky affair being christened anywhere else. Although I was only twelve months old, I still don't think I would have taken too kindly to being *touched* up by some dirty old *priest*. At least Baptist ministers have a healthy reputation for *not* being 'kiddie fiddlers'. I'm none too sure about them other mobs.

During the baptism, Mother asked the minister to hold my head under water for an hour or so. She wanted to make my christening more akin to a *sacrifice* to God. Thankfully, the minister refused.

I was at the beginning of my teenage years, thirteen, when I dropped out of school in grade four. I use the term 'dropped out' loosely, as it was more a case of being asked to leave. That, or be expelled.

'The boy is as thick as a tree, thick as a forest full of trees,' Mother would say. 'Damn disaster he is. Nothing good will come of him.'

Father was more understanding. He remarked I'd tried for a number of years to crack a *pass* level in grade four.

'Ten out ten for the effort, son.'

I found Father's comments positive and uplifting.

'Perhaps *learning* is not your forte in life,' he said.

My schoolteachers agreed. They couldn't see the sense of me learning either. From my perspective, I didn't care a hoot about some bloke Pythagoras running around bleating about his theorem. I'm betting he was a relative of that other bloke Euclidean. He did stuff with geometry. They both probably lived in a house looking like a three-sided right-angled triangle. Perhaps Hypotenuse lived with them?

Father thought it better if my *résumé* stated I had left school voluntarily, as opposed to being expelled. Hence he agreed with my leaving. You have to give credit where credit is due; they didn't come much smarter than my old man. No flies on him.

Mother was not a happy camper because my school career had come to an end. One of my aunties wasn't happy either. The woman did nothing but complain. I called her the *Whinging Aunt from Whining Hill*.

'Oh, the shame of it,' she would wail. 'How can it be, leaving the education system in grade four? People will talk about it, you know. I'll never be able to show my face in town again.'

Father believed the *Whinging Aunt from Whining Hill* was a certifiable loopy loopy control freak. He also thought she needed a good *root*.

'People who have good roots don't complain. You can tell! I've never complained in my life,' he would say. 'Remember, son, for later in life, always surround yourself with good roots. It's what keeps us men happy and contented and stops us from complaining. Whenever you need *solace, compassion* and *understanding* just go pull a good root. There's your solace, compassion and understanding, boy, right there.'

Later in life I understood what he meant, and what sound advice it was!

As payback for me dropping out of school, and to ensure I wouldn't have the entire family fortune to myself when my parents became *dearly* departed, Mother adopted two others. What escaped Mother's attention was the family fortune she was trying to protect fitted nicely into a small tuna can.

Father didn't like the adopted ones. So much so, he never spoke to them.

Sometimes I heard him mutter, 'It is not possible people exist as stupid as those two. Fuck me; there isn't a brain cell between the pair of them, not one.'

My adopted brother became Mother's favourite. He could lift heavy weights, but that was all he could do. I called him *Speed* because he was so *quick* on the uptake. In reality, he wasn't. *Speed* was never accused of being the quickest cab off the rank.

My adopted sister was *not* gifted with any form of intelligence – whatsoever. She was as dumb as dog shit. I called her *Wind Between Ears*. I felt the name did her fair justice. She annoyed me so much my arse would bleed when she came near me. Other times, just the sound of her voice would send me to the toilet with the bleeding shits. If you were scrapping the bottom of a barrel of stupid people, she *wouldn't* be there. She's so stupid she couldn't even get a gig at the bottom of a barrel full of stupid people. If all the stupid people in the world held a party only for stupid people, *Wind Between Ears wouldn't* be invited on account of her superior stupidity. She was never accused of being the sharpest knife in the cutlery drawer. But, she did have a *unique* personality – one similar to a house brick.

Wind Between Ears often referred to Centrelink, the local unemployment office, as her little Happy Reservation. It was here on Fridays, she gathered with like-minded people to collect their social welfare payments. They would dance and yell whoop-whoops together, and then rush outside to buy cigarettes, track suit pants, and go to MacDonald's.

'How's good's this shit?' *Wind Between Ears* would say as she spun around the Centrelink floor on her stupid head attached to her stupid body. 'They gimmee money for doing nuthfing, not a fing. This is the land of the free, orright. Free freaking handouts, man! Why would youse want to live anywheres else? Not me. I know which side of the road my bread is smeared with butter on.'

I'd throw rocks at her and she'd go tell on me. She'd sob in Mother's arms exaggerating the entire incident. At times, she became emotional because her unemployment benefits didn't last her long. Once, I tried to play the caring brother role. I took it upon myself to ease her pain, to console her.

I told her I knew of a way out of her misery. A place she could go to where she could get as many cigarettes, track suit pants, and big Macs as she wanted – all free. She broke into a burst of excitement as I slowly, but thoughtfully, suggested *suicide* to her. I explained it would end her suffering.

As *Wind Between Ears* thought about my kind suggestion, I solemnly added, 'You know I can get a rope, and you could use the tree out back.'

Three weeks later, *Wind Between Ears* cottoned on I was pulling the piss, when she caught me drawing a hangman's noose on her bedroom door. She told her obedient *Speed* to beat me up. He did everything she said. *Speed* ducked, weaved, threw punches, and finally broke the mirror. Dumb prick thought his reflection was me. With *Wind Between Ears* and *Speed*, Charles Darwin's Theory of Evolution had failed. They had not evolved.

Who hated me the most? Depended on the day of the week, and who could blame me the most. They blamed me for everything. The war in Afghanistan, climate change, global warming, too little rain, too many floods. They blamed me for the government and for taxes. They even blamed me for 'Home and Away' being on TV. They all wanted me dead.

Speaking of blaming me, Mother blamed me for her having

to get married. Early in her relationship with Father, they both threw caution to the wind and played doctors and nurses. You know the game? Similar to hide the sausage or letting the python out for run. Before premarital sex became par for the course, and having children out of wedlock became a norm of society, Mother and Father rattled one off, they did. I was born because Mother and Father failed to control their primal urges of mating. They failed to quell the flames of their passion, and most importantly, they failed to practise safe sex.

By the time the smoke had cleared from Mother and Father's heated, wild and crazy, screaming, sweating, pulsating, doing it this way, doing it that way, doing it any old way, getting their rocks off, 'was it good for you' lovemaking, I was swimming towards the womb of life.

Father would have been pounding his chest, bragging how his magical flute hadn't missed a note, because it was so highly tuned. Mother would have been lying there with her skirt up over her head and her ankles in the air, thinking to herself, how the Hell did that happen?

At the same time Father would have been saying, 'Yeh, that's what I mean – a bit of old-fashioned solace, compassion and understanding.'

Mother learned two things that evening. The bench seats of an FJ Holden had the room for two people to stretch out, and whilst Father may be taller, you're all the same height lying down.

'I never even felt you,' said Mother to Father.

'Your dick shrinks when you're highly tuned,' replied Father. 'It's well known.'

'You serious?' said Mother. 'Wow, you must have been super highly tuned.'

Often, to fend off Mother's criticism, I'd remind her of this incident. I'd remind her I was born, because of what she and Father had done, hence my birth wasn't my fault, and therefore she should lavish gifts and goodwill upon me. Mother wouldn't have a bar of it.

Instead, she would say, 'No, no. it's your fault I got pregnant.

You were the one who swam. You didn't have to, you know; you didn't have to swim.'

Father was different from Mother. What you saw is what you got. He was born during the Great Depression when there wasn't much of anything for anyone. This made him a man of few needs and wants. A noble tradition he *insisted* I follow whilst I lived at home. Father was originally a Catholic, but for reasons best known to him, he sacked the Catholic religion from his life and married my *then* pregnant mother in a Baptist Church. In case the Catholics misunderstood his message the first time, Father also became a Freemason. The Roman Catholic Church has long been an outspoken critic of Freemasonry; this suited Father. If the Catholics didn't like the Freemasons, then the Freemasons must be all right. Besides, Father never trusted a man who had never rattled one off, hence his distrust of Catholic priests.

'It's not right,' Father would say. 'It's not right at all. A man has to unravel his Johnston every now and again. Otherwise you get headaches. You know, play humpy humpy, trip the lights fantastic. A man who doesn't root and prefers to wear dresses is messed up in his head. He needs a good root to get it right.'

In my younger days, Mother made me read the Bible every day.

'You little tadpole impersonator, you. I'll learn you not to dart off to my womb,' she'd say. 'Now read and pray for forgiveness for your sins, you wicked boy.'

Before the Adopted Ones came into being, every Sunday morning Mother frogmarched me to church with her and Father. I had to sit in a pew with old people who smelled and dribbled through their oversized false teeth when they sang or spoke. I listened intently to the sermons in an attempt to understand the minister's weekly tale of enlightenment. Sermons, he had designed for all us sinners. Everyone was a sinner. How's that work? I didn't get it. The more the Church minister ridiculed sin, blamed the human race for sin, the more he mocked Hell, the more convinced I became I needed a piece of the *sin* action. The minister made sin sound like fun. I figured it had to be fashionable, as according to the minister, a lot of people were doing it.

I mentioned to the minister once, if Heaven and Hell were true, Hell would be my preferred destination. He enquired as to why. I answered him by saying, a party in Hell would have alcohol, girls, swearing, sex and sin, yeah, lots of sinning. Whereas, a party in Heaven would be what, a cup of tea and a lamington. The minister didn't see the same picture I was seeing.

As he walked away from me that morning shaking his head, I shouted, 'Why do you accept a belief system where you have to wait until you die to find out if it's true or not? It doesn't make sense, man. It's crazy thinking.'

Mother was trying to push me out the church doors as I continued with my wrath.

'Let's say you die, you end up facing the Pearly Gates, and some fat dude sitting on his butt with his legs crossed says to you, you screwed up man, Buddhism was the one. Now piss off! You're buggered, get my drift?'

The minister and Mother failed to understand my point. She took me straight home and made me read the Bible again as punishment. Once, I attempted to explain to Mother I didn't *believe* religious leaders officiating on behalf of somebody's God; we're all that smart.

'Blasphemy!' she hollered. You're a blasphemous little bastard, you are!'

I never believed that leaders of religion, no matter what religion they were, knew their subject matter – in their case, the Bible. That's why they have to read from it. They don't know it. Any numbskull can read from a book, and let's be honest, preaching is not like having a real job, like a technical job or a medical job. For those gigs you need many reference materials.

A person of the cloth uses one reference source *only*, a book, an old book. It's been around forever. The words in it haven't changed. The stories are the same. The characters in the stories haven't changed their names, and they're still doing the same stuff. The miracles are the same; no new ones added since the Bible was first written some 2,000 years ago. How hard is it to update the Bible, put out a new version as they do with other reference books? Put stuff in about what Jesus is doing now in Heaven? Is he working, or is still rattling on about his old man? Did God ever marry Mary, the mother of Jesus? Or do they live in sin? It, too, is fashionable these days. The Bible should also have an address in it for Heaven, so we can send birthday cards and gifts to Jesus. On Jesus's birthday, people give each other gifts. Why? Jesus gets nothing, no presents, no cards. That's very selfish. Religious people should be showing Jesus the love on his birthday. They should be singing him 'Happy Birthday', not giving each other gifts and saying 'Merry Christmas'. Jesus gets ripped off every year by a fat guy in a red and white suit, and it's not his birthday. It's the birthday of Jesus.

If religious leaders knew their subject matter better, they'd be able to *pass* onto their congregations the important messages the Bible offers.

For example, in 2 Kings 2:23-24 it states: 'Elisha left and headed towards Bethel. Along the way, some boys started to make fun of him by shouting, "Go away, baldy! Get out of here!" Elisha turned around and stared at the boys. Then he cursed them in the name of the Lord. Straight away two bears ran out of the woods and *ripped* forty-two of the boys to pieces!'

The message from this piece of scripture is simple enough to understand. Don't take the piss out of bald men; if you do, the bears will get you. This is the information the community needs to know. It makes sense; it's a good safety message. As God's preachers *failed* to pass on safety messages such as this to their congregations, people are still taking the piss out of bald men, and therefore, bears are still running about killing people.

I was fourteen, a recent school dropout, when I had a change of heart about my church attendance. I began to look forward to my weekly church sessions. By then, I knew enough of the Biblical shenanigans to run rings around the minister. It was fun watching him squirm as he tried to counter the logical arguments of a young teenager.

'Did you know,' I said to him once, 'if you repeated out loud every word Jesus is alleged to have spoken in the New Testament, it would take you two hours. That's it; that was the life of Jesus; you can tell it in two hours. Yet, you've been telling stories here every week, for how long? Your sermons go for an hour. You've gotta be making stuff up, man. Jesus didn't have that much to say. Two hours' worth. That's it, a done deal in two hours. What gives with you?'

The minister half-smiled at me and tried to talk to other worshippers.

I continued. 'Not only that, Jesus spoke in parables. Every parable he spoke in the *New* Testament, every one of them, was previously mentioned in the *Old* Testament – that's plagiarism, is it not?'

The minister was now outside the church trying to get away from me.

I let rip. 'The money donated by way of the collection plate is an interesting affair, isn't it? The donations are cash transactions, right? No receipts are issued, unaudited dollars, correct? The one person who knows where the money goes is you, huh? Who checks you?'

I kept following him. 'The Biblical authors were great, weren't they? We must praise them for sharing with us their limitless, vivid imagination in the ancient art of storytelling. The most repeated story from the Bible, the story used more than any other story to indoctrinate children, is the Ten Commandments. According to scripture, God summons Moses to go to the top of Mount Sinai to receive the Ten Commandments. Exodus 19:18 tells us, God arrived in a flaming bush to the summit of Mount Sinai.'

Question, Mr. Minister Man. Why would God arrive in a flaming fire?'

'What are you on about this time, Travesty?' he asked.

'If you're God,' I answered, 'wouldn't you just rock up and say, "Hey Moses, like man, I'm God; crack open a bottle of good red and let's talk about your behaviour? From where I sit, it doesn't look too good down here. I got a few rules for you, ten really good ones. Grab a rock and some slate pens." That's what God would do. He wouldn't send an old man climbing up to the top of a mountain looking for a flaming bush.'

And off ran the minister. Beaten by logic, brought down by fact.

I knew I was walking a thin line with the church before they expelled me. Yes, the bloody Baptists expelled me. I had a bad attitude towards God and his boy. The telling blow which tipped the bucket in favour of my expulsion was when I told a bunch of Sunday school kids that if they had their bags packed for the Second Coming, best they unpack; it isn't going to happen. I put my case forward as gently as I could, understanding the tender and vulnerable age of the young kiddies.

I said, 'After what we did to Jesus the last time he was here, do you really think he's considering coming back? There ended up being nails and stuff all over the place, bits of wood as well. Lots of crying too. We put him up on a Cross, left him hanging there, screaming his tits off in pain because of the nails we hammered into his hands and his feet. Blood and shit was all over the place. The Romans were laughing at him. One of them stuck a sword into his side. Come on kids, do you think Jesus is going to forgive us for that one? No way. He's probably scared of us. Hence, no Second Coming, and besides, based on the evidence I've seen, there hasn't *even* been a First Coming! It's all crap.'

The kiddies' little faces looked up at me and started to crumble as I told them, 'If Jesus is true, then I'm betting he *doesn't* love us; instead, I'm betting he hates us. We even made him carry his own big heavy Cross up the hill. And he was a king. Jesus wants us all dead, not in Heaven for eternal life with him. I'm telling you, Jesus has had a gutful of us.'

The little people were beside themselves with terror as I mentioned the pain Jesus would have been in when some flog slammed a Crown of Thorns on his head.

'Jesus is probably still carrying the scars on his forehead! Every time he looks in mirror he curses us.'

More importantly, as religious leaders do not understand the Bible, they've missed the real message Jesus was trying to tell us about his death.

'Don't you little snot gobblers go believing all this hogwash about Jesus dying on the Cross for the sins of mankind. That's not true. The message Jesus wanted us to understand from his death was that believing in God can be a painful experience. Sometimes you have to walk up hills carrying heavy shit. People can even die on a Cross from following God. Therefore, follow God at your own peril.'

The little joys of wonderment began screaming in fright with tears running down their faces and little bits of snot coming out their noses; a few did poo-poo in their pants. Parents heard their anguished cries and rushed over to shepherd their little lambs out of harm's way, right at the exact moment I said, 'And what is Christianity exactly? One woman has an affair, and every religious person in the world ignores it, and then quotes crap like "Thou shall not commit adultery". You dummies, religion started because of adultery. Get it together. And don't go taking the piss out of bald men; otherwise the bears will gobble up your sorry arses.'

I became the first person since Judas Iscariot (he stitched up Jesus at the Last Supper) to be expelled from a Baptist Church. This greatly embarrassed my mother. She never got over it.

'How could you do this to me?' moaned my wailing mother of the Baptist faith. 'I'll never be able to show my face around town again.'

Mother would rant, rage and call me a heathen as she made many phone calls to many people to see if they felt sorry for her because of my actions. Regularly, the *Whinging Aunt from Whining Hill* would appear with the 'feel sorry for me train'. On Mother would get, and off they'd go, whinging and whining and complaining into the distance. Toot toot!

I said to Mother, 'I don't understand why people put money into the collection plate every week; it's a con. They must be *stupid*.'

Mother snapped back, 'I put money in the collection plate every week.'

Sometimes life is more joyous if we say nothing. I smiled and let her comment pass.

Let Us Pray

....

Oh Lordy, oh Lordy,
I don't get this religion thing, mate
Like if you're true
Give me a hint
Which religion are you?
Amen

The Prophecies of Chapter One

→ If Jesus does return, remind him the Romans did him in; no sense in anyone else taking the rap.

→ Do not read the Bible to young children. It has scary bits in it.

→ Do not upset bald men unless you're wearing a bear-protective suit.

→ If you are in the woods and you happen to see a bald man in a bear-protective suit, keep your wits about you.

→ The next time you go to church, take your own plate and ask for a donation.

→ Bald men in the woods should wear hats and put sunscreen on their heads.

→ If you're enjoying nature by walking in the mountains and you see a bush on fire, trust me, it isn't God. Do the right thing, put it out or call the Fire Brigade.

→ Just to be sure, before you extinguish the fire, you could ask the bush if it *is* God. If God is true, you probably don't want to piss him off with a burst of cold water.

→ Stupid people are put on Earth to help entertain the rest of us.

→ Thank God for stupid people.

2

My fatal beating occurred many years after the Baptist church sacked me. At the time of my death, I was fifty-five and still living at home with my parents. I pioneered the 'living at home' concept long before the young folk of today got onto the idea. I should have patented it.

Once the Adopted Ones had moved out, it wasn't too bad living at home. *Wind Between Ears* had run off to somebody's happy hunting ground. It was a vacant block of land beside the local Unemployment Office. This gave me cause for great celebration and much happiness. I danced, and now it was my turn to yell whoop-whoops. I also tried to take scalps. The bright lights of my tepee shone for days and nights, acting as a beacon of warning to the world; *Wind Between Ears* had moved on to screw up other people's lives – beware.

Though appearing most challenged in the brain faculty department (steroids can do that to you), *Speed* had enough common sense to migrate to a country where the good old 'roids' were almost legal. I must admit, I did miss him. As he mostly grunted and moved about with his knuckles dragging close to the ground, as a Neanderthal would have done, I was able to hire him out to school kids to exhibit as part of their 'early man show and tell' projects. I also hired him out to companies that moved furniture on weekends. Not that he knew what day it was. But, with his departure, those little money earners dried up for me.

Unfortunately, the *Whinging Aunt from Whining Hill* was still ever present, or perhaps that was omnipresent. No, that couldn't be right, she was no God. She was the Devil masquerading as an interfering old busybody. I did miss my battle of wits with *Speed* and *Wind Between Ears*. Sure, it was unfair – they were always disarmed, but I still had fun.

As it was only me living at home with Mother and Father, I tried on a number of times to worm my way into becoming Mother's favourite. I would tell her the Adopted Ones had died of stupidity. I tried to convince her that the Adopted Ones had left the planet as they had been abducted. I even used the old, 'They were run over while trying to steal hubcaps from passing motor vehicles!'

Each time, Mother would call up the *Whinging Aunt from Whining Hill* who always informed her to take no notice of me.

'Travesty is simply jealous because he doesn't have Unemployment Benefits in his DNA and he can't bench press ten times his body weight; ignore him,' the Whinging Aunty would say. 'Ignore him; it's not as if he's ever going to be one of your favourites.'

Many years prior to my death, I discovered working for a living didn't appeal to me at all. I tried it once. I had a job, but I didn't think I was very good at it, so I quit. I also became ill. Sadly, I contracted *Workitis*. I couldn't shake it. According to the medical profession, the illness doesn't exist – but what do doctors know?

Workitis was as baffling then, as it is today. It can only be identified by the medical procedure known as *self-diagnosis*. Workitis is far more serious than *Mondayitis*. Workitis is with you every working day of every working week. Strangely, on weekends and public holidays, Workitis doesn't bother you. I know, I could never understand it either. Workitis is also incurable; hence it ruined any chance of me going back to work. But I did so want to contribute to something, even if it was only my own wallet. So I took to gambling; it was more fun, and more lucrative than work. Also, I could choose my own hours.

One of the early symptoms, which convinced me I had contracted this terrible illness, was the overwhelming need to sleep-in on most mornings. Mother blamed my laziness on the late nights of partying I did after my big gambling wins.

With time, my illness became worse. I found the very mention of the word *work*, sent my blood pressure into overdrive. This was always followed by a feeling of faintness and an over-powering need to lie down with the TV remote. Some mornings I was so physically drained, and so hung-over with Workitis, I had to stay in bed until way past lunchtime, watching TV or reading the magazines I kept under my mattress.

During these stressful times, I would scream, 'Damn you, Workitis; look what you have done to me!'

Upon hearing my screams of anguish, Mother would yell, 'Don't think for one moment you can get a ticket on the "feel-sorry-for-me train" that easily, you lazy, good-for-nothing, heathen scum! There aren't any seats left; some of your relatives have taken the spare ones. You'll have to wait for a couple of them to die. Toot-toot!'

'Oh, dear God,' I whispered, 'please hear my prayer...'

But, true to form, God never heard my prayers, let alone answered them. Shame really.

'Why don't you get off your lazy backside and get a job? You're a disgrace to the family name,' Mother would say.

'I need sympathy, not a job. How about showing me the love?' I asked.

'Fat chance,' Mother answered.

Despite my lack of enthusiasm for most things, apart from gambling, partying and sleeping, I did at times show the community I lived in that I was trying to soldier on despite my illness. Weak from a mere twelve to fourteen hours of sleep, I'd sometimes drag myself out of bed and prepare a chicken and champagne breakfast. I'd set up a small camping table and chair on the nature strip in front of our house and have my breakfast. People drove past me on their way to work, fighting the morning traffic and, later in the day, fighting the same traffic in reverse. To these people I would raise a chicken leg and a glass of champagne in salute, reassuring my fellow humans that I admired their work ethics, and I was trying my best to recover. People stared at me from behind their car windows with surprise and astonishment. I think they were shocked to see a man with my medical condition out of bed so early and attempting to get on with life.

Nice people acknowledged my effort by blowing their horns whilst yelling at me. The horn blowing made it impossible to understand the words they uttered, I assume, words of encouragement. I was happy. I was demonstrating to the people it doesn't matter how afflicted you are with Workitis, you can always get out of bed for a chicken and champagne breakfast.

One Sunday morning in God's universe or Charles Darwin's paradise, depending on your belief system, I had risen early from bed, pumped out two calf raises on my left leg, and engrossed myself in analysing the horse-racing form for the afternoon races. My unfair, but wonderful, expulsion from the Baptist church, had forced me to become a non-practising Baptist. Therefore, *not* to bet on a Sunday afternoon was being *irreligious* and disrespectful to all non-Baptist gods.

On this Sunday morning, as with every Sunday morning, those who believed in the *Almighty* had also risen early to eat and dress, as this was their day to attend church with other like-minded people. At church they would all pray, sing, be jolly and promise to love one another, whilst collectively ignoring the plight of the homeless and the starving. They would disrespect their own fathers, by praising someone else's father, who lived in Heaven. The sounds of my own father noisily clearing his throat in the bathroom filtered through to my bedroom.

Downstairs Mother prepared breakfast whilst merrily singing, 'Jesus loves me, this I know, for the Bible tells me so.'

I yelled, 'No he doesn't! He hates us, especially those Roman bastards! He's none too keen on them.'

Mother retorted, 'Hush your heathen mouth, you ungrateful bucket of pigs' swill! After all I have done for you, you treat me like this. When Jesus comes back, he is going to get you good, boy. I'm going to tell him you were expelled from church.'

I replied, 'Seeing as you're going to church, can you ask Jesus or his old man who they fancy in the fifth race at the Valley this afternoon?'

'You mock him at your own peril. Jesus died for our sins on the cross and you mock him; how dare you!' Mother fired back.

I responded, 'Do you know how stupid that sounds? How could he have died for *my* sins? He's been dead for over 2,000 years. I wasn't born back then. When Jesus was running about the place flogging his stuff like an Amway salesperson, I hadn't committed any sins. Bit different now though, the *sins* I mean. When's he coming back again? I may need him to die again'.

Laughter erupted from the bathroom.

'Besides, if Jesus did die for other people's sins, more fool him for taking the rap for stuff *he* never did.'

'You'll never get to Heaven, you blasphemous, free-loading, lazy bastard,' said Mother.

I replied, 'My definition of Heaven is a winner at 20/1, that's Heaven, especially if I've got a shed load of the folding stuff on it.'

'One day, just you wait. One day, the *Whinging Aunt from Whining Hill* and I will get your father's hacksaw and cut you up, you bad child,' threatened Mother. 'You, who insult and mock everything religious.'

'That's a tad unfair. I neither insult nor mock religion. I merely point out the bleeding obvious. Based on my observations, this life is the only one we get. There is no evidence to suggest we're getting a second crack at it.'

'I just knew I should have beaten you more when you were a baby. When I get to Heaven, I'm going to tell God not to let you in, ever,' Mother snapped.

'You'll never get Heaven,' I said.

'Why not?' Mother asked.

'Because I'm *not* going to tell God you died,' I answered. 'I won't even tell the police or the church minister. I'll leave you where you lie. God won't know you died. How'd you like them apples, baby?'

Ahh, there is something special about the sound of silence.

My God-fearing parents ate, dressed and came up to my room to tell me they were leaving to commune with the great Creator. Well, Father did. Mother came up, spat at me, and mumbled something about how I was destined to go live with the Devil.

The backfiring and the rattling of the family FJ Holden (yes, the same car), told me I had the house to myself for a few hours. I settled back into my form analysis.

Within thirty minutes, I had finished and placed my bets for the day via the internet using my online-betting account. With my parents gone, and to help me unwind from the rigours of thirty minutes of gambling analysis, I usually made a call each Sunday morning to the agency, and asked for a home delivery. One of the benefits of being a successful gambler is one has the ready flow of cash to be able to participate in whatever the agency offers.

On this morning, her name was Karen; at least that's what she told me when she arrived. But, you never know with agency girls; it could have been a false name. Karen was younger than I was. Slim and tanned, she was. Her light, yellow dress, with the hemline falling discreetly at upper thigh level, fluttered in the morning breeze as it gave way to a nice pair of legs. Her long auburn hair fell loosely over her shoulders and her eyes displayed a vacant look of 'Here we go again'. I figured her good-looking cleavage had to be part of a great set of boobies. In one hand she carried a bag, which housed the products she used for her specialised trade.

Whilst chewing a big wad of gum, Karen warmly, affection-ately, lovingly, and showing I mattered to her, asked, 'What'll it be love – cash or credit?'

'Cash,' I answered.

Karen told me she was twenty-one. The age gap between us didn't appear to bother her. Money never discriminates. We went upstairs and into my room. I saw the racing form guides I had been working on earlier strewn over my bed. I suggested to Karen we adjourn to another bedroom for my *horizontal* folk-dancing lesson.

I placed an AC/DC CD in the player on my table, cranked up the volume, and then we went into my parents' bedroom. I knew Karen found my finely honed athletic body an attrac-tion as when I undid the belt of my trousers, and my stomach hit the floor twice, before bouncing back into place, her face went pale and she was lost for words. I was a sight to behold. I briefly explained to her that *once* I'd had big chest muscles, but my Workitis illness had made them slump to my stomach. Her face still stayed pale.

Karen never found any words until I removed my shirt. As she looked, she declared loudly, 'Look at your man boobs; you've got bigger tits than me!'

We climbed into the bed of magical times, and I told Karen of my fitness regime. My two calf raises each morning on my left leg is what makes a body like mine I pointed out. Yep, I thought, as I tried to find my penis for her, Karen was one lucky woman to have me for an hour. I had read the day before in one of my magazines that sometimes the man should pleasure the woman. I think Karen was most flattered when I asked her where her G-spot was.

The look of shock on her face told me this could be the first time a man had taken the time to *consider* her pleasure.

She hesitantly answered, 'I'm not sure; maybe I didn't bring it.'

Karen, who by now was helping me to locate my penis, was most grateful when I reassured her it was OK, she could bring her G-spot with her the next time I called up the agency and they selected her to visit me. The tears of happiness that welled up in her eyes signalled to me how much I had come to mean to her in a short time. A few moments later, we both gave up trying to find my penis and Karen reached into her bag and handed me a strap-on.

In a hurry to have me, Karen from the agency said, 'Stand up, look in the fucking mirror, lean backwards, find your dick, put it in the plastic and let's stop mucking around here; I'm a busy girl.'

I did as instructed. Some women like to take charge in the bedroom. It gives them power I've heard.

Karen whispered, 'Hurry, be nice and quick,' confirming my earlier suspicions. She was smitten with the big fellow.

My parents arrived home suddenly. I didn't hear the car. AC/DC music was still reverberating throughout the house.

Karen was also moaning in my ear, 'Please, please, never mention this to anyone, ever!'

Both my parents mistook my choice in music for the noise a cat makes when its tail has been jammed in a door. Given we didn't own a cat made their assumption puzzling to me. They rushed upstairs to rescue the cat we didn't have and caught me in the act – the unfinished act. For a moment, I thought things were going well. They stood, just stood, and looked at us; both appeared gobsmacked as the blood drained from their faces.

Father broke the icy silence first. 'Way to go, my boy! That's how to pray, the good old missionary position. I hope you've got someone underneath your stomach!'

I'm not sure what upset Mother the most. Catching me doing the deed, catching me doing it in their bed, or Father seemingly granting his approval for the activity I had now began to pursue with great haste, in the hope that I could finish before Mother fully recovered from her shock. I knew she was going to over-react to a situation which could be sorted with good manners, diplomacy and another couple of minutes (for my sake). But, I should have known none of this would be forthcoming.

My plea of 'Can you come back later? I haven't quite finished', went unheeded and merely served to make Mother hysterical.

There is nothing worse to a man in his mid-fifties than the sound of his mother becoming hysterical whilst he's trying to finish shagging a twenty-one-year-old prostitute named Karen. It's off-putting, and to be honest, rude. I think Karen was most upset by the proceedings.

Mother moaned, 'We came home for my Bible. I forgot it! What do I find? I find this disgusting, vile, inappropriate filth happening. You don't even use your own room, and you're on my side of the bed, you filthy little heathen man!'

'Mother,' I said. 'Lighten up, grab your Bible and go back to church. I'm nearly done here. I'll tidy up afterwards.'

Mother wailed, 'Why, why, why? In my house, why do you resort to lust? God forbids lust! The minister warned us last week about lust; it's sinful.'

In desperation I argued, 'I had a vision God wanted me to share the love – that's what I'm doing.'

Whilst Mother and I conversed by way of the spoken word most loudly, Father kneeled on the floor beside the bed, not to ask God for my forgiveness, but to gain a better look at Karen, under the guise of asking her what footy team she supported. Mother grabbed him by the scruff of his jacket and sent him flying backwards.

'Pick yourself up, man,' Mother hollered to Father. 'Pick yourself up and beat him with the ironing board (who keeps one of them in their bedroom?), the heathen sex maniac he is.'

Father grabbed the ironing board and commenced pounding my body as I yelled, 'She has a twin sister!'

'Really?' replied Father.

He stopped beating me and put down the ironing board.

Karen decided whilst two was OK, three's a crowd, and four's a big crowd. She therefore decided to withdraw from further participation in my horizontal folk-dancing lesson, by crawling out from underneath me. She grabbed her clothes, complimented Mother on her Sunday dress, and made her getaway by the time-honoured way of the *bolt*.

No such bolt for me. Mother yelled at my father to keep pounding as she fell on her knees and prayed for the sin of my deeds not to be held against her.

Karen yelled as she ran out the front door, 'Don't you ever call me again! You lot are loopy! Plus, I have two sisters, we're triplets.'

What is it with women who play hard to get?

I yelled after her, 'Wait for me! I want to come with you.'

Karen hollered back, 'As if I'd ever get off with a fat prick like you!'

'Give me back my money!' I hollered.

Father said, 'I'll chase after her – for your money.'

Mother said, 'No you won't. You will stay here and continue to beat his body, otherwise you'll be restricted to nookie-nookie on your birthday, and Christmas Day *only*.'

Father looked at me in one of those father-to-son ways as if to say, 'Sorry son, but if I only get laid twice a year, I'll end up complaining like the *Whinging Aunt from Whining Hill*,' and he commenced the pounding again.

Mother, now leaning over me and attempting to push the iron, in its entirety, into my mouth, began to quote scripture on *why* having sex out of wedlock is for sinners.

Spitting out the iron, I yelled, 'Sex out-of-wedlock must be allowed! Look at Adam and Eve. They never married and they had kids!'

'They would have been married!' Mother declared.

'Who married them? There were no other people on the Earth. On the sixth day God only made those two. It says so in the Bible,' I replied.

For a moment, I thought I might have won the round on a technicality, as Mother stopped with the iron and the scripture. But, she was just catching her breath as she stretched out her free arm, and attempted to place one end of the iron cord into a power point.

She yelled, 'God must have married them in the Garden of Eden!'

'Rubbish!' I replied. 'Show me where God is in their wedding photos?'

'Don't be stupid, boy!' responded Mother, as she gave up with the iron and threw it to one side. 'Everybody knows Adam and Eve never had a photographer.'

'Then where's the proof they were married? No photos, no God saying he married Adam and Eve, no witnesses, and nothing on YouTube about it. You have no argument! God wasn't there and neither were Adam and Eve, and there was no Garden of Eden either. Besides the Bible is full of crap. It wants us to believe that Adam stood next to a naked woman and went for a piece of fruit instead. Come on, you can't take it seriously. Anyways, you and Father did it before you got married; I'm the proof of that. I'm the best thing that has ever happened to you.'

Mother went still, quiet, momentarily confused perhaps,

unsure how to react. She sighed, a long sigh, turned and walked deliberately, purposefully to the bedroom door. Here she stopped, and shut it. Father, witnessing the change in Mother's demeanour, stopped pounding me and backed away, placing the ironing board in front of him, as if for protection. Mother turned, faced me, sighed again, and then went fucking ballistic. She went straight through Father's security board, knocking him over. Out of the haze of pieces of shattered ironing board falling to the bedroom floor, emerged something I had never seen before. Mother had flames coming out of her nostrils and her ears; she made loud guttural sounds I could not decipher, and *this* was hurtling towards me.

I said loudly, 'Oh, bugger!'

Father, covered in the remnants of what had once been an ironing board, looked up at me from the floor and declared, 'You're buggered!'

To escape the mother of all cruise missiles, I rolled sideways from the bed and bounced along the floor on my stomach. I stood up to run to the closed door, but stumbled over Father's slippers and fell. I tried to get up whilst Mother started to kick the living crapper out of me.

Suddenly, Mother realised she was witnessing my fully exposed, naked, fifty-five-year-old body, as I rolled to try and get away from her madness.

'Hang on; hang on a minute. What do we have here?' she screamed to Father. 'Look at him; look at him! He's got the curse of the donkey! He's suffering from donkeyitis!'

Father looked and I do recall him saying, 'Wow! That's an impressive-looking Johnson, you've got there, son. You're just like your daddy!'

Intent on moving with the same electrifying speed as a Tour de France cyclist does on illegal drugs, I staggered to my feet whilst hollering, 'It's a strap-on. I'm wearing plastic; it's a fake!'

Seeing me trying to escape, Mother went stark raving crazy; her hair stood on end and began to smoke. She started to froth at the mouth, and the veins in her neck looked as if they were going to pop out. Herein lies the problem with my escape plan. I had staggered almost upright to run as fast as a deer would do after coming face to face with a lion. As I did, one of my feet stepped on the strap-on. The elastic band holding the strap-on in place stretched right out and then, as if possessed by a force, the likes unknown to humankind, the plastic doodle holder sprang back with a twanging sound. The strength behind the recoil was exceptional. It was so powerful, it knocked me over backwards and once again I fell. Except this time, the back of my head came to rest on the pointy end of the iron.

My parting thought. Bugger! I wonder if death is a fatal beast.

Let Us Pray

Hey God
If you're there
I think I'm dead
Just thought I'd let you know
I've always believed, really I have; I love your work
Amen

The Prophecies of Chapter Two

→ Living at home when you're fifty-five is probably overrated.

→ Beware of Workitis; it can strike at any time.

→ Paying up front for services can often lead to disappointment.

→ If you're still living at home, use your own room for certain activities.

→ If buying prostitutes, see if you can pay half now, half afterwards.

→ Do not leave irons lying around; they can be dangerous to people's longevity.

→ The force behind the rebound of a strap-on brings tears to your eyes.

→ Try not to get your mother hysterical.

→ If you see a person doing the Indian dance for unemployment benefits, give *Wind Between Ears* my regards.

→ You'll know her the moment you try and talk to her. She can't put a complete sentence together, without stopping and thinking in-between phases.

→ Better still, say nothing. Throw rocks at her instead.

→ Love only hurts when your parents come home early and catch you at *it* in their bed.

3

You may not be able to put your finger on it straightaway, but when you die, you do realise, almost immediately, something has gone sadly amiss in your life. An early clue to your death is finding yourself floating in a sea of grey mist above your lifeless body. I've never been big on surprises, so when I peered below and saw my dead body lying on my parents' bedroom floor, I was surprised. Most surprised indeed!

Mother rolled me over, removed the iron from the back of my head, and complained, 'Look what he's done; he's gone and died, he has. Never any good that boy; he can't even die without a making a mess, painful boy.'

Just as I was thinking the Adopted Ones will gloat as soon as they find out I'm dead, the *Whinging Aunt from Whining Hill* appeared in the doorway.

Standing up with her hands on her hips, Mother said, 'What a mess he's left. Messy boy. I always told his father that. Messy because he's lazy. Blood and gunk over the iron and the carpet. Hopeless lad. Such a bad child; we could have done so much better than him. If only he had been more like the Adopted Ones.'

The *Whinging Aunt from Whining Hill* moaned, 'I suppose I'll have to do all the cleaning; no one else ever helps me do anything, you know.'

I waved my hands and called out, 'Up here!' Then I yelled, 'I'm up here.'

'I suppose I'll have to buy another ironing board,' Mother complained, as she surveyed the shattered pieces lying on her bedroom floor.

'The carpets will need a clean as well; forever costing money he was, useless boy. He used to do it with women, right in his parents' bed. No respect for anything that boy. Ah well, maybe the iron still works.'

'That'll be left up to me, won't it?' said the *Whinging Aunt from Whining Hill*. 'It'll be me who has to go and buy the new ironing board.'

'Up here!' I yelled again.

I received no response.

Those below could not hear or see me. What a strange predicament I found myself in, floating in an upright stationary position, unable to be seen or heard. I could turn my head from side to side, move it up and around, and move my arms, but that was it. There was no grey mist below, only daylight.

I stretched my arms out into the grey abyss, but could feel nothing. Hang on, I thought. How do I know I'm dead? This was confusing; dead people couldn't think, could they? If you were dead, you were dead – weren't you?

I looked down upon my lifeless body, and could understand how I might have died. The big hole in the back of my head showed me. Not being a religious man, I was under the opinion that when you die, it's all over red rover. No afterlife, no floating in space or grey mist or whatever; when you die, the lights are out, and there's no one at home.

I rationalised, perhaps I'm only a little bit dead, you know, partially dead. That must be it. I'm partially dead and I'm floating in an unconscious state. Wait, ludicrous thinking. Soon, my eyes will open; I'll realise I was having a dream and was never dead, a little bit dead or even partially dead. But what if I wasn't dreaming? I strained my ears to listen for the sound of blaring sirens. Mother, Father, or the Whinging Aunt, one of them at least, would have surely called an ambulance. The ambulance by now was hurtling towards our house at breakneck speed, ready and able to dispatch its highly trained paramedics to bring my lifeless body back to life.

In death, as in life, the mind plays funny tricks on you. What if I was dead? What if I was wrong and there really was a God in Heaven, and a Devil in Hell? Could I be, right now, in Hell?

The grey mist surrounding me could be smoke from the Devil's furnaces. Though, it didn't smell smoky; there was no smell. And where were the other dead people?

Did the Greenies convince the Devil to only fire up his furnace every few days instead of leaving it on all the time, polluting the place and contributing to global warming? Is this why I was floating in a stationary position. The Devil is waiting for furnace day. Furnace day must have been yesterday, the other dead people already collected. This could explain why I was here on my lonesome; I was waiting to be collected.

I couldn't hear any sirens, people! Did they call? If not, why not? By all accounts, Jesus didn't need an ambulance, a hospital or a doctor.

He popped up a couple of days after he died and uttered these famous words: 'Hello world, I'm outta here; this Earth gig is like, way too hard for me. Did you see the size of the Cross I had to bear? Damn heavy, I'm telling you.'

Did my parents not call the emergency number because they believed I was Jesus, and had taken it upon themselves to crucify me for my sins – and everyone else's? Is it possible I was not just the black sheep of the family, but had become the Baptist sacrificial lamb? The Bible is full of sacrifices to God. Perhaps I'm another one. I could be onto something here, about me being Jesus. I remember as a kid whenever I did something wrong, someone would yell, 'Jesus, what have you done now?' Other times they yelled, 'Jesus bloody Christ, look at the mess you've caused!' I always thought this was a weird request. If I had already created the mess, why did I need to look at it?

In my younger years, I believed Jesus existed inside me. On occasions, I was threatened with, 'I'm going to knock the living bejesus out of you, boy!'

My first few days at kindergarten were a disaster. The teacher asked my name and I answered, 'Jesus Bloody Christ, Miss!' Kinder detention is embarrassing for a young child.

I again screamed out to remind Mother and Father we had private health insurance, and hence there would be no cost to revive my life. I got nothing. Mother shone a torch into the gaping hole in the back of my head where, not long before, the pointy end of the iron had come to rest.

'What are you doing?' Father asked.

Mother replied, 'I think I was correct, no brains in here.'

The Whinging Aunt laughed.

'I told you he took after your side of the family,' Father casually remarked.

Mother snapped back, 'Given he wears a strap-on, shows he takes after your side!'

The Whinging Aunt laughed louder.

Above me and behind me, in the abyss non-reality, a strange whooshing sound became audible. Stranger still, there was the sound of a bell ringing and a voice, a monotone human voice, saying, 'Bring out your dead; bring out your dead.'

This must be somebody from one of the Monty Python films. He'd know what's happening. But, no matter how hard I looked through the mist, I couldn't see anything.

'Don't tell me; don't tell me,' Mother groaned, 'we'll be spending more money on this dumb child for a funeral. He's dead and still he costs us money. Brainless, good-for-nothing, never amounted to anything, piece of rot he became.'

Through the greyness, a faint glow became brighter. The glow was heading my way. Could this be the source of the whooshing sound? Oh, golly gee, I wasn't happy about this. Perhaps the Devil had a mobile furnace. I needed to pee.

'Hey, you lot below, where's the ambulance? Call one now; I promise I'll move out of home.'

The fear of the unknown is the worst fear; if one knows what's going to happen, one can plan, but with no knowing comes no plan, oh gawd! Fear had gripped me and the grip was getting tighter.

I yelled again, 'I'm serious, call the ambulance and I'll move out of home and go to church again. I'll show God the love.'

I remembered being scared once before. I was fourteen or fifteen.

A woman asked me if I knew what fellatio was.

I answered, 'No.'

She replied, 'Come over here and let me show you.'

So I did, and she did. Nervous, scared at first, yes. But, I soon relaxed and settled into the rhythm of things. If the outcome this time around was going to be a similar experience, I had no cause for concern. I should just hang in my dream and let whatever was going to occur, occur. Bingo! I had it now. It suddenly dawned upon me. I was having a wet dream! No need to panic; I had it under control. Soon I'd be waking up and enjoying the day. Slumber on, my man. Whatever you are going to receive, may you be truly grateful.

But, the seeds of doubt growing in my mind would not go away. What if I wasn't having one of those pleasant, fun-filled dreams? I'd had wet dreams before and none of them involved a glow of light, whooshing sounds, bells ringing and a voice saying, 'Bring out the dead.'

That thing was getting closer. I could see to my right a light, no, a circle of many coloured lights, which gave off a faint glow. Nothing good could come of this. What if they weren't lights and were instead the eyes of a monster coming to gobble me up and down and around. My mind clicked over from the state of a wet dream to a state of panic. I peed. Oh golly gee! I'm in freaking trouble here with a capital T; the fuck-up fairy has come and paid me a visit.

'Come on, you lot, it's not funny anymore,' I hollered to those below. 'Get me out of here!'

My panicking mind had begun to think perhaps the Greenies had convinced the Devil to close his furnaces down altogether, and instead use a recycling monster. The monster eats us via the front end, and provides fertiliser via the back end. That's a Greenie thing, environment stuff. Then again, the Devil would not be so stupid as to take advice from the Greenies; they've been away with the pixies since they first fell out of the trees.

The Devil probably only talked to them when he said, 'Come on now, hop in the fire, don't mess me around, be a good Greenie, in you go.'

Cautiously, nervously, I looked above, half-expecting to see the ugly beast that had floated up from the depths of Hell to devour me. A prayer, that's what I needed. A prayer, just in case the Religious Ones were correct. I'd better hedge my bets. I'll shoot a quick prayer up to God, and he'll come save my arse. I delved deep into my memory banks as I tried to remember prayers from my time in church.

Dear God,
As I lay me down to sleep
To dream of cuddling a breast so fine
If you make my dream long enough
I'll cuddle the other one in time.

No, no, that wasn't right, that prayer was for something else. Gad oh gawd, come on God; give me a hand here! I don't want to be lunch for the monster. I then imagined the snarling and the gnashing of the monster's saliva-splashed teeth piercing my skin and tearing the flesh from my bones as it set about devouring the body of this great athlete with gusto. This didn't make sense; my body was still on the floor below, yet I was the grey mist. I looked down again; bloody Hell, I'm naked!

From the mist, I heard a voice again. Not the same monotone voice as before; this time it was a jovial, bouncy voice.

This is what the voice from the mist said: 'Hey numb nuts, up here!'

'Go away,' I screamed in terror. 'Go away, you talking monster creature gonna-eat-me-all-up thingy. I don't want to look at you, let alone talk to you.'

The voice replied, 'I'm not a monster, numb nuts. I'm going to help you.'

'Did my prayer work? God, is that you?' I timidly, nervously and hopefully asked.

'No, I'm not God. I'm Roger. I'm your Spirit Guide.'

Then I saw him, to my right and slightly above me. Roger was human in appearance, immersed in a glow of white light. He was wearing a white sheet.

Roger smiled as he floated down to me and said, 'Welcome. Welcome to death. You're gonna love it, man. It's a real hoot.'

Printed at chest level on Roger's sheet in bright red, were the words 'Spirit Guide'.

'Beware of the monster!' I called out. 'Or monsters; there might be more than one judging by the number of eyes I have seen.'

'There are no monsters up here, little dick. The lights are from the entrance to the *tunnel* to Heaven,' said Roger.

He was munching on a hamburger and carried an old battered suitcase which had seen better days. The sauce and juices from his hamburger had dripped onto his white sheet. He also carried a bell. Roger wasn't big; wasn't small either. Perhaps average height and build. He had short cropped black hair. On first impressions, he appeared to be in his late 20s, early 30s. His blue eyes seemed to dance as he spoke and portrayed a more mischievous side to their owner.

'So you're not God?' I stuttered.

'Nope, I merely work for the guy. It's his world; the rest of us are just living in it,' answered Roger. 'How's that "bring out your dead" bit? I call it my Spirit Guide sense of humour.'

I didn't call it anything, I was frightened and confused.

'Don't worry about the mist; on first appearances it looks ghoulish.

The mist is to *Heavenise* you; clears away the Earth bacteria,' mumbled Roger in between mouthfuls of his hamburger.

This can't be good; no way was this happening.

'I do so like my hamburgers,' Roger said as he licked his lips. 'Especially when the meat is juicy and tender so it melts right in your mouth. To be truthful, I have to level with you here; it's not so much the meat that makes the burger. It's the nutritious fresh salad on the top of the meat; this completes the burger. The aromas from a fresh salad smell are so delightful.'

Let's take stock. I winced as I thought of the rebounding strap-on. I fell backwards. I'm dead, well deadish, perhaps. I still haven't figured this one out yet. I have an alleged Spirit Guide talking to me about hamburgers. When I wake up, no one is going to believe me when I tell 'em about this dream.

Roger continued to consume his burger whilst informing me of more culinary delights that go towards a good burger.

'A good burger makes your tastebuds dance with delight and do cartwheels in your mouth. Your mouth waters and dribbles like the mouth of a hungry dog just before it's given a bowl of food. But, the salad is the one that allows the texture and the character of the ingredients to escape from between the two buns and right into your mouth. The sauce simply tops it all off. Not the meat as some people would have you ...'

'Roger!' I screamed. 'Enough of the hamburger lessons. I'm not caring for food right now. I need to know, what's happening to me? Am I dreaming?'

'Nope, from my point of view, you're pretty much dead,' replied Roger as he opened up his suitcase, placed the bell he was carrying inside it, and pulled out papers and a pen.

Roger, my Spirit Guide who eats hamburgers, told me that as I had died, I was now qualified for being dead. I was hanging around in the *'Waiting Zone'*, the hiatus between Earth and Heaven. Once Roger had completed the paper work and the mist had completed its job, I'd be engulfed in a white light, an aura he called it. Then, into the tunnel and off to Heaven we would go. The aura was to protect me until I reached Heaven. It sounded so simple. Dumbfounded, I looked on as Roger fumbled.

'Who fills out paperwork when they're dead?' I yelled. 'And, I don't believe in Heaven and Hell, so how can I be going to either of them, let alone Heaven?'

'I fill out the paperwork and you, as the applicant, sign to acknowledge I've answered the questions correctly on your behalf,' answered Roger. 'As far as Heaven and Hell go – best you start believing.'

Disbelieving, I looked on as Roger mumbled to himself as he commenced to fill out the paperwork.

'I never even went to church,' I blurted out.

'I know. They were fun mornings for you,' replied Roger with a wink and a chuckle.

'Did you know your name means disaster?' he asked with a grin.

'Yes, yes, I know!'

Reading the questions from his papers, Roger mumbled to himself, 'How did applicant die?' In the same breath, he answered while he wrote, 'The applicant stepped on his penis and fell backwards onto the pointy end of an iron.'

'Strap-on!' I hollered. 'I'm not so stupid as to step on my own dick; I was wearing a strap-on!'

Ignoring me, Roger continued. 'The applicant's religion is? The applicant is *not* religious, but he was baptised in a Baptist Church. That's all he needs.'

'The applicant's skill set is? The applicant's skills are limited to gambling, drinking and the purchasing of prostitutes.'

'What value can the applicant add to Heaven?'

It was here, at this very question, Roger paused, stopped writing, scratched his nose with one end of the pen, looked at me for a moment and continued mumbling as he wrote. 'Hard question to answer as the applicant probably can't add much value. But, we have to take him because of his Baptist baptism ... I don't make the rules!'

I interrupted. 'Roger, old chap. A question or two, please, if you have a moment.'

'Sure, fire away.'

'Roger, Rog, do you mind if I call you Rog? Listen, old mate, I missed something in the hullabaloo that's been occurring, which mostly involves me. Can you level with me, mate; who and what are you exactly? Why are you here? What is happening? What's with the applying stuff? Am I really going to meet my maker, or is this a dream that will end soon?'

Rog, my Spirit Guide, answered, 'Bloody Hell, man, you're dead! Get over it, you need to move on. Death happens every day. How many times do I have to tell you? No wonder your mother thought you were stupid. But at least you're not as stupid as *Wind*

Between Ears. You ortta hear what her Spirit Guide says about her. Dumber than dog shit she is.'

I could only fully endorse his comment.

'As you were baptised in a Baptist Church when a youngster, you qualify for Heaven. God's law is: *once* a Baptist always a Baptist. It doesn't matter to him if you're a practising Baptist or a non-practising one. God only discriminates against the other religions.'

'What garbage is this? God discriminates against the other religions!' I retorted.

'It's true,' replied Rog. 'God only allows the Baptists into Heaven; he frigging hates the other ones.'

'How's that work?' I asked.

'Someone will explain in due course,' answered Rog. 'I only do Spirit Guide stuff, the pick-ups, and the checklist.'

'Rog, let's just say, for the sake of argument, I do believe you, and you are my Spirit Guide. Speaking of which, if you're my Spirit Guide, why didn't you warn me about my impending death?'

'I could have warned you, I guess, but at the time I was in a long queue to buy a hamburger. I didn't want to lose my spot. I did get to you as quickly as possible.'

'But as a Spirit Guide, by definition, aren't you meant to guide me away from danger and death, possibly *spirit* me away?'

'Technically that's a maybe at the moment. Our Trade Union is looking into the issues around the whole death and Spirit Guide relationship thing.'

Astonished, I responded, 'What Spirit Guide is a member of a Trade Union?'

'We all are! Spirit Guides are members of the Spiritual Guide and Associated Death Trade Union, SGAD for short.'

'You serious?'

'Yep.'

'Unfreakingbelievable,' I muttered.

'The way it stands at present, we're not supposed to interfere in the 'dying come death' process. If God and his executive team want us to issue an early warning to people so as we can prevent their death, then God and his executive team are going to have to hit us up with a few extras.'

'Who would have thought?' I replied.

'Hence my *maybe* comment; sometimes we do; sometimes we don't. There's no official direction on it at the moment,' said Roger. Then he added, 'Righto, we 'bout done; we need to go.'

'No, we're not 'bout done!' I said as I raised my voice. 'I haven't finished!'

'Yes, I know,' smiled Roger. 'I did see Karen running out the door as I was waiting in the queue!'

'Everyone's a comedian,' I replied.

'Your questions will be answered soon enough. Here, sign this,' said Roger, as he handed me the checklist.

A moment later, a light descended from the tunnel and engulfed me. Roger gave me a gentle push and we both floated up to what was no monster, but instead, as reported by Roger, a tunnel entrance. Shortly, I was floating in a circle of lights beside Roger. I was naked. He was dressed in a sheet, carrying a suitcase containing a bell and paperwork for God. Soon, I thought, not long now, any moment now, the police will come and I will be arrested. The dim lights highlighting the entrance to the tunnel became bright. I found out later, the tunnel lights always dim when approaching a dead person in the Waiting Zone so as not to scare them.

I did mention on hearing this, 'It doesn't work.'

From below, the sounds of Mother's wailing drifted upwards: 'Oh woe is me and dear is me. Whatever will the neighbours think now he has gone and died on us? They will blame my cooking for sure, I know they will. Where's the telephone? I need to see how many people feel sorry for me.'

The *Whinging Aunt from Whining Hill* moaned, 'I don't know what you're complaining about. I have to do everything!'

I saw Father in my bedroom rifling through my contacts book in which I had rated the agencies I used. Father put the book in his pocket as he lifted up my mattress and removed the magazines.

Mother justified my death by saying, 'Any person who has sex in his parents' bed is not worth saving; he's lost to the Devil. I'll have to wash the sheets now. I know I should have got his father's gun and shot him years ago. The Adopted Ones never liked him, you know.'

Mother kicked my lifeless body, stormed out of her bedroom and headed towards the telephone. At the same time, Father left my bedroom with my contacts book and magazines.

Roger, watching the scene play out below, enquired as to whether the magazines were any good. I nodded and he shot downwards at the speed of light, returning moments later clutching a few. He opened up his suitcase, put the magazines in, and looked at me.

Then he burst out laughing. 'I nearly forgot; cover up, man.'

He handed me a white sheet. The sheet, as it turned out, was not a sheet. Instead, it was clothing apparel made of soft cloth, the likes I had never felt. I wrapped it around me and could not help but think my appearance was now more akin to one of a Greek philosopher, not the Adonis I assumed I was.

My sheet had the word 'Newbie' embossed on it. 'You look better when you have clothes on,' Roger declared, breaking my thoughts.

'You're not the first person to have said that,' I replied.

Roger gave me a smile and told me the word 'Newbie' stood for New Arrival to Heaven. He gave me a pat on the head and let me know he'd catch me in Heaven; others were going to look after me now. Then he was gone, up the tunnel. And then it was just me, standing in a circle of bright lights, wearing a sheet.

'This cannot be normal behaviour!' I shouted after him. 'I am so going to jail when they arrest me.'

Let Us Pray

Yo God, God I say
I hear you're the man
Your boy has even been to the Promised Land
I hope you're true, and Heaven is as well
If it is and you be nice to me
I can hook you up with three
All you have to do is let me in
Then we can begin
Amen

The Prophecies of Chapter Three

→ No matter what your age, detention sucks.

→ If you die and you see a tunnel appear above you – surprise!

→ If you die and you don't see a tunnel appear above you – you're buggered.

→ If you get a heads up about dying, take a book with you. You could be hanging around for a while.

→ Yea, and a pair of sunglasses too. There are a lot of bright lights to contend with.

→ There should be a law against kicking dead bodies.

→ If you see the fuck-up fairy – run.

→ You're not lost to the Devil if you have sex in your parents' bed. But, it is best they don't find out.

→ Do not hide porn magazines under your mattress. Every father knows that one.

→ The way it stands now, Spirit Guides do not guide.

→ Love only hurts – when your parents come home early.

4

A short time after Roger, my Spirit Guide, who doesn't guide but does eat hamburgers, had left me standing in the entrance of the tunnel to Heaven, I heard another voice say, 'Welcome aboard the tunnel to the Kingdom of Heaven. I am the Golden Angel Jacquetta. We will be departing soon. Please sit and fasten your seat belt.'

Out of nowhere, a chair suddenly appeared in front of me. I know, you had to have been there. I looked for the owner of the voice. I couldn't see anyone.

'Please sit, we have to leave,' the same voice said again, more firmly.

I sat in the chair and tightened up the seat belt. The lights outside the tunnel disappeared. There were no lights inside. I was in total darkness and I was none too happy about it. I became aware of other presences floating around me. I felt as though I was in a coma, a conscious coma, if that's possible. They poked and prodded, and a few touched my sculptured left calf muscle. I tried to respond, but I couldn't.

Someone said, 'Will you get a look at the size of that? This boy can't be human – he's more beast.'

Someone else commented, 'Nah he's wearing a strap-on. Take it off.'

They drew straws to see who would take it off. Once my strap-on had been removed, another presence suggested I wear a strap-on for a reason. They all laughed. They laughed again when it was mentioned my name means disaster.

If this was the flight crew to Heaven then they needed to readjust their manners. Luckily for them I can't get out of this chair, otherwise I'd give them what for. I won my last fight by 200 metres. As if one switch had turned off and another turned on I suddenly felt calm, relaxed. I was surrounded by beautiful presences in a place where tranquillity, peace and happiness had collided together and engulfed me. The sounds of soft harp music playing in the background soon had me asleep.

I had no idea how long I had slept, but I do remember waking to music from 'Dancing with the Stars'. The darkness had disappeared, replaced by a faint glow existing throughout the inside of the tunnel. From what I could observe around me, which wasn't much, I appeared to be the only person travelling. I saw a strange message scribbled on the ceiling of the tunnel. It read, 'Bring your own linen'.

My body started to change. The flowing locks I had religiously streaked with grey dye each morning were turning black. No longer would women be able to call me the Silver Fox. Come to think of it, they never called me anything; they never called. I had to do the calling. My stomach became trim and taut, I felt muscles, which had long gone to sleep, begin to awaken. Some muscles I had forgotten I owned, emerged from their hiding place. Oddly, there was no change to my sculptured left calf muscle, developed enough, I guess.

I took stock of my situation again. According to Roger, my Spirit Guide, who in the main was useless to me, I was dead and going to Heaven because I was baptised as a Baptist. This is despite the church expelling me many years prior. Throw into the mix I'm a non-believer, and you have to agree, my résumé for getting into Heaven wasn't strong. But what if Roger was correct in everything he said to me. On the off chance God was real, what did he look like? More to the point, who was God? What was Heaven like? Did it have racetracks? Did it have Agencies? I searched for signs on the tunnel walls to inform that angels really did *do* it better.

As if by magic, she appeared before me carrying a tray of drinks and food. This was no ordinary flight attendant; this was an angel of magnificent beauty. I knew she was an angel because she'd introduced herself as the Golden Angel Jacquetta. She was stunning, as if a child of God or someone from the Heavens. In another time and place, my wee-wee might have gone all hard. She was hot. On her sheet was embossed the words 'Golden Angel Jacquetta'.

'How are you travelling?' she enquired.

'I'm travelling pretty well!' I answered. 'I must compliment you on your wings; they're so golden and most spectacular.'

'Thank you,' she smiled as she offered me something from the tray.

'How soon until we arrive in Heaven? That is where we are going, right?' I asked.

'It won't be long, and yes, Heaven is our destination,' the Golden Angel Jacquetta answered.

'What's the go with Heaven? Why is it only Baptists are allowed to enter, or was my Spirit Guide pulling my leg?' I enquired.

'No, he wasn't pulling your leg,' the Golden Angel Jacquetta smiled.

'Only the Baptists are granted entry into Heaven because we are the Chosen Ones.'

Baffled, I asked, 'How's that work?'

'You'll find out soon enough,' she replied.

'So I keep getting told.'

Desperate to engage her in conversation, I continued to make small talk. She was mysterious and evasive in her answering, as when I enquired if she was married or dating; she half-smiled and ignored me. I repeated my question. This time she was more forthright in her answer. She told me to mind my business, and with no half-smile. An agency man myself, to be confronted by this hard-to-get attitude was something new. The Golden Angel Jacquetta sat opposite me in a chair, which as per the last one, just appeared. For a fleeting moment, ever so briefly, I thought I might have weakened her rock-solid defences and in doing so, dealt her harsh 'don't-mess-with-me attitude', a lesson. But, it was not to be. Once she had rearranged the food and drinks on the tray, she stood up and, without a word, floated back in the direction she had come.

'Will I see you again?' I called out. But, she didn't hear me, as she didn't respond.

I was tempted to scream out, 'Can you take off your top?' But given she didn't hear my previous question, I doubt she would have heard this one. Hence I sat, and wondered, imagined if you like, what it would be like. We men are prone to do at times, you know. My wondering only stopped when my thoughts were interrupted by someone instructing me to remove my seat belt and stand upright. I would automatically float out of the tunnel. I did as instructed and bang, I hit a wall with one heck of a thump.

The same voice apologetically said, 'Bugger! Sorry about that!'

I picked myself up to discover I was standing near a gate, a small, grey gate, which was part of a grey wall. In days long past, the wall and the gate might have been white, but not now. All of it needed a decent scrub. The wall stretched upwards and lengthways. I couldn't figure out where it finished or even started. No way in this world, or any other, these could be the Pearly Gates. If they were, there was nothing pearly about them.

'Are you all right?' enquired the Golden Angel Jacquetta, who reappeared near me. 'We need to get the tunnel ejection process fixed, and the pilot is new.'

I nodded in agreement.

'Ring the bell and someone will come and escort you inside,' she said.

'Can you escort me inside?' I asked hopefully.

'No, I can't,' she replied, ever so politely.

'Any chance of your phone number then?' I asked, ever so hopefully.

'No, not really, none,' she answered, and she floated towards another gateway located under a neon flashing sign that read: 'Accepted and Approved Residents Only'.

'Perhaps we can catch up for a drink sometime?' I asked, being really hopeful now.

'One day, perhaps,' replied the Golden Angel Jacquetta, without turning back.

Ahh, hope is restored.

'Are you serious?' I hollered after her.

'Yes, yes, perhaps one day, maybe, who knows, if I'm not busy, I'll see,' she answered impatiently over her shoulder.

'No, not that,' I yelled. 'The drinking bit! I can drink up here?'

The Golden Angel Jacquetta turned, gave me a short, piercing stare, didn't answer me, turned again and floated through her gateway with a shake of her head.

Roger popped up and frightened the living crapper out of me. He was carrying a sign and a hammer. He commenced to bang the sign into the edge of the cloud. The sign faced towards the grey wall and read, 'Steep Drop'. Whoa now; I was standing on a cloud! A freaking cloud! You cannot bang anything into a cloud, can you?

'Rog, old chap, another question if I may. What are we standing on? It looks as if it's a cloud, but it can't be, can it?'

Roger replied, 'Yep, sure is. But fear not, everything belonging to Heaven has a silver lining, otherwise Heaven and those who live up here would fall right through the clouds.'

I agreed – it made sense.

'The tunnel will disappear soon; stay away from the edge; it's one heck of a drop.'

Roger reminded me to ring the bell on the gate as he bid me farewell. He then disappeared through the same entrance as the Golden Angel Jacquetta. Again, I was alone. Why is it when you die, you keep finding yourself alone? Given nothing was happening on the outskirts of Heaven, I went to seek out the inskirts. I found the button on the gate and pushed the bell whilst reading the sign beside it: 'At times, it can be busy up here. Therefore, on thy busiest days, please ringeth the belleth and waiteth thou turneth.'

Fuck that, I thought as I rang the bell again. It's not busy.

A voice on the other side answered my summoning bell. 'Who is it? Who is the impatient one?'

What a stupid question to ask. I've been killed by my parents, left hanging and scared witless in a place called the Waiting Zone, sent up a tunnel by a hamburger-loving Spirit Guide, ignored by a Golden Angel, spat out into a wall and now some knob on the other side of the wall wanted to know who I was!

I replied, 'You should know who I am. You're God!'

The voice replied, 'Idiot. No wonder you're dead! I'm not God, I'm John the Baptist.'

I noticed a spy hole in the gate, at chest height. I bent down and squinted though it. I couldn't identify an eye belonging to the voice on the other side, yet I could hear him talking to others.

'Where are you?' I asked.

'Right here,' John the Baptist answered.

'Where, I can't see you through this thing. Stand up straight, will you?'

The dirty grey gates opened inwards and allowed the sound of laughter to escape. A person wearing Ray Bans and a sheet similar to mine approached me. The dude was short, seriously short; he had a potbelly and his wild crop of hair looked as if it was trying to escape from his head. Behind him stood two huge angels dressed in spooky black sheets and helmets. Dead set, these blokes must have seen lots of milk, popping whatever and pumping all sorts of heavy weights to get to their size. They nodded at me and I returned the nod, noting nodding must be the universal form of greeting. Beyond them was a long cloud, going on forever by the looks. Its colour was the same as the wall and the gate.

One of the big lumps commented, 'Top joke that – about standing up. He was!'

The other lump said, 'Yeh, John Boy's so short, for exercise he crawls underneath snake's bellies.'

'Enough!' interrupted John the Baptist angrily.

He motioned to me to enter with a wave of his hand. The moment I took a step to walk through the opened gates, I was stopped; not stopped by the short one or the big boys, but by an invisible force. I could not move a fibre, let alone a muscle. Motionless, locked in place, unable to move, I heard a long beep.

'You can move now,' said John the Baptist.

The angels nodded at me again, said goodbye to John the Baptist, spread their enormous wings and flew off. Those two big boys were Guardian Angels; part of God's Police Force. Had I not been baptised in a Baptist church, an alarm would have sounded – a series of short beeps, instead of one long beep. Look out if that happens. The Steroid Heads will immediately grab you, take you back out the gates and throw you over the edge of the cloud with the silver lining. A straight free-fall to Hell. This is one of a number of security checks to ensure whoever comes through the gates is the real deal, a verified Baptist. It is also a check on the Spirit Guides to make sure they get things right in the Waiting Zone with the checklist.

John the Baptist approached me with a wine cask under one arm and two glasses in his hands. Embossed on his sheet were the words, 'John the Gate Keeper'. Later I learned most people have the word 'Heavenite' embossed on their sheets. This means they had successfully contributed to the 'Betterment of Heaven'. The exceptions to this rule were people who have a specific job. Everyone else, including me, had 'Newbie' embossed on their sheets.

'Congratulations on getting through the tunnel and the gates,' he mumbled in a way that implied he had seen it too many times to be interested anymore. 'As you've gathered, John the Baptist is my name; starting the Baptist religion is my fame. By the way your aura is gone. No longer required, just in case you're worried. I know you bleeding heart Earth people are so precious with auras and the titles on your business cards.'

He suggested I call him John Boy, as everyone else did. I went to introduce myself but John Boy waved me away and said, 'I know who you are; you're on the manifesto. I have Roger's paperwork.'

'Who the Hell gives their child a name which means disaster?' he asked.

Before I could answer, he looked behind me and further asked, 'Did you bring your own linen?'

'No, I didn't realise I had to until I saw the sign,' I answered.

John Boy shook his head and muttered how things were so much easier in the old days.

'In the old days everyone travelled with a change of underwear and fresh linen. They listened to their grandparents.'

'You serious?' I remarked.

'No, not at all,' responded John Boy laughing. 'The sign is a joke. It's a good one, isn't it?' He poured me a glass of red and said, 'Follow me.'

Looking at how short John Boy was, and not to be outdone by his attempt at humour, I enquired of him, 'I'm guessing your Baptisms were done in shallow water, huh?'

'They were at that. How did you know?' he answered.

'Merely an observation,' I replied.

The mode of transport in Heaven is floating, as in you float. The further you lean forward, the faster you are propelled forward. The further you lean backwards the slower you go. Standing upright causes you to stop, to float in the one place.

'If this is Heaven, mate, it's a tad disappointing,' I said. 'There's not a lot here except a long cloud; there has to be more. Where did the Guardian Angels fly to? Where are we going? Will I get to meet God and his lad, and why do only Baptists get into Heaven?'

John Boy told me to be patient as he waved away my questions. He put the headphones of his iPod into his ears and signalled for me to follow him. I followed, drink in hand. Every so often, I caught sight of Guardian Angels flying above us, sometimes in pairs, sometimes in groups of four. They were patrolling the skies, making sure the perimeter was secure and no one from any other religion, apart from Baptist, had discovered a way to breach the tunnel, the wall or the gates. We continued floating. John Boy was more interested in listening to his iPod than talking to me.

Eventually we ascended and I bore witness to a most incredible sight. Compared to what I was now seeing, John Boy and I had been travelling on a dry and dusty road through a parched barren countryside. The oasis of the Pearly Gates stood before us. No mistake, the real ones: huge, shiny and totally spectacular. A waterfall of shimmering gold ran down all twelve gates. Each gate was made from one large pearl. Underneath the gold waterfall was the glitter of precious stones.

The family crest of 'God the Almighty' adorned the top of the gates. It was a simple crest: God sitting on his throne, looking very much the benevolent ruler, and the motto, 'We're no fools – the Baptists Rule', was inscribed underneath.

As we approached, trumpets pierced the air, the Pearly Gates opened and in front of me lay Heaven in all of its splendour and glory. For a man who never believed, I have to tell you, I was beginning to have a change of mind. The evidence before me was compelling.

'What a marvel, a phenomenon, a paradise, a Godadise,' I hollered to John Boy.

Angels on either side of the gates blew trumpets and played harps to herald our arrival.

John Boy pointed to his ears as if to say, 'Now you know why I wear headphones.'

A single angel broke into song:

> *Hark, the Herald angel sings*
> *Glory to him*
> *It's grand he's one of us*
> *And not one of those religious other things*
> *Otherwise, I wouldn't get the chance*
> *To have a sing*

As we floated through the enormous gates, I immediately noticed the streets were made of gold. Yet no one used them as everyone floated. I saw a sign saying, 'Welcome to Kingdom Come'. I wondered why they never finished the sentence. It doesn't sound right, does it? Kingdom Come. But from whence does it come?

The aroma of herbs, mixed with the scent of fruits like oranges, apples, lemons and mangoes, struck me. There was also a plethora of other smells, new to my senses. Together, they gave off a wonderful perfume fragrance. White fluffy clouds, big and small, square and rectangular, were everywhere. Happiness resonated; people were floating, playing games and relaxing. The sound of crashing waves on a beach was audible. In the distance, I could make out the bluish tinge of mountain ranges.

Around me and below me, there were lakes and streams, with water cascading over more precious stones. Some waterfalls generated their own splendid rainbows in colours I had never seen.

The grass beneath me looked lush and deep green and there were lots of trees, shrubs, and colourful flowers spreading out as far as I could see. The sky above and in between the clouds was deep blue. I remember thinking if this was the Kingdom of Heaven, don't change the decor; I love it just the way it is!

The further we travelled inside Heaven, the duller became the sounds of the trumpets, harps and singing from the Pearly Gates. John Boy took out his iPod headphones and explained to me that people lived in some clouds and socialised in others. Other clouds were set aside for Heaven administration. John Boy informed me we couldn't hang around too long as I was booked in to see God. The surprise must have shown all over my face as he added quickly it was no biggie, meeting God. God met every new arrival. John Boy made it sound rather boring.

'Always bloody God this, bloody God that! I got so fed up with all the crap I became an atheist,' uttered John Boy despairingly.

'Whoa now, Captain of Baptisms,' I uttered, alarmed. 'Atheist? Not possible! You're here with God and his boy and angels and clouds and the Pearly Gates and stuff. You can't be an atheist; it doesn't fit the business model for Heaven.'

'It's a complicated story,' he replied.

John Boy, the short one, the atheist, proceeded to tell me he was an atheist because he felt as if he had not received enough special acknowledgement for being the first ever Baptist.

'Jesus was not a Baptist until I bloody well messed with him in the water.'

Valid point, I thought. John the Baptist did baptise Jesus in the Jordan River. This by rights has to make him, John Boy, the first Baptist, and Jesus the second one.

'Mr Fancy Sandals Jesus gets the credit all the time for everything because he's the son of God,' said John Boy sarcastically. 'Me, I am just a lonely gate keeper who threw the King of the Jews into the water and baptised him. To appease me they named a religion after me. Apart from that, I hardly rate a mention; no holidays named in my honour, no prayers prayed to me, no hymns sung about me. Jesus gets everything. King of the Jews, my arse.

When he came out of the water he was spluttering, crying and carrying on, as does a little child who can't get its own way. He's a self-proclaimed King! I gave him everything, I made him, and I never even received a thank-you. You'll become famous, I was told. Famous, my arse; all I got out of the religion deal was a piddling disciple appointment, which I had to beg to get. A job for life he told me, and what a job it is, being a freaking gate keeper for his old man!'

I had to agree with John Boy again. The points he raised appeared fair and valid.

'I should have been the person in charge of the Baptist religion. I should have been the *superstar* with my name in lights and people singing their praises to me.'

'Don't be so hard on yourself,' I said. 'Look at it this way; you have to be the first atheist to exist in Heaven! That's no small feat. Kudos to you for pulling it off, mate.'

John Boy stopped. 'You're right!' he said excitedly. 'I am at that! I am the first atheist in Heaven – way to go!'

Many people passed and greeted us with the friendliness Heaven is renowned for. They all appeared to be quite young, even John Boy himself looked young. Short, yes, in need of weight control measures, yes, but young looking all the same.

I asked him, 'Why is it so?'

'In Heaven, everyone is thirty,' John Boy answered. 'In the tunnel your body is rejuvenated back to when you were aged thirty. The cloth you're wearing helps. If you die younger than thirty your body is aged to thirty. The process is completed once you enter through the grey gates.'

'What, me as well? I'm thirty again?' I asked.

'Yes, you are,' replied John Boy.

John Boy floated downwards and I followed him. We stopped above a pond and I saw my reflection. Bloody Hell, I looked so young.

'How is it so?' I asked.

'It is so, because it is the way of Heaven.'

Let Us Pray

....

Hey Big Fella
Are you the man
The one from up above
The one who only knows of love
If that's true
Then reading your Bible is not for you
It's full of people being killed
That's no thrill
Amen

The Prophecies of Chapter Four

→ To die as a non-practising Baptist and still manage to gain access to Heaven is one of life's more impressive feats.

→ Led Zeppelin got it wrong; there is no Stairway to Heaven. It's a tunnel.

→ Don't mess with the Guardian Angels.

→ It doesn't appear you can mess with Golden Angels either.

→ If you're pre-warned you're going to die, and you are a practising or non-practising Baptist, pack a stubby cooler.

→ Karen, if you're reading this book, I'm now thirty, trim and taut and I can see my penis.

5

John Boy eventually managed to stop me from admiring my youthful looks in the pond. After all, if one has a meeting with God, it's best not to be late, especially on your first day. As we floated off to catch up with the 'main man of the land' I noticed clouds housing Baptists, fellow non-practising Baptists and places of work and play. All work done in Heaven is a part of God's 'Betterment of Heaven' program. Mind you, you only work if you want to – you can do nothing if you wish. I felt I was most qualified at the 'nothing' one.

I saw a hospital, medical research centre and a multitude of laboratories where specialist doctors and scientists, who had died on Earth as Baptists, could continue their work, if they wished.

I asked, 'Why hospitals in Heaven? Nobody is meant to get sick here, are they?'

John Boy informed me the people who worked in these places, worked on projects for God. God had to defend the Heavens, the Earth and the other planets against the Devil. Hence, he needed to make sure his defensive capabilities such as anti-plague medication, fire-retardants, anti-hot fork spray and his Police Force of highly trained and well-equipped Guardian Angels were up to standard to meet such threats.

'Wow, he seems to have his bases covered,' I said.

'He has to,' replied John Boy as he pointed to a massive white cloud up ahead, 'The Devil can strike at any time with anything. God has to be prepared to save the Baptists.'

'And the others?' I asked, 'The non-Baptists on Earth? What happens to them?'

John Boy shrugged his shoulders and said, 'I guess they can

put their heads between their legs and kiss their butts goodbye. God only loves the Baptists.'

We came upon the House of God. A man and a woman were sitting on the deck surrounding this large cloud. They both recognised John Boy and greeted him warmly. John Boy introduced them as Mary, the mother of Jesus, and her husband Joseph. Didn't that just blow me away?

Upon ushering us into a couple of deck chairs, Mary ambled inside to inform God I had arrived. A short time later, she returned with refreshments and told me God would see me soon. I settled back and waited. Mary made small talk and mentioned God was not in the best of moods today. He had a backlog of work to get through; he'd caught Joseph in the kitchen again playing with his donkey, and God's haemorrhoids were giving him grief. I immediately cast my mind back to the biblical story contained at Genesis 19:23 – 25. God freaked out and destroyed the twin cities of Sodom and Gomorrah. The story illustrates what a powerful skill set God has, and how upset the boy can get. Not the kind of person you want to meet when he's having a bad day. I offered to pop back later, but Mary insisted I stay.

'He'll be OK, eventually,' said Mary. 'He works too hard. He probably needs a good hobby and other interests; he never takes a holiday, you know.'

John Boy and Joseph became engrossed in a conversation on how the Roman Empire spectacularly fell and Mary and I idly chatted away. The view from the deck of the House of God was spectacular. God's House was the highest cloud in Heaven. Sitting on the deck and drinking a cool drink was the first opportunity I'd had since Roger picked me up, and sent me tunnel bound, to reflect and appreciate what had happened to me. I took a deep breath and sighed; it had been one heck of a day. One moment I was jumping Karen's bones and the next, I was meeting God. Bloody Hell, now I felt nervous. Mary, no doubt understanding my predicament, tried to ease my fears by pointing out various landmarks.

She was a plump woman, who dressed modestly for the mother

of the Son of God, reassuring in her manner and possessing the grandmotherly charm of one who fussed over little things to make sure everything was as it should be. Joseph was taller than Mary, and slimmer. In the few words I had with him, I worked out he liked donkeys, but not Romans.

The longer I waited, the more I wondered about the goings on inside the House of God. Mary, her husband Joseph, and God, all lived together in the same abode. Interesting, to say the least. Kicking back on the deck, I did begin to wonder who the real father of Jesus was. Was it God or Joseph; surely, not the two. Perhaps God and Joseph *both* accepted responsibility for the kid. If Jesus had two fathers, he'd be able play one off against the other to gain the best deal.

Given his birthday falls on Christmas Day, I also wondered if he received two lots of presents from his dads: one lot for Christmas and another lot for his birthday. If I was Jesus and didn't receive two lots of presents, I'd be feeling ripped off. Like it's not his fault he was born on Christmas Day.

I did hope Jesus didn't receive a nickname like *Two-Dads* at school. Kids can be cruel. Come to think of it, did he go to school? There is no mention of him going to school in the Bible, but he must have gone to school. He was a carpenter. You *can't* be a qualified carpenter, and do carpentry stuff, unless you do an apprenticeship first. To get an apprenticeship, you must have some form of education. Carpenters aren't dummies. They have to know how to bang stuff loudly, very early in the morning, so as they can annoy every person who is trying to sleep. Carpenters also have to know how to yell out to their work mate, who is standing right beside them, just to wake up those people who didn't hear the banging. Too, carpenters must have some knowledge of how to drop stuff so it makes a loud noise, just to piss off any shift workers trying to get a bit of shut-eye in the surrounding suburbs. And, they have to learn how to swear and not read architects' plans.

The only place you can learn most of the skills required to be a carpenter is in the school playground. Besides, you can't have the King of the Jews being uneducated. I bet he went to a posh private school. With both his dads working, his family would have been able to afford the fees.

Later I would learn, the living arrangements involving God, Mary and Joseph were a wee bit uncomfortable at first, between the men of the household. The usual chest beating, sulking acts, my willy is bigger than yours, and 'I'm not going to talk to you again' type of stuff that us men do. Over time though, the relationship has worked itself out.

The only one who has a problem with two dads is Jesus. He has to get two Fathers' Day gifts each year.

Out of the Heavens, a great voice boomed, 'I'm ready.'

Oh bugger! Stone the crows, here I go.

'Follow me and come forth. Don't fall over or you may come fifth,' said Joseph as he burst out laughing.

I managed to force a smile as butterflies fluttered madly in my stomach. I'm sure my legs were shaking under my sheet. I followed Joseph inside and immediately noticed the inside of the House of God took on more of a labyrinth appearance. We floated through rooms, around corners, up corridors and into other hallways. Inside the House of God it was a mess. Various tools, paint cans and brushes were strewn about the place. In some hallways, a ladder was leaning against the wall. Other areas there was scaffolding still erected. Joseph told me God had nearly finished his renovations. God had been renovating since the beginning of time, but the end was in sight. Joseph ushered me into a room and told a man sitting behind a big timber desk I was here for my appointment. Joseph then left me.

The room I was standing in looked as if a bomb had gone *boom* in it. The place was messier than where the renovations were happening. The room would have been a spacious office if it had been tidy. Books lay in piles on the floor. Battered curtains hung haphazardly across a couple of windows. The faint whiff of stale cigar smoke lingered in the place. Papers were strewn about.

The person behind the desk was black; so black he appeared to be shining. He could have used one of his arms as a shaving mirror. He was wearing a stripy, coloured sheet, which looked more like pyjamas. He was wearing sunglasses, I kid you not. This dude was wearing sunglasses inside a cloud – where there is no sun. He reminded me of the wanker brigade on Earth who wear sunglasses inside shopping centres because it makes them look *cool*. He had long black hair which was gelled and in two long plaits, one falling across each shoulder. His hair was resplendent with yellow highlights. He had a grey patch of hair on the top of his head. It looked as if low flying seagull had crapped on it. He wore an earring in his left ear.

Here we go, another bloody yuppie wanker, I thought. Yuppies. They've been giving Earth the shits since the first one was born. They live their lives on credit. They wear the latest fashions in clothing, drive the fanciest cars, drink the most expensive wine and eat at the flashiest restaurants, all done to impress. Bloody yuppies, they can't go out their front doors unless they've had a bubble bath, spent three hours on their hair, and done their nails. They go to all this effort to try and outdo their friends. They think they're hipster-dufsters. Wouldn't be half a brain amongst them.

On Earth, I found most yuppies belonged to Happy Clapper Churches. Happy Clapper Churches have *also* been giving Earth the shits since the first one was established. Happy Clappers should just own up and admit they can't clap, can't sing, can't dance, and can't do any bloody thing! Truth be known, God probably hates them because they bothering him with their noise and singing and constant clapping out of tune. That, plus their stupid screaming *hallelujahs* would be enough to give anybody haemorrhoids.

I wondered if this was what sat behind a desk in front of me. A bloody yuppie. That's why he was ignoring me. I'm not good enough for Mr. Yuppie Wanker.

To break the silence, I said, 'Ur hum, I'm here to see God.'

'I know,' replied Yuppie Wonder without even granting me the courtesy of looking up from whatever he was reading. 'Pull up a pew.' A glow of light covered him. I thought this odd, as John

Boy told me you lost your aura of light as soon as you stepped through the grey gates. My aura had disappeared. Maybe yuppies kept their aura of light so everyone knew who the tossers and wankers were.

'Ur hum,' again. 'I'll just stand here and wait for God, shall I?' I asked.

'Stand, sit, jump, squat, lie down – who cares, do whatever,' answered Yuppie Wonder.

Arrogant shmuck, I thought. No wonder I used to try to run you pricks over on Earth. Bloody oxygen thieves.

'Didn't see the seagull?' I asked.

Mr. Shiny Black Yuppie Wonder ignored my question, which reinforced my already formed view. Arrogant schmuck.

I sat on a couch. In its younger days it may have been white but now it was more of a grey colour, similar to the gates and wall at the front of Heaven.

'This Heavens a bit of all right,' I said.

'Yes, it's a bit of all right,' Yuppie Wonder replied.

Trying to get a conversation happening with this bloke was like trying to change a baby's nappies when it first starts to eat solid food. There are some things that bring tears to your eyes. My anxiety had not abated and in times of nervousness, the mind can play funny tricks on you, Heavenised or not. Perhaps Yuppie Wonder was reading my church records and making notes for God, prior to our meeting. I hope he takes into account the church expelled me. Therefore, my record of non-attendance shouldn't be held against me. Maybe, he might take my expulsion as a black mark against me.

I pre-empted any questions concerning my church attendance by declaring, 'I didn't go to church much as I often fell sick on Sundays.'

'No, you didn't,' said Yuppie Wonder as he kept reading and making the odd note.

Bugger! God had a smart Personal Assistant Yuppie Wonder – I wasn't counting on that. A waste of my time talking to him; I'll put my case forward to God when I meet him. God, after all, was a person of compassion, love, peace and goodwill. I'll be fine if he's over his crankiness and in one of his let's-love-everybody moods. I'll make mention to God to get on the backside of this guy. His office was a disgrace. First impressions should be positive ones, right? Nothing positive about this mess or the Yuppie.

Seriously, his office was a fire risk. It was cluttered and had paperwork lying around in untidy piles. Against a wall were filing cabinets overflowing with stuff trying to escape. A computer sat against another wall and an old-looking whiteboard stood in a corner. It hadn't been vacuumed in years by the looks of the carpet. Untidy offices mean the people occupying them are unprofessional. Unprofessional people are not worth a cracker.

Yuppie Wonder turned off his desk lamp and the glow, which had surrounded him previously, disappeared.

At the same time he said, 'Right, I'm God. Welcome to Heaven.'

Of course you are, I thought. I knew that.

'A very busy-looking, but beautiful office you have,' I said.

'Yes, yes,' said God. 'Busy office, busy God. Always busy. Crap everywhere. I'd like to get Mary in here more often to clean the place. But it's hard. These liberated woman more or less tell you to *fuck off*, and you have to find time to do it yourself.'

God apologised for not standing. He said he couldn't as his haemorrhoids were playing up. He was sitting in a bucket of ice. I suggested there was no need to explain further. I had the picture.

For people who go to church and are religious, it would be *no* biggie to be sitting in a room with God. After all, is that not the aim of going to church and praying and placing your 'hard earned' in the collection plate – to ultimately end up sitting in a room with God? But, for a bloke who didn't believe, this was some biggie. I now realised the argument, 'there is no God', had become unwinnable. I became overwhelmed with religion, godliness too. Had I now become a believer? Had I finally seen the light? Am I changing my opinions? I think I am.

I stood up quickly, clapped my hands and yelled, 'I'm born again! Praise the Lord! Let's go and see your brother Hallelujah!

Sorry, I mean Hallelujah Brother. I'm a Jesus lover. Where's Jesus, I want to show him the love, I want to wash his feet or whatever it is I should be doing! I want to apply some ointment to his nail holes. He still got them?'

God got such a fright, he and his shiny black arse fell backwards out of the bucket of ice. He began screaming in pain and cursing the Devil. In two bounds, I moved from the spot where I had stood up, to be beside God. I yelled for Mary as I grabbed a folder off the floor and tried to scoop the ice back into the overturned bucket. He may well be God, but no way was I putting my hands into the mess that had exited his bucket. Mary came rushing in and took charge of the folder. We righted the Big Fella in the bucket and Mary gave him a stern lecture on proper sitting posture when your backside is in a bucket of ice. I suggested to God to listen to what Mary was telling him. It was important stuff.

'This correct posture thing when sitting is taking off on Earth,' I said. 'It keeps lots of OH & S people employed.'

God moved his butt around in the bucket and stared at me. I think he was in shock. Once the cooling effect began to numb his bum again, he half-smiled.

'You're not born again,' he finally said. 'How the bloody Hell can you be born again, you numbskull? Once a Baptist, always a Baptist, and I don't have a brother called Hallelujah. Now sit down, shut up, and let me focus on some pain relief!'

Remember my earlier reference to the sin cities of Sodomy and Gonorrhoea, the two cities thrashed by God. Let me add more to the story. God instructed Lot and his family not to look back as he went about nuking the two places. In Genesis 19:26 it tells us Lot's wife failed to heed God's good advice and she looked back. God freaked out and turned her into a pillar of salt.

'That'll teach the heathen bitch not to listen to me,' he roared. 'How dare she? I'm bloody God.'

The lesson I took from the story was this. If I ever met God, and he told me to do something, for example 'sit down and shut up', then I was going to do exactly what I was told; I didn't want to mess with his skill set on a good day or a bad day, or on any day.

When Mary left the room, God held up the magazines Roger had taken from my father, the ones that had originated from under my mattress, and said, 'Thank Heavens Mary didn't see these sitting on my desk; she would have kicked my arse big time, haemorrhoids or not.'

I burst out laughing; more so from the relief of discovering God had *not* been going through my church records. In fact, he could not give a toss about them. The notes he had made were website addresses he had discovered in a couple of the magazines.

Praise the Lord and hallelujah to somebody's brother!

God spoke; I listened. 'You're dead, so enjoy it, no sense stressing over the small stuff.'

During our brief, but enlightening, meet and grief, God put more flesh around his Betterment of Heaven program. He had developed this program eons ago, originally to appease dead Baptists who had spent most of their lives on Earth working. In the main, these people had chosen to spend the bulk of their time working instead of being with their family and friends. As such, they had limited social skills and very few interests outside of work. God's logic was if these people wanted to work in Heaven because they weren't skilled enough to enjoy the fruits of the afterlife, they might as well work at making a Heaven a better place.

Some of these unfortunates arrived in Heaven in a distressed state. They'd realised on death how much they'd missed out on by not having quality family time with their loved ones. They also realised their few friends weren't really friends, more like acquaintances. These acquaintances were only people they had met on their journey of life, who had stopped and swapped a yarn or two, before moving in a different direction. In many cases, these workaholics had foregone opportunities to be a part of their children's lives, instead opting for their own self-interests. Little wonder their children didn't know them. This is what happens to people whose priorities in life are wrong. I made it a practice on Earth to avoid people who were more interested in the daily task of making a living and earning a living instead of *living* a life. They were no fun. I for one had never supported giving too much of myself to work. I was more of a living kind of person.

I had never gone to a funeral on Earth, where someone from the company at which the deceased had worked, had stood up and said what a great bloke the deceased person happened to be. The people who did stand up, were the deceased person's family and friends. Truth be known, six months after you've left a job, no one remembers you, let alone what you ever did. Your family and your mates will always remember you, long after you become dearly departed. What does that tell you?

But, as the program for the workaholics had worked well, God decided to expand the program to allow anyone who thought they could offer something, anything at all to the Betterment of Heaven, a chance to do so. It was *not* compulsory.

New arrivals into the Kingdom of Heaven reside at the bottom of the Heavenly corporate ladder in the Newbie realm. A Newbie can stay in this realm forever and a day, it matters not. But, if the Newbie has an idea which assists with the Betterment of Heaven, and that idea is implemented and does make Heaven better, the Newbie will gain a promotion to Heavenite. As on Earth, some people in Heaven are big on status.

Status was something that never interested me. People, who are into the status thing, tend to be *up* themselves. This was never for me on Earth. I preferred to exist in a world full of mates and fun. In Heaven, if you achieve Heavenite status, you wear a sheet with *Heavenite* embossed on it in your favourite colour. So freaking what! If you were a bit of gun and you continued to have great ideas approved and implemented for the Betterment of Heaven, you gain promotion through to the other realms. Such as Prophet, Saint, Angel and finally, Archangel. Above the Archangels sits Jesus and finally God Almighty. Becoming an Archangel is the highest rank a Newbie can achieve in Heaven.

As God created the Heavens and the Earth, creating a small

committee called the 'Heavenly Spiritual Society' to support his betterment program was no biggie for him. The Heavenly Spiritual Society first approves your idea for making Heaven better. God is the Chairman of the Board and has the final approval for all Betterment Plans. Once you had an idea you wished to pursue, you informed the Heavenly Spiritual Society. They appoint a representative to meet with you and discuss the idea. If the representative believes your idea fitted the criteria for the Betterment of Heaven program, you then present your idea to a full meeting of the Board of the Heavenly Spiritual Society (God in attendance).

Should the Board approve your idea, a Spiritual Overseer is assigned to assist you. The Spiritual Overseer's role is to guide you through the process of bringing your idea to fruition. These good souls were tremendously gifted people. They had planned, project-managed and implemented every Heavenly project on time. They come from the planet, MyAnus. MyAnus is the sister planet to YourAnus. Both planets are part of the celestial body which orbits Heaven. Nobody gets to see MyAnus, but you can see YourAnus anytime.

If you have nothing to contribute to Heaven, you're not black-banned or thrown over the edge. You just don't get a sheet embossed with the word Heavenite. Once again, so what? I agreed the concept of contributing something to make Heaven a better place was good, but I didn't spend a great deal of time thinking about what I could offer. If it wasn't broken, why fix it? The Newbie lifestyle was 'cruisey' enough; why mess with something that's working fine? Besides, I still had my Workitis, and let's be honest, I had come to Heaven with a long history of never having had any ambition whatsoever. Now that I'm in paradise, why spoil it?

I did ask God why only the Baptists make it up here. But, he fobbed me off.

'I don't have time to fill you in on all that stuff,' said God. 'I have other appointments, more dead Baptists to interview, and my haemorrhoids are starting to be a pain in my arse again.'

He needed to have the ice in the bucket changed. God told me I could read all about the history of Heaven, and more, in the official records on Heaven, held in the *Heavenly Hall of Historical Facts*. These records informed the reader of the background of Heaven, creation, the interesting Periods of Accidental Evolution, Relativity and Natural Selection. The official records also explain why *only* the Baptists make it upstairs.

I told him I would take his advice (like who wouldn't) and with that, our time was up. I stopped at the door as I was leaving. I looked at God and said, 'A black God, who would have thought?'

'Yep, I'm a black man,' he said. 'Most people on Earth portray me as being a white honky. A white honky, who looks old, grand-fatherly, with long white hair and a white beard. Who said God has to be white? Black is beautiful, baby. We're so beautiful we shine. And, to prove I'm not a *racist*, I hooked up with a white woman. Ain't that something to rap and jive to?'

I guess it was.

Let Us Pray

....

Hey God, you old numb bum you
Sorry about the fright
I didn't mean to scare you none
I only wanted brownie points
I thought I may need a few
But if you say I don't
Then I won't
Pull that 'born again' rot no more
Amen

The Prophecies of Chapter Five

→ If you know when you are going to die, try to get a good night's sleep beforehand, especially if you're a Baptist. There's a shed load of information to take in on day one.

→ Don't scare people with all that 'Praise the Lord, Hallelujah Brother' stuff.

→ Never judge a cloud until you've been inside it.

→ Likewise, never judge a yuppie until you know him.

→ There is sufficient evidence to suggest if you piss off God, you could end up in a world of hurt.

→ Too much work, too little play makes for a crap life.

→ You can strain your eyes if you keep looking at YourAnus.

6

I took God's advice and spent many a day in the Heavenly Hall of Historical Facts trying to understand all there was to know about Heaven. I'd always had a keen interest in history, so reading and learning from a time long ago was a joy.

The Heavenly Hall of Historical Facts is the biggest library in the universe. It houses books of every size, shape and content. The most important book it houses is the *Chronicle of Heavenly Records*. God personally keeps this book updated. The Chronicle documents the entire history of Heaven and the planets, including Earth. And, it's not as if we've been led to believe on Earth.

For example, the first sentence in the Book of Genesis in the Bible states, 'In the beginning God created the Heaven and the Earth'. This is *partly* correct. God did not create Heaven. Heaven was already created. God was living in Heaven long before he went down the creation path for the rest of the universe. Besides, God's creation of the universe was more by accident and good luck than planning on his behalf. Following creation, evolution and population of the Earth by people naturally followed.

If God had not had his accident, there would no Earth, no universe, no humans, no animals, and no beer. According to the Bible, evolution was quick. From nothing to people in six days. The biblical stories of Genesis tell us God created the universe in five days. On the sixth day, he created Adam and Eve, and on the seventh day, he rested. This is *not* true.

This is what is written in the Chronicle of Heavenly Records. Once, Heaven was the only place in existence. There were no other planets, no suns, no moons and no stars. There was no other living thing in existence, only God. God used to get bored out of his brain on a regular basis. He developed fireworks to help ease his boredom, and often he engaged in some good old-fashioned fireworks displays. He found such activities *brightened* up his nights. He lit sparklers and waved them around. He'd also ignite other pyrotechnics, which lit up the sky around him. He'd have a wow of time watching the pretty flashes and vibrant colours exploding in the sky around him. One could say it was in Heaven that God saw the light.

God has no idea how it happened, but happen it did. One evening, whilst entertaining himself with a fireworks display, a spark got into the box of fireworks and it exploded with much noise.

God states in the Chronicle of Heavenly Records, 'The whole box went off with one heck of a *Big Bang*! It freaked me right out, near turned my skin pale. I could have ended up being a white honky.'

The Chronicles vividly described the deafening noise, the flashing lights and the ensuing mayhem. Acrid smoke blacked out the sky. The explosion from God's Big Bang sent bits and pieces of fireworks and Heaven flying in every direction. Many of the pieces hurtling out into space were on fire. Suddenly, the darkness in the nether regions gave way to the light of the many fires. God panicked and reacted by slamming on his fire hat, grabbing his hose and commencing to douse the flames, all the time saying, 'Oh bugger me, and bugger me again; this can't be good.'

In amongst the fires, the smoke, the debris, the water, and subsequent slush, God had an idea, which, unbeknown to him, would have ramifications for the entire universe. He decided not to quell *all* the fires, not to put them all out. He saw how the lights from the fires brightened the universe. Yes, God saw the light again, and it impressed him. He also enjoyed the warmth coming from the many fires, some he called suns, and he especially enjoyed the beauty of the stars and the shining moons. Long after the Big Bang occurred, the remnants of God's accident on that day can still be seen. Check out the Milky Way at night. That's not cloud you see, its fireworks' smoke residue.

The learned academics on Earth seemingly *agree* with the

Chronicle of Heavenly Records, as they too state the Big Bang was the *singular* cause for the creation of the universe. But, they fail to give God the credit for causing it, if only by accident. Our learned friends do however, correctly inform us the Earth was originally a planet of molten lava. But, they fail to identify it was only a planet of molten lava until God cooled the planet with water from his hose. Unbeknown to God, this act of cooling the planet with water, was the precursor of life on Earth.

Even dummies understand that if you have a puddle of water which doesn't evaporate, eventually stuff will grow in it. Stuff like mould and fungus. The bigger the puddle, the more stuff grows in it. You don't have to be an Oxford University Graduate to savvy this. Due to the water lying around from God's valiant firefighting duties, the Earth had many puddles. Some big, some large. Some puddles were as big as lakes and oceans. Other puddles joined themselves together and formed creeks and rivers. Where ever there was water, mould and fungus were soon to visit. From this, little organisms and molecule thingies began to grow. These little organisms and molecules grew and multiplied into other thingies, which inhabited the waterways. After many eons, a number of them that didn't like having web feet, moved out of the water and adapted to dry land.

They were ugly creepy crawly things. On land, they kept right on evolving until a few of them got it together and evolved into Adam and Eve. They too were ugly, so don't place too much credence on Genesis 1:27 where it states, 'God created Adam and Eve in his own likeness or image.'

No proof is required for the Period of Accidental Evolution, as it's written in the Chronicle of Heavenly Records as occurring, so it must be true. But, Charles Darwin did go some way to confirm it in his 1859 book called, *The Origin of Species by Means of Natural Selection, or the Preservation of Favoured Races in the Struggle for Life*. Darwin states in his book, originally, thingie things did grow in the water and eventually migrated to land. From this, life forms developed and evolved. Eventually, prancing through the forest, came man and woman.

With the arrival of Adam and Eve, the Earth entered a new period. In the Chronicle of Heavenly Records, this period is called the *Period of Relativity*. It is important *not* to confuse this period with Albert Einstein's theory of relativity. The two are different. One relates to population growth and the other relates to physics. It was during the Period of Relativity, the family tree belonging to Adam and Eve grew many branches, as the Earth became populated with more people.

I warn you now, some readers may find the Period of Relativity a tad yucky, unpleasant even, and somewhat hard to accept. Hard to fathom it is – there is even disgraceful behaviour – but accept we must. To be brutally honest, the Period of Relativity was deemed so disgusting, it is *not* spoken of in religious circles (apart from by the Catholics).

The Period of Relativity fully devotes itself to population growth. You don't have to be a Rhodes Scholar to understand the basic principle of population growth involves utilising the best practice methodology of throwing the leg, humping the hubby, letting the ferret out for a run, jumping her bones, banging her like a dunny door in a cyclone, and so on. I'm sure you understand my point.

Genesis 1:28 in the Bible states, 'God said to Adam and Eve, "Have a lot of children. Fill the Earth with people."'

To put it bluntly, God wanted Adam and Eve to get down and get it on. Herein lies the inherent problem with population growth when it begins with only two people. The children of Adam and Eve also had to get along exceptionally well together... if you know what I mean.

Without getting into the sordid details, I will only mention that the Period of Relativity was essentially a period where teams of relatives, initially brothers and sisters, got it on and were at it day and night. To put it bluntly, and from what I've read, the Period of Relativity was all about rooting your relatives. The term *rellie rooting* was coined by some. A lot of it occurred. So much so, Adam renamed the Garden of Eden, Fornication Central. As time moved forward, Fornication Central became overcrowded.

This had good and bad points. The good point being, by having more people around, and in the one location, folks who didn't want to hook up with their brother or sister anymore, could now hook up with cousins, or Aunts or Uncles, as they were all relatives. Freedom of choice was as powerful back then as it is today. The bad point of having so many people involved in *rellie rooting* was the noise levels.

Over time, Adam had become old and cranky and set in his ways. He became annoyed with the constant noises of huffing, grunting, and puffing. The screams of people enjoying themselves began to bug him.

'My goodness, you're a great brother!'

'Did the Earth move for you, Sis?'

'Ahh man, who's your daddy, who's your daddy?'

'Come on Aunty, one more time before Uncle gets home!'

All of this served to irritate Adam more with each passing day and night. Eve was OK with everything. She mostly sat around, watched, made cups of tea for everyone, and offered fruit and encouragement.

'Go on, Son, give her another one!'

'Wow, you've done your entire family today; top effort, Tamar!'

'You did your grandmother? Wow! Brave man. She's been dead for five years. Remember it's better for population growth to *do* the living.'

Eve also chastised people who she thought were getting away from the principles of population growth.

'Oi you, Barabbas, put the duck back in the pond.'

'Jedoiada, I know you prefer goats, but for fuck's sake, boy, put it back in its pen and grab your niece. I want the goat for dinner.'

'Abel, is that your brother? You dirty mongrel! You just wait until your father wakes up, he's going to be pissed with you, boy. And, you'd better look out Cain doesn't kill you when he gets out of the stock you've got him in.'

'That is not your sister, Rueben, it's a pig. What is the matter with you, man? Oops, sorry, my mistake. Carry on.'

One day Adam spat the dummy big time. He told his large

extended family to bugger off and get the Hell out of Fornication Central and let him and Eve have some peace. Genesis 5:5 informs us Adam lived until he was 930 years of age. I imagine in the later years of your life, the last thing you want is a bunch of noisy great, great, great and so on grandchildren in their crappy, smelly nappies pulling on your hair and beard, and sticking their pooey fingers up your nose. After Adam's dummy spit, his extended family had a sulk, packed up and moved away from Fornication Central. Finally, Adam had his peace. He renamed the place back to its original name of the Garden of Eden.

The Period of Relativity officially came to an end when Adam and Eve's, by now, very large family migrated to other areas. Though, in some countries, the family practice of rellie rooting is still followed. Too, in some of those countries, a goat or a sheep is regarded as family. In those countries, it's probably better not to eat meat. Just to be on the safe side, if you can see my point.

Let Us Pray

....

Hey God, you guru of accidents
If not for you
The Earth would never have been made
People never laid
I like your world; it's kinda neat
Sure beats being alone between the sheets
Amen

The Prophecies of Chapter Six

→ Be careful when playing with fireworks.

→ Be wary if your sister or your brother asks you away for a weekend.

→ Shagging your sister or brother may be against the law in some countries.

→ Prior to participation, check with your lawyer.

→ If either Adam or Eve, or both, had been gay, the world would not exist as we know it.

→ You weirdos, leave your goats alone.

→ Many people are glad the world has passed through the Period of Relativity. I've seen some of their sisters, bloody Hell!

→ Doing dead people is *so* wrong on so many fronts.

→ The term Hallelujah Brother may well have originated during the Period of Relativity.

7

There was something I was missing in my reading of the Chronicle of Heavenly Records. Something I didn't get. I may not be the brightest spark in the electricity station, but I knew something wasn't adding up. I sat at a large wooden table in the Heavenly Hall of Historical Facts, thinking, absorbing. In the Earthly Bible, there is no mention of the Period of Accidental Evolution or the Period of Relativity. But, both periods, according to the Chronicle and subsequent references, did occur. God made the entries in the Chronicle himself. So happen they did.

On Earth, religious people believe the Bible is the word of God. If we were to accept this as truth, the gospel truth even, then surely God would have mentioned the Periods of Accidental Evolution and Relativity. I believe it took around one thousand years to pull the Old Testament together, most of which was in the Hebrew language, though, a few chapters in the prophecies of Ezra and Daniel, and one verse in Jeremiah, were in a language called Aramaic. The New Testament was originally in the Greek language.

From the original writings, the Bible was translated into 2,300 different languages. Maybe the periods I refer to became lost in the translation process. Or, perhaps the translators missed those two periods on purpose. The translators may have decided the rellie rooting was a bit hard for the Religious Ones to come to grips with, to accept. Perhaps the translators thought comments such as, 'Take off your top, grandma,' were a bit crude for the Bible. Like, if you're trying to convince people to follow God, and the only reference you have to assist you is the Bible, then perhaps you fiddle with history a bit, not add everything in, to make the Bible appear to be nice and proper. A possibility perhaps.

In my opinion, the Periods of Accidental Evolution and Relativity were too significant to be lost in translation, or deliberately ignored. Without the Period of Accidental Evolution, there would have been no Period of Relativity and without rellie rooting, no family tree. People's family trees commenced with rellie rooting. I was beginning to have seeds of doubt about the authenticity of the Bible. Ringing in my ears was what the Religious Ones wholeheartedly believe, 'The Bible is the word of God.' If the Bible is the word of God, he would have made sure the translators entered the details of both periods. Otherwise he would have fired broken broom handles up their butts. He is God.

Another nagging thought was growing in my mind. There are so many different versions of the Bible getting about they can't all be the word of God. Back in my church days on Earth, I thought it odd for every religion to have its own version of the Bible. I read that this occurred because no two religions could agree on the biblical content, or the number of books the Bible should contain.

The first religion to accept the belief of 'the one God who lived in Heaven' was the religion of the Judeans, Judaism. Their Bible, the Jewish Bible, the first-ever Bible, contains twenty-four books. The Mormon Bible consists of sixty-five books. The Holy Qur'an (meaning recitation) has one hundred and fourteen chapters spread over thirty volumes. The Protestant Bible contains sixty-six books, and as per normal, the Catholics always have to go one better, they have seventy-three books in their Bible. I can only assume they required more books because the Roman Catholic Church had to explain why they think women are incompatible with the Christian faith and not allowed to be priests. Priestly ordination is reserved only for men. Most sexist of the Roman Catholic Church.

One of the reasons the Catholics cite for this ridiculous ruling is contained in 1 Corinthians 14: 34-35. It states in part,

'It is disgraceful for women to speak in church.' Sad but true. No wonder God doesn't allow the Catholics into Heaven. They discriminate against women, sexist pigs.

'You look lost,' said the Golden Angel Jacquetta as she floated past where I was sitting. I was most surprised to see her again and *this* time my wee-wee did go all hard.

'Yes,' I stuttered as I slapped it, and whispered, down boy.

'I see you're reading the Chronicle of Heavenly Records,' she said.

'Yes I am. I'm trying to get my head around all this Heaven stuff,' I answered.

'Which part?' she asked, as she sat opposite me and placed the books she was returning to the Heavenly Hall of Historical Facts on the table in front of her. I explained I was fine with the Periods of Accidental Evolution and Relativity. They made sense. I got those periods. But, I was struggling to understand how the Bible could be the word of God, and if it was, which Bible was the word of God? And, if the Bible was *not* the word of God, then who wrote it, and why. Surely, it wasn't written for mental stimulation.

'Impressive, Travesty, impressive indeed,' replied the Golden Angel Jacquetta. 'I didn't take you for a thinker when we first met.'

I smiled.

For the next hour or so, the lovely Golden Angel Jacquetta sat opposite me in the Heavenly Hall of Historical Facts and we discussed the Bible. Could it be, I suggested, the Bible was a disciplinary tool for children?

'Why do you think that?' the lovely Golden Angel Jacquetta asked.

'Well like, some parents could threaten their children by telling them to go and tidy up their rooms or God would send down a big flood to drown them. That's not thunder and lightning you can hear and see; that's God coming to get you for not doing your homework! Man, he's going to thump you big time!'

She smiled.

'Or how about God just called and said if you back answer me once more, I have to sacrifice your two kittens to appease him.'

She smiled.

What about, 'I couldn't care less if you're sick. I'm not Jesus and can't heal you. Get to bloody school!'

She smiled and made reference to the fact that I'd lost the plot well and truly.

The lovely Golden Angel Jacquetta did burst into loud laughter when I further suggested that just maybe, the authors of the Bible wanted a means to promote sexism, genocide and slavery.

By way of evidence, I presented to her 1 Timothy 2:12. It states a blatant case of sexism as it reads, 'Not to permit a woman to teach or to have authority over a man, she must be silent.'

'The writers of that were woman haters,' she said.

A frightening endorsement of genocide is contained at 1 Samuel 15:3 where God is alleged to have said, 'Go and attack the Amalekites! Destroy them and all their possessions. Do not have any pity. Kill their men, women, children and even their babies.'

'Sickos wrote that,' she said.

God's boy Jesus gets a jersey from the ancient writers for allegedly approving slavery and violence. At Luke 12:47 it states Jesus said, 'If servants are not ready or not willing to do what their master wants them to do, they will be beaten hard.'

'That's not true either,' she said. 'The Jesus I know is too soft to be recommending beating people up. He's like a big teddy bear.'

The lovely Golden Angel Jacquetta shook her head and told me, the Bible wasn't written for any of the reasons I'd mention.

She asked, 'Are you hungry?'

I nodded and she returned her books to the counter. Interestingly, the entire time the lovely Golden Angel Jacquetta and I had been conversing, my wee-wee had not retired. The thought of lunch had convinced me that it was not going to retire for some time.

I thought I heard my wee-wee say, 'Go on, ask her to take off her top. Like give us a gander at what she's got.'

I slapped it again, and whispered, 'Whoa now Captain Happy Face; you just bide your time and behave. This is no agency girl.'

We floated to a nearby café called the Yin & Yang Asian Cuisine Café. Over our lunch of sweet and sour prawns and steamed rice, all washed down with ample cups of green tea, this is what the lovely Golden Angel Jacquetta told me: 'The ancient writers of the Bible were *Boat People*, Roman Boat People to be precise, illegal asylum seekers to be more precise.'

'What?' I managed to say, 'How can it be? How did that happen?'

The lovely Golden Angel Jacquetta enlightened me, eased my anguish of not knowing, cured my curiosity and educated me as to *who* really wrote the Bible. It took her some time to explain, so much so, my wee-wee gave up, called me gay, and retired back to his usual sluggish self. This bit is going to rock your socks, blow your minds, and may even convince some of the Religious Ones to convert to atheism.

In the year 770 BC, entrepreneurial Romans decided to try their luck on 'easy street' by seeking *asylum* in Judea and living on the country's handouts. In their own country, Romans had to work for a living. They didn't like it. They had heard of an easier life in other countries, a life where living off that country's taxpayers, was a given. Instead of applying for immigration to another country as was normal, some Boat People decided to jump on a boat and sidestep the legal process of immigration. It is thought the Roman Boat People got the idea from a book they read about Noah. Early Boat People are believed to have worshipped Noah as the first ever boat person. Once the word got out about Judea having hopeless Border Security, Roman Boat People flooded into Judea. They eventually became Judea's biggest recipients of government financial grants, as this was how the Judean government rewarded queue jumpers. They arrived with nothing, and got a lot, for nothing. This practice by Boat People would continue until Judea had a change of government.

The Judean government at the time, the one which employed hopeless Border Security, had no money of their own, only taxpayers' money. Most taxpayers' money came from punishing the working class with shady taxes, disguised as really shady taxes and covered by the one Judean law which said, 'tax the people to the max.' Judean taxpayers were none too happy to see their taxpayer money spent on Boat People, and any money left, spent on the high salaries of politicians and their rorts.

The Judean government of the day hailed the new 'Give the Queue Jumping Boat People Everything They Want Policy', a huge success. And it was. Roman Boat People began flooding in. This policy worked in nicely with another one of their policies, called the 'Open Border Security Policy'. Meanwhile, the poor Judean people were scratching their heads and were left wondering why their government was so helpful to the Roman Boat People, but couldn't care less for some their own people who struggled to place three meals a day on the table, because of crippling taxation. Their own government ensured all Roman Boat People were housed and fed, but couldn't have cared less about Judeans who were homeless and hungry.

The Judean people told their government it wasn't fair, but the government told them to 'shut the bloody Hell up' and instead of complaining about having nothing, adopt a Roman boat person or two and try to borrow money from them. After all, if you can afford to pay for passage on a boat, you must be wealthy. Importantly for Roman Boat People, once they arrived, they were able to recoup all of their finances by way of free handouts offered by the government. Unbelievably, most Boat People couldn't speak the language of Judea, hence they couldn't get a job; so they spent their entire lives living on taxpayer-funded welfare.

The government of Judea said, 'Hey boaties, that's OK; we'll just continue to give you money until you die. This makes us look good in front of the United Nations Human Rights Committee (UNHCR). The UNHCR considered Boat People as very special. They didn't give a hoot about anyone else.

I couldn't believe what I was hearing. The Judean government bent over to ensure Boat People were given preference over the homeless, the veterans, and the disabled. They gave them free housing for life. Free furniture too. Judea ended up having entire suburbs of Boat People all living off the poor battling taxpayers.

The lovely Golden Angel Jacquetta continued. After many decades of living the high life, courtesy of Judean taxpayers' money, some Boat People came up with a plan to obtain even more money for doing very little. A number of them discovered if they claimed to be university lecturers, they could get large financial grants for something called *research*, as this is what university lecturers do; they make stuff up in the name of research and get money for it. Despite the very valid point that most Roman Boat People couldn't spell the word 'research', let alone pronounce it, the government was not deterred. Once again, the Judean taxpayers funded the research grants. On receiving the extra grants of money, the Boat People banded their money together, wrote stories, sticky taped them together and called their completed work a Bible.

I was like a stunned mullet. I sat at our lunch table in the swanky Yin & Yang Asian Cuisine Café in Heaven, with the lovely Golden Angel Jacquetta, unable to fully comprehend what I was hearing. Happy Face popped up again and asked if we were done talking. I dropped a plate on him, and he turned into sad face and was gone for the rest of the day. No doubt sulking.

'Bloody Hell,' I said, 'I guess that explains how the Bible had so many authors.'

Later, with the grant money left over from writing the Bible, the Roman Boat People bought land and houses in Judea, which they rented back to the original inhabitants, and then the Boat People spent the rest of their lives doing nothing, except for collecting benefit money, and rent money. Eventually, the Judean taxpayers ran out of money and the flow on effect was the Judean government also ran out of money. To solve the problem, the government gave Judea to the Boat People. By this stage, Boat People outnumbered the original Judean inhabitants and they owned most of the country. It wasn't too long before the Judean people became second-class citizens in their own country.

The Roman Boat People became very wealthy and bought up

all of the food in Judea. The Judean people had to beg for food in the streets. When they asked a wealthy Boat Person for a hand-out, they were told to, 'Piss off and eat from rubbish bins. If you don't like it, jump on a boat and go live elsewhere.'

The Judean people began to pray to their god, the one God in Heaven, for help. But as he never answered their prayers, they *forsook* him and either starved to death or ran into the pastures and ate grass with the cows. Sad, yes, as this can happen in any country, but at least I now knew who wrote the Bible and their reasons for doing so. Boat People wrote it, Roman Boat People wrote the Bible. They did so to con *more* money out of the Judean government by way of research grants. Eventually, Judea would have a change of government, and the Boat People would be stopped.

In between cups of green tea, the lovely Golden Angel Jacquetta and I continued to talk. Too soon, she had to leave. I thanked her for the benefit of her knowledge and watched as she floated away. As for me, I went back to the Heavenly Hall of Historical Facts to continue my own research. I did this research *without* a financial grant.

This day in the Heavenly Hall of Historical Facts was most fortunate for me. It was the beginning of many meetings and discussions with the lovely Golden Angel Jacquetta. She was a regular at the Heavenly Hall of Historical Facts as she was researching her family history. I don't believe she *received* a financial grant either.

Let Us Pray

Hey God, you listening to me
Thanks for sending the Boat People our way
It's not fair, mate
I can't claim social welfare payments in their land
But they can come to mine
And straightaway they can put out their hand
Yeh, mate, thanks a bloody lot
Amen

The Prophecies of Chapter Seven

→ Blame the Roman Boat People for everything; it's easier that way.

→ Despite what Jesus said at Luke 12:47, in some countries it may be against the law to beat your servants. Check with your legal adviser first.

→ Be nice to Boat People; one day they might own your country.

→ Your government would like you better, if you come from another country.

→ World leaders – ignore the lessons from 770 BC at your own peril.

→ If you are receiving government handouts, use them to your advantage. If in doubt, check with your local Boat Person representative.

→ Hard wee-wee can be embarrassing at times and annoying.

8

The Roman Boat People ruled Judea with an iron fist, oppressing and over-governing the underfed and poor Judean people. They introduced a Federal Government, State governments and Local Councils. These Roman Boat People politicians all lived off the gravy train courtesy of the Judean taxpayers. To pay for their reforms, (which were only for Boat People), they raised taxation levels (only for the Judeans), as this is what Boat People *do* in government. The Roman Boat People changed the laws and changed the religion of Judea. This too, is what Boat People do in government.

The Judeans had every right to feel as if they had been abandoned by God. The very people who began the religion of Judaism, the very people who began the belief in the one God in Heaven, now believed their God had forsaken them. Perhaps, there was no God in Heaven. The Judeans reasoned if there was a God in Heaven, he wouldn't have allowed so many Boat People to seek asylum in their country, and eventually take over the country, would he?

Eventually, the Judeans said 'bugger God in Heaven', and they began to worship the pagan gods the Boat People had brought with them. After all, the Boat People had been well looked after by their pagan gods; they now owned everything Judean. Unbeknown to the Judeans, God had not forsaken them; he was just busy. Once he caught up on his backlog of work, he checked in on his creations, the Earth and its people, to observe how both were developing. He was not happy with what he saw. He looked down and he saw sin, a lot of sin, and he didn't like it one bit. It wasn't the rellie rooting that bothered him. God was used to that; the Earth did have to populate. Besides, rellie rooting allowed

God to add to his home movie collection. The swingers' parties didn't bother him either. God understood ugly people had to get laid as well. The sins that made God's blood bubble towards boiling point was when he saw people worshipping not one god, but many gods; all false gods, all pagan gods. The people had become polytheistic heathen scumbags for they had forsaken him and forsooken him too. The people had a God for this and a God for that, a God for every bloody thing.

God's first thoughts were, 'Well now, this crap will never do! More than one God, and none of them me – what is this nonsense?'

God believed he should be shown respect and love for creating Earth and its people, even if by accident. The people should be showing him gratitude for him allowing them to fornicate amongst themselves. God thought he was a good God, an understanding God. So what if he never answered any prayers. Had he not ignored the brother and sister acts? Had he not cast a blind eye towards the brother and brother acts? Was he not impressed with the sister-to-sister acts? God appreciated the arts. Some sister-to-sister acts he applauded loudly and wolf whistled too. God appreciated the arts. He was a gracious God, and now he found the people have forsaken him for multi-god worshipping.

As the real God, he had a reputation to uphold. He should be the only god the people worshipped, not the wind, the rain, the sun, the moon, the stars, the trees, the harvests and figurines carved from wood and stone. The more God looked down, the more sin he saw. The more sin he saw, the more upset he became.

Most men do what, when they're upset? Take it from me, when men are upset they seek solace, compassion and understanding in the arms of a good woman – though, it can also be a bad one. To be honest, it doesn't really matter, so long as it's a woman. It needn't be one woman either. It can be two, or three, depending on how much solace, compassion and understanding is required. More than five, you're being greedy and should seek help from a counsellor. No one should ever get that upset.

God was no different when he was upset. He ventured forth

to seek solace, compassion and understanding in the arms of a woman. For the sake of the woman's privacy, and to protect her from the media, I shall call this woman 'Mary', as I feel Mary is a good name for a bit of fluff. God had himself a night of godly passion he did, a romp in the sack of mega proportions. Thunder crashed in the skies above, lightning cracked overhead, the Earth moved, and people wondered what the heck was happening. What was happening was Mary was appreciating godliness and she knew he was a good God in the sack, because she screamed louder than the sound of the thunder and lightning, 'Oooohhhhhh God, God, my God, good God.'

God woke up in the morning and Mary made him breakfast before he hightailed it back to Heaven. On leaving, God thanked Mary for helping him out; he also thanked Joseph for Mary, and then he did what most men do after a one-night stand – God did a runner. God arrived back on his home turf much happier, no longer upset, no longer requiring solace, compassion and understanding – for the time being at least.

With the cobwebs blown out of his system, God was able to think more clearly and come up a plan on how to deal with all the false god worshipping occurring on Earth. His new motto became, 'Revenge is the sweetest thing I'll ever taste.' It worked well with his other motto, 'Forgiveness is for the weak and soft cocks – I'm not either.'

The Big Fella believed those who worshipped false gods were not to be trusted, not fit to be fed. They had no loyalty, ethics or morals. The heathens were as soft as mashed potato and as weak as a bloke who couldn't piss straight into a light breeze. God was going to destroy them and their stupid gods.

Early one morning Mary called God in Heaven. She woke him up. But he was soon wide awake when she informed him she was pregnant.

'What, how did that happen?' asked a surprised God.

'If you don't know by now, then you're stupid,' answered Mary.

'How did you get my number?' God asked. 'I had it changed when I got back to Heaven.'

'A 'News of the World' Boat Person journalist gave it to me,' she said.

'They can do phone taps as well.'

God cursed the media, and reacted the same way most men would react when they're told by a woman who was the subject of a one-night stand with them, that they're pregnant. God told Mary birth control was not his responsibility, and as she was now pregnant and going to get fat, he certainly wasn't interested in her. He asked if Mary had a sister. Mary said no, and God hung up the phone. God didn't hear from Mary again. Well, not until she gave birth to a strapping lad in a stable in Bethlehem in the province of Judea.

After Mary gave birth, she called God again. 'Hey sugar daddy, you'd better pop back to Earth so as we can hook up for coffee and discuss names and child support payments.'

God replied, 'Pig's arse! I'm busy up here.'

Mary said, 'Then you'd better get unbusy, God boy, and get your butt down here, or I'll tell everyone you're lousy in the sack.'

God replied, 'Bloody Hell, woman, don't nag. You were a one-night stand! I'm not ready for commitment stuff. I'm God; I have to share the love.'

'You gotta pay child support, and fix up the bills from the stable,' said Mary.

'Be buggered I will!' replied God.

'If you don't pay up, I'll put your scrawny God arse in a Family Law Court and take you for everything.'

'Bloody Hell, woman, you cannot be serious!' replied God.

'Yep,' replied Mary.

'Jesus H Christ!' said God.

'OK, I like that name. That'll do for him,' said Mary. 'Now you and your pimply arse get down here so as we can discuss the monthly payments.'

God was probably thinking about what the bad publicity could do to him if he didn't pay Child Support. I bet he was also thinking Mary was turning into the most expensive one-night stand he had ever pulled. By all accounts, Joseph wasn't happy at first with Mary being pregnant. He did what most men would do in such a situation. He gave Mary the silent treatment for a while, and ran away with his donkey for a few days. But, once the child support payments commenced, he was OK.

Jesus H Christ was to grow up to become the apple of both his daddies' eyes. Unbeknown to him, he would also play an important role in God's master plan of squaring up with the false god-worshipping heathens.

Let Us Pray

Hey God
Oh joy oh joy
You've got yourself a little boy
You dirty bugger
Next time wear a rubber
Amen

The Prophecies of Chapter Eight

→ Remember, Boat People want to change the world – starting with yours.

→ When upset and seeking solace, compassion and understanding

→ – remember the limits. Don't be greedy.

→ If you're male, and you're about to engage in a one-night stand with a woman – wear a condom.

→ If you're male, and you're about to engage in a one-night stand with a woman, and she undresses, and *she* puts on a condom – guess what?

→ If you're going to mess with a woman, bear in mind she may mess with your bank account later.

→ Come to think of it, it's probably best not to give a one-night stand your real name, telephone number, or address. Better to play it safe.

→ When in doubt, blame the Boat People.

→ No matter how broke your government becomes, do not allow them to hand your country over to Boat People. It's not right.

→ Just because a woman starts screaming out, 'God, oh God,' during sex, does *not* mean you are him. Lose the attitude.

→ Asking a woman if she wishes to be the mother of your children, during sex can be a mood killer. Especially, if your kids are already teenagers.

9

G ranted, the Bible states Jesus is the Son of God and achieved many great things on Earth. But, Jesus did not achieve his greatness as the folklore in the Bible states. It is a mystery as to why the writers of the Bible even made Jesus the central figure in the New Testament. According to the Bible, Jesus was supposedly born in a stable of a virgin, and executed at the age of thirty-three for criminal behaviour. Surely, if your old man is God, you'd be born in five-star accommodation, or a private hospital, not a stable. Your health plan would be the best ever. You'd have all the extras. So why write he was born in a stable? And of a virgin, please!

In between his birth and his death, Jesus never travelled more than 150 kilometres from his birthplace and he never owned anything. He didn't write on paper or papyrus, instead he wrote in the sand. Jesus commanded no Army, yet the Bible states he was a King. A King of what, exactly? King of the Jews, some say. But the Jews, the Judeans, had sold their country out to Boat People. Therefore, Jesus was a King of squat. Jesus did no kingly type work. He preferred to hang out with a bunch of long-haired layabouts who spent their time bopping around the countryside trying to convince people he (Jesus) was a wonder-worker. You do not achieve greatness this way.

What the Bible fails to tell you is, because Jesus had two fathers, he grew into a spoilt, cheeky young man who thought he could get away with anything and everything.

'Give me an extra doughnut and the latest edition of the Judean 'Big Titties' magazine, or I'll get my dad to fire a couple of lightning bolts right up your arse, Mr. Shopkeeper.'

'Yes sir, Mr Jesus, sir, please take whatever you like. And my daughter is out the back as well, Mr Jesus sir.'

The Bible also wants us to believe Jesus was executed by way of a couple of good floggings dished out by the Roman Boat People, and finally put to death on the Cross. Let's think about this. The Bible states at John 3:16, 'For God so loved the world he gave his only begotten son...etc., etc., and etc.' And then what, we sent him back to Heaven all beat up and dead. If that occurred wouldn't God be a tad annoyed. God would have freaked out. He would have paid Earth a visit. Not a seeking compassion, solace and understanding type of visit either. God would have arrived with his kick-butt Police Force, and I'm telling you, there would have been none of that forgiveness stuff. He would have levelled the planet.

Jesus did achieve greatness, but not as the Bible states. Jesus achieved greatness by other means. As mentioned, the birth of Jesus gave God an idea. God decided to use Jesus to iden- tify those few who still worshipped him, the strong. He would reward these good people by allowing them to enter Kingdom of Heaven and have everlasting life. These people he called his *Chosen Ones*.

'I'll teach the heathen bastards now; I got me a plan I have,' he hollered from the Heavens.

Later in time, Matthew confirmed God did have a plan. He says at Matthew 5:5, 'Jesus said, blessed are the meek, for they shall inherit the Earth.'

'Let the meek and the weak inherit the Earth,' screamed God. 'The Greenies and their dumb-arse policies are going to screw the place up anyway. I only want the strong in Heaven.'

One evening, I told Happy Face to behave himself and I met up with the lovely Golden Angel Jacquetta for dinner. Over a meal of roast beef and baked vegetables washed down with a couple of glasses of fine red, she told me how Jesus had achieved his great- ness. Jesus had been badgered into completing an apprenticeship as a carpenter by Joseph, just in case one day he had to pay child support to someone. But, despite his trade qualifications, Jesus couldn't land a job. He always got fobbed off in his interviews, as the Boat People running Judea were racist.

'You're a bloody carpenter, man – we build brick places.'

'You've just completed your apprenticeship – we need more qualified people here.'

'You've just completed your apprenticeship – you're overqualified for this role.'

'You can build boats for us you say, why? We don't need them anymore; we've got your entire country!'

'Jesus Christ, man, only *one* of your fathers can vouch for you – you're telling me the other one lives in space. You're a right little Judean nutter, aren't you? Piss off.'

Little wonder Jesus became frustrated applying for jobs and being knocked back because he didn't have Boat People heritage. Jesus was discriminated against in his own country, as this is what Boat People do when they take over new lands. Jesus complained to the Judean Human Rights Commission, but the commissioners told him to bugger off as they were all Boat People.

Nobody knows what made Jesus snap around 30 AD. Perhaps it was because Mary and Joseph had decided to stop his pocket money as Jesus had reached thirty years of age. Jesus could have because God wouldn't help him get a job.

'You need to get a job based on your own merits, boy,' God preached. 'I can't be seen wiping your arse and blowing your nose. I expect my son to work. It'll teach you values and you'll learn to appreciate stuff. And yeah, always wear a condom, will you?'

Jesus pleaded, 'I'm trying here, but it's too hard; it's getting me down. I feel so bad, oh woe is me, and woe is me!'

'Then try harder,' God responded.

Mary would defend Jesus by making him a hot chocolate, rubbing his feet, and telling God to get off his case.

God replied, 'I'm the one paying child support here, woman. I want value for my money. Tell him to get a bloody job instead of hanging out with them long-haired layabout friends of his! They're no good, bloody louts, they are.'

The final straw came when Jesus went out one morning to buy a bladder of goat's milk, minus the goat, for Mary.

A Boat Person yelled out in broken Judean, 'How come one of your daddies lives in space; is it 'cause your mama's ugly?'

Jesus was under pressure from many quarters. He couldn't bag a job in carpentry, and so he decided he didn't want to work with wood, preferring instead flowers. He wanted to be a flower arranger, but Joseph would hear none of it. Jesus also had God on his back and Boat People insulting him; he'd had a gutful of the lot of them. Against his mother's wishes, Jesus at the tender age of thirty, ran away from home and kept right on running into the wilderness of Judea. This wilderness bordered the fresh-water Sea of Galilee.

Jesus ran through the bushes and scrubs of Tamarisk, the rhododendron, the Agnus Castus and the Apple of Sodom, all of which grew along the banks of the Jordan River, which ran into the Sea of Galilee. He stopped only to smell some bushes and wild flowers and occasionally hug a tree. Imagine Jesus's surprise and alarm when he was suddenly confronted and crash-tackled by the *Wildman of the Wilderness of Judea.*

Much had been written in the *Judean Times* about this short, smelly, pot-bellied, hideous-looking creature. Some believed he didn't exist and was merely an old wives' tale, a figment of people's imagination. People who swore they had seen him, described him as a food thief with a hairy back. Others stated he wore a large nappy and was prone to jumping out of the bushes, picking his nose and flicking the contents at them. Witnesses who had seen the Wildman of the Wilderness in action, said he would rush out of the bushes whilst they were enjoying a picnic, take off his soiled nappy and throw it at them whilst swearing profusely. As they ran away, the Wildman would steal the food (the bits not soiled) and bolt back into the bushes. Sometimes, he left his business card behind. 'Yogi and Boo-Boo thank you.' In truth the Wildman of the Wilderness of Judea was nothing more than an unemployed Judean bum, who could no longer get welfare benefits under the new Boat People government. Welfare was only for Boat People.

When this law came into effect, Wildman spat it big time. He told the welfare people they should go back where they came from, and take their stupid girl's blouse religion with them. Deeply insulted, the welfare people shut the doors to their office, and went on strike for five weeks. Hence, no Boat People could receive their welfare entitlements. As the death threats rolled in, Wildman headed to the forest to hide out. Apparently, he'd been there for ten years, prior to flower-sniffing Jesus bounding into shrubbery.

Worst of all, so the rumour goes, Wildman was once having sex in the forest, by himself, when the branch of a tree dropped on his head. When he awoke, Wildman believed he was a reincarnated greenie and this convinced him not to live amongst the people again. He wanted to hug trees, have sex alone, or with small animals that sometimes fell out of the trees when he hugged too hard.

One story about Wildman tells us the boat person Governor of Judea, Fat Boy Pontius Pinecone, and his family were picnicking in the woods. They laid down their nice picnic rug, placed their baskets down and went for a leisurely walk through the bushes. Unbeknown to them, as they walked, the Wildman struck. He stole their food and left filthy nappies over their picnic rugs, along with his business card. Governor Pinecone was pissed off to the max. He ordered the Military Legions of the Roman Boat People to go into the woods and kill every bear that ever was, especially those who had gathered there for a certain occasion, you know the teddy bears' picnic.

The Military bear hunt made it risky for Wildman to expose himself, so he hid. He had no access to food and this made him cranky. Fortunately, the Military never found the Wildman, or Yogi or Boo-Boo. They eventually gave up and returned to their barracks. Not long after this episode occurred, Jesus came running along a camel-track road wearing his backpack. The Wildman came screaming out of the bushes hitting Jesus hard, so hard he knocked the wind clean out of him. Wildman began screaming for food and trying to get into Jesus's backpack whilst

Jesus was lying on the ground, attempting to deep breathe and simultaneously scream his lungs out in sheer fright.

Wildman hollered at Jesus, 'Gimme your food before I thump you into next week! I haven't eaten for ages.'

Jesus spat back, 'Nick off hairy back, short arse!'

This comment riled up Wildman. He rubbed a soiled nappy into the face of Jesus, called him a shit head, and proceeded to kick the crap out of him. Weak from the pain of the beating, Jesus told Wildman he had no food left and even let him look inside his backpack. Wildman looked and saw no food. He started to jump up and down on Jesus in an attempt to force him to regurgitate his last meal.

Jesus managed to struggle to his feet by crawling between the legs of Wildman, grabbing a hand full of his dirty, sweaty back hair and pulling himself up. But, the Wildman proved to be a worthy opponent. Despite being weakened from no food, he was still strong; he bent over and Jesus rolled over him. As Jesus got to his feet to run, he slipped in a large pile of camel poo and fell over again.

Wildman leaped at Jesus who was trying to regain his footing in the slippery camel poo, and they both hit the ground together, rolling repeatedly down the embankment, through the thickets, prickly pear bushes and finally coming to rest with a splash, as they had both rolled into the Jordan River.

Wildman began to scream like a girl and yelled he was going to drown as he couldn't swim. Fright is a powerful ally; in times of fright people can do amazing things to survive. Whilst Wildman may have been in fright, so was Jesus. The difference being, Jesus was the Son of God. Jesus stood up, yelled to Wildman that now was probably a good time to learn to swim and with that, Jesus began to walk on the water towards the riverbank, towards freedom.

Wildman looked and said, 'How the bloody Hell can you do that?'

As Jesus approached the riverbank, he yelled, 'Look out for the piranhas!'

The Wildman of the Wilderness looked around nervously and promptly shat himself. Mistaking his turd for a piranha, the Wildman panicked and jumped up to discover the water was shallow. This changed the entire game plan for Jesus. Wildman chased after him again. Jesus was buggered from running and the beatings and therefore easy prey for Wildman, who caught him just as he reached the top of the riverbank. Down into the water they both rolled again.

Jesus managed to break free, and then he did it again. He walked on water; this time he walked to the middle of the river where the water was much deeper. He began poking faces at Wildman and calling him names.

Wildman got to the riverbank and threw stones at Jesus. Bruised and battered, Jesus surrendered. Both men, completely knackered from their physical endurance, collapsed and lay in the mud on the riverbank. They had no more energy. Strangely, a white seagull appeared above them. Wildman yelled at the bird to go away as he didn't have any hot chips to give it. But, the seagull spoke. This is what the seagull said as it fluttered above two grown men, one who had a hairy back, which glistened in the sun as it dried, and one who could walk on water.

The seagull said, 'Bugger me, Jesus. I've always told you to lead with your left when you're in a scrap.'

'I was trying,' replied Jesus. 'But I was weak from running.'

'Then stop bloody running and sulking and man up,' said God.

Wildman, startled by a talking seagull, began to throw stones at the bird and very nearly succeeded in hitting it. The seagull suddenly turned into a size 18 boot and kicked Wildman right up his Khyber Pass with a delivery so hard, Wildman ended up back in the river. Jesus burst out laughing as Wildman emerged from the water spluttering.

'Bloody Hell, I've been out here too long; I'm going loco,' said Wildman. 'I heard a talking bird, which turned into a boot and kicked me. You see that?'

Jesus replied, 'It's only one of my dads jerking around.'

Jesus now found himself in the river, also the recipient of a size 18 boot.

It was now Wildman's turn to laugh. From pain comes pleasure, and from pleasure can develop profound friendships built on nothing more than mutual understanding and the shared experience of a kick up the butt. Jesus and the Wildman of the Wilderness now had something in common. Both been kicked up the date by a hovering boot. This made them both feel happy, really happy.

They hugged and they danced on the banks of the Jordan River and smelled some flowers on a bush. They then threw off their muddy garments and *frolicked* together in the water in the nude.

God looked down through his bird eyes, shook his beak, and said, 'Bloody Hell, get a load of those two, will ya?'

They jumped around in the water and splashed each other and laughed, and showed each other their willies to see who had the biggest.

God, sitting in a tree, didn't know what to make of the carrying on, but at least they weren't fighting anymore. John the Baptist told Jesus he was happy to have found a friend as living alone in the wild can be a lonely experience. Jesus thought for a moment and informed John that the lonely bit probably came from being by yourself.

John nodded his head in amazement and said, 'You're such a deep lateral thinker, profound too, and smart as well.'

The two of them continued to Frolicin the Jordan River. Jesus and John even showed each other their bottoms to compare the red marks from the boot of God. At one stage, Jesus told John about his dad in Heaven.

John thought, 'Heck! I thought I was loco, but this Jesus bloke is messed up real bad, a right nutter he is!'

Jesus had an idea: 'Let's start a club for nude swimming in the Jordan River.'

Jesus and John the Baptist both agreed it would be fun to Frolicwith more like-minded people.

'We could charge a membership fee and make a lot of money,' suggested Jesus.

'We could have cafés selling coffee and buns and other stuff on the banks of the Jordan,' said John.

'And franchise the business further upstream and make more money,' said Jesus.

'And downstream as well,' said John.

'Picnic baskets. We could sell picnic baskets full of food,' said John.

Whatever God was thinking, he now stopped, as he suddenly had an idea so big it should have been photographed.

'Whoa now, you Captains of Industry,' said God. 'Let's have ourselves a little chat about this for a tad.'

John immediately thought, 'Woo bugger me, the talking seagull is back. I'd better sit back down; otherwise, the boot might kick my arse again.'

God said, 'I've got an idea that's better than all yours combined. We can pull a few loose ends together; I can help you and you can help me. Here's what I'm thinking. Seeing as you two get along so well, I want both of you to start a religion, a religion that will worship me as the *one* and *only* true God, because as it stands, I am.'

God explained to Jesus and John the Baptist that by starting a religion, they'd both have employment for life. Whoever heard of a minister of religion made redundant?

'I haven't,' answered Jesus.

'What's a minister of religion?' asked John the Baptist.

God informed them they could both become famous if they worked hard and the religion took off – far more famous than owning a few cafés. They could also combine their religious duties with their frolicking ways. This would enable them to meet many like-minded people. In return for forming a religion, God promised all who followed their religion a place in Heaven for eternity.

'Wow!' said John. 'What a hoot. Count me in. I don't care if I am agreeing with a seagull, but eternity sounds like a really long time.'

Jesus thought briefly and said, 'It must be one that can pull women.

We don't want to start one of those anti-women religions like them cursed Boat People.'

'I know!' said John, 'We could call our new religion the 'Loopy Ones who Frolic!'

'Loopy Ones, I don't like,' replied Jesus. 'It sounds like a breakfast cereal.'

God suggested they both put on their thinking caps and come up with a decent name for their new religious group. This name had to be different from the pagan religious names and false gods spreading across Judea.

'The 'Religion of the Frolickers' might work,' said Jesus. 'Or 'Frolicking Good Fun Religion', suggested John.

'For Pete's sake!' said God. 'Dead set, you two are brainless. The youth today baffles me. Listen up.'

On this day, as opposed to other days, on the banks of the Jordan River, God chaired his first religious conference. He was a seagull. The other attendees were both naked. The outcome of this conference had ramifications that resounded across the world because at this conference, the Baptist religion was born, so named to appease John the Baptist, as Jesus had won the leadership vote, two to one. After all, blood is thicker than water.

God gave the boys a pep talk as to what he expected from his new religion. In doing so, he wanted all new converts to the Baptist religion to follow a simple ritual, one easy to follow yet different from other known rituals practised by the pagans. The lads and God tossed around many ideas before deciding all new Baptists should be initiated into the faith by way of a Baptism. Baptism is the ancient Judean word for naked frolic. The boys thought this was good, as they had met in the water and had celebrated their friendship by having a Frolicwithout their clothes on. In some parts of the world, due to the shortage of water, the Frolicchanged to splashing a small amount of water on people's bodies.

On paper, God's plan was a masterstroke. He had his son installed as the head of the Baptist religion, and its followers, and only its followers, were allowed to enter Heaven. Those who wanted to live for eternity in Heaven had to toss aside their pagan beliefs for a new belief in the Baptists. It was the Baptists who commenced the belief of the one God who lived in Heaven, who had a son called Jesus, who became the Head Honcho of the Baptist religion, yada, yada, yada.

God finally had a method to square up with the multi-god worshipping heathens. This was his *Period of Natural Selection*. Once again, Charles Darwin mentioned *Natural Selection* in his great book. His view on Natural Selection is much supported by eminent scientists throughout the world. For reasons which I find difficult to understand, God received no credit for naturally selecting the Baptists as his Chosen Ones. This is despite Matty confirming for us, in the Bible at Matthew 28:19, that it was indeed the Baptist religion that became the preferred religion of God. It states: 'Jesus said to all of the disciples, go to the people of all nations and make them my disciples. Baptise them in the name of the Father, the Son and the Holy Spirit.'

It is important to note from this biblical text, Jesus said, *baptise*. Jesus did not say Catholicise or Happy Clapperise or Mormonise or Presbyterianise or Anglicanise or Lutheranise or Methodistise or Pasteurise or Homogenise or whatever other religionise there is or was. Jesus said *baptise*.

Let Us Pray

....

Oh great philosopher from above
Thank you for making us Baptists the Chosen Ones
A bloody Baptist through and through I am
I love sneaking up behind the Happy Clappers
And yelling Boo!
Amen

The Prophecies of Chapter Nine

→ Please note that the magazine titled, 'Judean Big Titties' is out of publication.

→ If you're Baptist, the evidence is irrefutable; you're going to Heaven.

→ The Baptists invented skinny-dipping.

→ To be a member of the Baptist religion is the most moving, thrilling, exciting... Aw, who am I trying to kid?

→ Never throw stones at birds; you just never know.

→ Not all short people have hairy backs.

→ When swimming, remember what you see may not be a turd; it could be a piranha. Either way, don't touch.

→ If you're *not* Baptist, then I'm guessing the last chapter didn't please you.

→ Before taking off your clothes in public to participate in the frolic, please check with your legal adviser first.

→ Personally, I love the Frolic.

10

Theologians, academics and followers of the ancient religious texts pay scant homage to the significant Period of Natural Selection in history. Long after Jesus had been baptised by way of the Frolic in the Jordon River, baptism is still the rite of admission into the Baptist Church. Interestingly, most religions today, especially the Christian ones, have copied the *baptism* as means of initiation into their church. They also copied the Baptist belief in the one God who lives in Heaven, who had a son called Jesus, who became the Head Honcho of Baptist religion, yada, yada, yada. God doesn't like the other religions. He calls them copy cats, dirty rats.

The Baptist religion was to spread rapidly throughout the land of Judea.

The Roman Boat People rulers saw this, and knew the Baptists must be onto something big, perhaps a new way to get more money. They rounded up Judean labourers from the cow paddocks and made them build bathhouses with heating for warm water, so they too could to participate in the Frolic. Unfortunately, they did not become Baptists. They enjoyed the naked Frolic so much they became gay. Hence, the Roman Boat People eventually died off and were replaced by other kinds of Boat People. Today, in parts of the world there are some ancient Roman bathhouses standing from this era. They stand to warn us – look out for Boat People. They ruin your country and they build shit to shag in – dirty Boat People.

The fame of Jesus spread throughout the land. The Judean people saw the error of their ways and began to throw away their statues of false gods. 'Having a Frolic and listening to a really smart guy banging on about his dad in Heaven, has to be better than praying to a dumb-arse statue that doesn't talk to anyone,' was one comment found inscribed in stone.

Jesus became a hit. He was in such demand he had to hire staff. He was busier than a Union leader's shredder prior to a corruption hearing. Jesus needed a wardrobe assistant to do his washing. When travelling on the road he required a sandal maker and the services of a full-time chef. Preaching at night, he required a candlestick maker. He employed a personal assistant to take care of the venues and bookings, and Jesus found that a hairdresser and a makeup artist came in handy. Jesus also hired two big, burly security men to be with him in the water when he was participating in the Frolic, as people kept trying to touch his willie. Finally, Jesus took on a public relations manager and a spin doctor. In total, Jesus had twelve employees, including his original frolicking friend, John the Baptist.

Jesus called his little gang, *disciples*. This was easier than having to remember their names. They travelled across the land preaching from the sides of hills, on the roads, in towns and anywhere else Jesus could muster a crowd close to water. Many people attended Jesus's sermons to see his tricks. On occasions he did so many tricks, he went overtime and had to order in fish and loaves of bread to feed the masses. This created a flow-on effect of more people giving up their beliefs in the false gods and signing on with the Baptist boy. The false gods couldn't make food fall from the sky.

'Oh, thy tricks are tricks of magnificence and wonder,' said one happy camper as Jesus signed autographs in the afternoon sun.

'You are truly an all-round family entertainer,' said another.

'Do you do children's parties?' yelled one woman.

Jesus looked at her for a moment, and replied, 'Go away, stupid woman! Every entertainer knows you never work with animals or children.'

Jesus preached about the evils of those who sought to imitate him and his religion. He instructed his followers to forsake those who copied.

'This guy is good,' someone said. 'He preaches, he frolics, he does tricks and now he forsakes! Jesus is truly gifted; he should turn professional.'

In another sermon, this one on a mount, Jesus warned again of those who sought to copy him.

'The unscrupulous dogs who copy from the Baptists and make up their own shadier-than-thou religions are without good deeds and only know sin. They will go to Hell for what they do!'

The people Jesus was referring to were those who took parts of his teachings and added to them their own ridiculous bits to make their religion and church more appealing and appear different. Most had copied a shortened version of the baptism, and the belief in the one God, as the foundation for their quick trick scheme. And that's all they were. Some religions introduced nonsense like having their church leaders dress in frocks and robes and funny hats. Some religious leaders carried rods or smoking canisters and expected large donations. Financial greed was perpetrated by those who sought for themselves, not the needy as Jesus preached.

Jesus was different. Jesus never charged for his preaching and his tricks. He was a man of honour and integrity. He never wore fancy robes or frocks to preach. He wore his day clothes. He never wore a tall hat that made him look stupid. When he preached, Jesus didn't carry a rod impersonating a court jester. Jesus did not employ any stupid rituals to go with his Ministry of Baptists such as walking among his flock waving a smoking canister. Jesus knew very well the dangers of passive inhaling. There was no music when Jesus preached.

'You can't preach to Dad if you've got music blaring away,' Jesus would say.

Annoying organ music was bad enough, but some copycat religions went so far as to introduce handclapping, which they tried to intertwine with pathetic attempts to dance while they screamed out for their lost brothers who were all named *Hallelujah*. Most of these people didn't even have a brother! They were making it up.

Instead, Jesus would thoughtfully advise his worshippers by

saying, 'If you do have a brother and he's lost, stop mucking around in church screaming for him. Get your arse out of church and go look for him.'

The crowds love him. His words are not only *truth*, but *common sense* as well. Wow, two for the price of nothing. And he's an honest leader, who would have thought that could happen. That's three for the price of nothing.

Jesus required no flashy church to spread his word. He was a nature lover and an outdoorsman and that's where he preached. Jesus rode around on a donkey named *Eeyore* who brayed *hee-haw*. He needed no flashy car with an expensive sound system in it. Jesus wasn't greedy. He never asked for donation money to fund his lifestyle. Jesus was different: he never took; he gave. Try attending a church service today and not stumping up the visit with cash. They won't want to know you the next time.

Time did what it always did; it moved forward. And over time, the copycat religions began to add more and more to what they had already copied from the Baptists. The Baptist religion was founded on simplicity, with its fundamentals not changing since its founding fathers, namely God, Jesus, and John the Baptist, invented it on the banks of the Jordan River. Over time, the copycats added so much rubbish to their religions they had become complicated. For example, where did the Catholics pull the confessional box from – Dr Who?

In the confessional box, you tell the priest of the sins you have supposedly committed, and he in turn instructs you on how to redeem yourself in the eyes of his God, which is not the real God. The Catholic God is vastly different from the Baptist God. The Baptists don't do the confessional box. Jesus didn't have a confessional box. Jesus and his disciples never told people to go into a confessional box and repent.

The Baptists first coined the phrase, 'What happens on the field, stays on the field.' In other words, if you've screwed up somewhere and made a mistake – why tell anyone? If no one finds out, good for you! Confessional boxes are for sinners. The Baptists are the Chosen Ones; no sin for us.

Once Jesus told a gathering that religions that make use of a confessional box should install a pay telephone in it. He was always complaining about the lack of phone boxes on his travels.

'Oh Jesus, thou one-liners are as good as thou tricks. You're really very good.'

If you're the type of person who must do the confessional box, the next time you're in it and the priest opens up the little sliding grill to speak to you – pee through it.

Then say, 'Wow, thanks Father. That was such a relief to do confession with you. Can I check back in a couple of hours?'

Jesus and his work went on to please God. History has recorded him as a man who achieved greatness as he preached the good word about his dad in Heaven and performed the most amazing tricks ever witnessed. Not only did Jesus make it rain fish and loaves of bread for crowds of people at short notice, but he also turned water into wine and healed the sick. In his spare time he kept up his fitness by playing tag with his disciples. It used to annoy them when he walked on water.

They'd cry out, 'It's not fair!'

Jesus would respond by saying, 'Get a tissue, dry your eyes and blow your nose, you big Nancy girls.'

God would look down upon his boy with great pride and it made him happy as Jesus finally had a job, and God finally had a religion where its followers worshipped him and him alone.

Despite his carpentry apprenticeship, Jesus never built anything. His apprenticeship was a total waste of time and money. God reminded Joseph of this many times.

Let Us Pray

....

You up above
Great wonderment of love,
Your boy is good
The stuff he could pull
How he did it we will never know
But man, could he put on a show
Amen

The Prophecies of Chapter Ten

→ If you find a confessional box that flies – don't give the credit to a priest.

→ If your name is Hallelujah, perhaps you're lost as your parents dumped you because of your stupid name.

→ If you're male, when participating in the Frolic, don't try to touch other men's willies. It's unhealthy and not very helpful.

→ If you're female, go for it!

→ If you're female and can hold your breath under water whilst touching male willies, you're going to a popular Baptist.

11

Love is *hard* to find some would say, but I'm telling you, every time I saw the lovely Golden Angel Jacquetta, *hard* wasn't the issue. I continued to put my best foot forward in my attempts to impress. We chatted often in the Heavenly Hall of Historical Facts. Sometimes I caught her sneaking a glance at my sculptured left calf muscle. Sometimes times I caught her raising her eyes in disbelief at my comments.

I began putting in the big leaps and bounds to break down her defences. I played my trump card. I oiled and polished my sculptured left calf muscle. We met up more regularly over meals or coffee to discuss Heaven's history. She was the fount of all things knowledgeable about Heaven. Despite my persistence, the lovely Golden Angel Jacquetta was *not* biting back on my line of love. I flicked a prayer off to God seeking help.

One morning, I was explaining the many benefits of gambling to another Newbie by informing him that on Earth you don't pay any taxes on your winnings.

'So why the heck do people work?' he asked.

'Because they're stupid,' I said. 'Winners are grinners and losers can please themselves.'

During our discussion, I heard a loud yawn behind us. I turned around and lo and behold the Big Kahuna, God himself, was kicking back on a log and listening. Surprised at seeing him, I nodded a greeting in his direction and inquired as to his haemorrhoid issue.

'No issue now,' God answered. 'I had them out. I'm one happy camper of a God. Praise me or somebody or whoever.'

God continued to yawn as I continued to discuss the benefits of gambling.'

'It was too easy to make the folding stuff on Earth,' I said. 'Anybody could do what I was doing. Work your own hours even.'

Later, and as the Newbie farewelled God and me, he said, 'I wish I'd known what you know about gambling when I was on Earth. It's something special. Imagine putting some of your profits back into the *business* of getting laid.'

I sat on the log opposite God and mentioned perhaps one way to battle his yawning was to have a break from the job of being God. Everyone needs a break to recharge their batteries.

'It has to be a monotonous gig being God, boring as well,' I said. 'Take a holiday. Go somewhere nice and hit the beaches and allow the godly body to take in the sun's rays and punch up the Vitamin D levels.'

God immediately dismissed my idea. 'Mary says that to me all the time. Look at it from my point of view: there is no one else who can run Heaven, manage the universe and read the prayers,' he moaned.

From what I'd gathered, prayers prayed to God arrived on his HeavenPrayer computer via Prayer Mail. Prayer Mail is similar to Microsoft Outlook Mail, except Prayer Mail works all the time and doesn't contain computer viruses. The Newbie who designed this unique system is now a saint, the 'Saint of All Things IT.'

God struggled to find the time to do all his God stuff. Another of God's time-consuming problems involved Neville the Devil. Even though banished from Heaven, God still had to keep an eye on him. Neville was very annoyed at having to live in the outer regions of the universe. Neville had always been a bad egg, but the final straw with him came when he developed a firebug problem. God had to sack him from Heaven. After listening to God give me all sorts of excuses as to why he couldn't go on a holiday, I pulled up a log opposite him, and took it upon myself to offer up a few suggestions.

'Why not delete the prayers. Non-Baptists aren't coming upstairs anyway, so bugger them. The practising and non-practising Baptists will get here eventually, so why read their prayers while they're on Earth? You'll see them when they arrive.'

'That does make sense,' mused God as he rubbed his chin. 'It's not as if I've ever answered any prayers, but I've always felt it godly to at least read them.'

'A god in your position needs a stand-in God,' I added. 'If you have one, your god work will still be done whenever you take time off. How hard is it to be God? From what I've seen so far, your role is managerial in nature; you're not on the front line. You're not a doer, but more of an ideas and delegation god. You're the Big Kahuna, the Big Fella, the boss behind the whole outfit.'

God agreed with my board-brushed summary of his role. I offered up Jesus's name for the stand-in role. I thought he had the right qualifications being his son, and I did point out, most dictatorships are usually handed down from father to son.

'No, he's not interested,' answered God. 'Jesus is through with responsibility. Those Roman Boat People messed him up big time.'

The look of despair across his face, made me think this was an issue of concern for him.

'Rather interesting,' mused God as he changed subjects. He was looking at the white board displaying my graphs and notes from my previous discussion with Newbie.

'The gambling thing – it makes money you say?'

'It did on Earth,' I answered. 'Those were the days.'

I prodded God. I said, 'If Jesus has to suddenly attend to serious God business, he'll be OK. It's not as if people down below don't know who he is. They still talk about him down there, and he left, how long ago? Ignore his non-responsibility beef.'

'No, it can't be Jesus,' God replied firmly. 'He's too hooked on the weed to manage his own life, let alone the lives of others. Bloody kids today!'

'What? Jesus is on them reefer things?' I asked. 'Bugger me.'

From what I had read on Earth about Jesus, I had always thought him a bit loopy if he did pull off the things they say he did. I'd further thought if you believe he pulled off those things, you're probably loopier. Some religious people go about telling all who will listen, that gay sex is unnatural, and yet the same people try and convince us that Jesus walked on water. Hello! You trying to tell us walking on *water* is natural? I'd seen Jesus in Heaven a few times and we had a couple of chats, but at no stage did he give me the impression he was on the Happy Grass.

'I blame the innkeeper in Bethlehem for not having a ventilated stable,' said God sadly. 'I also blame the Three Men, and the Boat People. They didn't help one bit.'

This is what God, with the marijuana-addicted son, told me. Jesus was born in a stable in Bethlehem, as there was no room at the inn. (I never understood how Jesus could be born in an inn. If your old man is God, wouldn't you be going five star all the way?) But I let God continue without interrupting him. According to him, what isn't well known is whilst in the stable, three men on camels turned up to hide out for a while. The Bible inaccurately refers to them as the Three Wise Men. It turns out they weren't so wise, and they most certainly didn't follow any star to Bethlehem to give presents to baby Jesus as the Bible depicts. The Three Wise Men were well-known narcotics traffickers.

On this day, they were nearly caught running drugs out of Phoenicia. Members of the Roman Boat People Police Force (RBPPF) who were patrolling, spotted them sneaking across the border. They gave chase. The Three Wise Men bolted as fast as their camels managed to run. They outpaced the RBPPF who had no camels or horses but instead carried a boat around with them in the desert, just in case they heard of a country, with larger tax payer handouts. The boat, combined with the heavy armour the RBPPF wore, including their swords and shields, hindered their ability to move quickly, and hence, the camels outpaced them. Truth be known, the camels were more than likely smarter than them as well.

During the chase, the Three Wise Men paused briefly on the top of a sand dune, stood up in their saddles and bared their butts at the RBPPF and screamed:

'Roman Boat People smell like camels, Do dah, do dah
Their women have got hairy armpits too, Oh doo dah day.
Roman Boat People are uglier than camels,
Their women start to shave at ten,
Do dah, do dah, Oh doo dah day.'

After finishing serenading the RBPPF with more insults, the Three Wise Men high-tailed it to Bethlehem to hide out. They knew they had to lie low until the heat died down. It just so happened, this was the night baby Jesus was born. The camels carrying the Three Wise Men came stampeding through the stable doors just as Mary went into labour. In pain, she began screaming as if there was no tomorrow.

The Three Wise Men, not wanting any noise to attract the pissed off RBPPF, told her to shut up. A woman in labour, can be an angry woman. Mary swore at them, and asked Joseph why three donkeys were talking to her. Realising they needed more than a 'shut up', to keep her quiet, one of the Three Wise Men cracked open a package, rolled Mary a smoke and told her to suck on it hard. The reefer eased Mary's pain and before they knew it, Mary was as high as kite, flashing her boobs at three donkeys, cracking dirty jokes, and had forgotten she was in labour, until Joseph hollered, 'By jingo, it's a boy!'

Mary laughed and said, 'It's not yours.'

Now they all laughed … except Joseph.

To celebrate the birth, the Three Wise Men got into the rest of the package they had previously opened, and had themselves a big smoke. Joseph too, as he needed something to console him.

In recognition of Mary, the lads rolled a big joint and called it the 'Mary J'. Marijuana, in some circles today is still referred to as Mary J. The doors of the stable were closed at night to keep the animals safe, so the billowing reefer smoke had nowhere to escape. It wasn't long before the other people and the animals were up there flying a kite with Mary. Newly born Jesus was lying in the hay, passively inhaling. Shortly, he too became as high as a kite. Jesus was three hours old and trying to crawl up the walls of the stable and do algebra. Joseph thought the kid was showing potential, but Jesus wasn't showing anything except for a stupid grin on his face. Jesus had become addicted to the Happy Hashish.

Poor God, I thought. No wonder he looks like he stressing out a bit over his lad.

'Then again,' said God, 'I also blame the Boat People for ruining Jesus.'

Later in his life, and apart from working for his dad as the leader of the Baptist religion, and still addicted to the *good* stuff, Jesus played football for the Nazareth Old Boys. He believed raising his profile would increase his religion's followers. Jesus had his one and only bad game for the club on that day, and he is blamed for the loss. Some say, rightfully blamed.

Apparently the ball was kicked high in the air by the opposition, and as Jesus looked upwards to see if he could catch the ball, he was heard saying, 'Wow, look at all those pretty clouds in the sky. So psychedelic and colourful. Look they keep changing colours. I wonder if I can jump up and catch one for Mother.'

Now, as Jesus was the captain of the team, all the other Nazareth Old Boys stopped and looked up. By the time they realised Jesus was 'off his face' again, the opposition has rushed though, regained the ball and scored the winning points. Jesus had to leave Nazareth because the Roman boat person, Governor, Fat Boy Pontius Pinecone, had placed a number of gold coins on the outcome of the game. He backed the Nazareth Old Boys. Furious with the result, Pinecone ordered the club to tear up Jesus's contract. The media's campaign of ridicule against Jesus was relentless. They crucified him in the daily press. Headlines etched in stone plates screamed out daily abuse at him.

People yelled at him in the street, 'Get a haircut, you long-haired lout.' Others yelled, 'I'm no fool, come and try to walk across my swimming pool.'

One afternoon, as Jesus was entering a beauty shop to have his nails done, a Boatie hollered, 'Ya big Nancy boy, you can't catch, you can't kick, you can't do anything. You gotta be your Nazareth Old Boys' cheapest buy!'

Jesus, once again as high as a kite, copped this abuse on the chin, smiled back at the Boatie and said, 'I slipped your daughter, Laurentenia, a good old fashion Baptist length. We don't have foreskins, unlike you filthy bastards.'

The Boatie was stuck for words as he tried to understand where it had gone so wrong for him.

Jesus added, 'Your wife is next on my list; I'm gonna breed the boat travel shit out of you lot. Bludging free loaders.'

The Boat Person was beside himself with rage. He ran around gathering as many Boat People as he could find. For his safety, Jesus ran into the wilderness again, as fast as his Baptist legs could carry him. Whilst in hiding, Jesus's old frolicking partner from days gone by, John the Baptist, dropped by and gave him the latest news and food. Sometimes late at night, they'd sneak down to the Jordan River and have a Frolic together, just like the old days. John knew all the shallow spots by this time.

John Boy's updates informed Jesus he was continually mocked for his one bad football game. The RBPPF were after him as well, to charge him with slipping Laurentina a Baptist length. In those days, the Boat People had a rule: no cleanskins allowed, only foreskins for our women.

In the interest of his longevity, Jesus decided to leave Nazareth and head elsewhere. Prior to leaving and disguised as a travelling family entertainer, Jesus sneaked back into Nazareth to close his bank accounts, pick up his mail and say goodbye to a few people. He reeled with shock and anger when he read his Nazareth Stock Exchange Report, which told him his share market portfolio had dropped massively in value. Jesus had lost a fortune. Already under pressure from the local media and the RBPPF, Jesus went troppo from the stress. By the time, he hit his broker's office, Jesus was fuming and spitting chips. He started abusing the living daylights out of his broker.

The broker tried to explain to Jesus the only reason his share portfolio had lost so much value, was because Jesus had insisted on only purchasing shares in companies that started with the letter *A*. Jesus worked on the principle if he couldn't make money from companies beginning with the letter A, it was pointless to invest and buy shares in companies that commenced with other letters like B and C and so on.

Jesus's verbal attack on his broker was deafening. He yelled out so that everyone could hear that his broker spent a part of each day stealing people's turds from toilets. Fearing fistie cuffs, someone called the RBPPF as Jesus began overturning desks, emptying drawers and boxes, and throwing chairs through windows. Whilst Jesus was trashing his broker's office, he came upon a box of stolen turds. He opened the box and threw them at the broker. The RBPPF burst through the door, ran back outside, put on their gas masks and burst back through the already-burst door.

Whilst this was occurring, Jesus, using his skills from his non-*high* football days, crash tackled the broker to the ground and commenced smearing turds over his face while screaming out, 'Cursed heathen poo-poo head'.

The RBPPF separated the two and listened to both sides of the story. For a while, it was difficult for them to understand the goings-on, as they didn't speak the language of Judea. Once the RBPPF had established, by way of an interpreter, what had happened, they issued Jesus a warning for destroying other people's property and told him next time he did it he would go to jail. The RBPPF charged the broker with the misappropriation of other people's turds, and ordered him to return them to their appropriate toilets.

In amongst the commotion, one of Jesus's friends from an office across the hallway recognised him and greeted him. The very mention of the name Jesus alerted the RBPPF, who turned to arrest him. Quick thinking Jesus grabbed a couple of RBPPF evidence bags containing stolen turds, opened them and commenced throwing turds at them. The RBPPF kept running into each other and falling over as their gas masks became covered in crap. This was the cue to escape that Jesus needed. He ran again, harder and faster than ever before and when he could run no more he did what most people would do; he stopped running. Jesus realised the RBPPF charges against him were mounting up and if they ever got hold of him, he'd end up in a world of hurt. As such, a low profile in hiding became the order of the day.

Word about Jesus's warrants spread quickly via the camel-train routes. Jesus had become a wanted man. He realised if the Boat People eventually spread throughout the known world, he'd be screwed as the RBPPF would be everywhere. Out of options, Jesus knew his time on Earth had finished. He summoned his merry band of mates to meet him for a final Frolic in the Jordan River. He told them Earth was giving him lots of grief. Therefore, he had decided to head upstairs to have some father and son time with his other dad.

Luke asked, 'Will you come back again?'

Jesus replied, 'You kidding me, no way, man! The RBPPF want to kill me!'

Jesus's merry band, disappointed their little money earner was heading for the blue skies of Heaven, organised a farewell party for him. The party started early with much alcohol and food consumed, much shit smoked and many party girls enjoyed. The girls were brought in from 'Nariel's Naughty but Nice Topless Dancing Studio' in Nazareth (they were cheap and supplied their own poles). The lads couldn't afford the more expensive girls, as they too had backed the Nazareth Old Boys to win.

Too much drink too early in the day made Jesus far too cocky for his own good. Oblivious to the outstanding warrants for his arrest, he staggered around to the Nazareth Stock Exchange where he ran amuck yelling and screaming as if he was a lunatic. He tipped over the tables of the Roman financial advisers, the share market brokers and the money changers. He urinated on the slate pallets that displayed the current stock quotes in chalk and then he kicked them over so they broke. A similar story is loosely told in the Bible at Matthew 21:12.

The financial hub, which drove the economy for Judea, was attacked and the state thrown into financial meltdown. The Contract Trade Notes that recorded the daily transactions were scattered; no one had any idea who had traded what sheep for what wheat and who owned what goats, cows, camels or corn. The place was described by one astute Roman boat person broker as being a complete and utter fucking shemozzle. To make matters worse, as Jesus ran away he let the goats out of the holding pens. Goats, being goats, began to eat the Contract Trade Notes scattered on the floor with the spilled wheat.

Brokers tried sticking their hands down the throats of goats attempting to retrieve their Contract Trading Notes. A couple of brokers tried to chase Jesus, but no one could catch him as he kept changing direction when running, as apparently that's what being drunk does to you.

'Think of me kindly,' Jesus yelled to the gathering crowd standing outside the Nazareth Stock Exchange. 'I have left you a parting gift of Contract Trade Notes and animals.'

When the people heard of this generous gift from Jesus, they couldn't contain their greed. They ran into the Nazareth Stock Exchange and helped themselves. In the backs of their minds, each had thought if they could gather enough of the remaining Contract Trade Notes, animals or both, they'd be able to sell them, obtain a passage on a boat and thereby get away from the Roman Boat People. The word spread like wildfire throughout Nazareth. People who once owned nothing, suddenly owned a lot.

People who once owned a lot, suddenly owned, as one financially ruined Roman Boat People trafficker wailed, '*Nothing*! I invested my money from trafficking and now I've got nothing!'

The new owners of the Contract Trade Notes produced them, collected whatever the note entitled them to, say ten goats, and immediately sold them for cash.

The Judean economy strained and buckled to handle the mayhem; to quote yet another Roman Boat person broker, 'Somebody had pulled the plug and the economy was going down the gurgler.'

Another said, 'It was like being bent over a desk and having a large greasy pole rammed up your butt; we were well and truly fucked.'

The Governor, Fat Boy Pontius Pinecone, was beside himself

over what he viewed as an act of treachery. The Governor's yearly financial bonus was tied to the economy. If the economy did well, so did he. If the economy didn't do so well, neither did he!

Fat Boy Pontius Pinecone once again ordered the Legions and every spare RBPPF person out on the hunt to find and arrest Jesus. They looked everywhere: in the bathhouses Jesus liked to frequent, they questioned the ladies of the night he visited, they strip searched people they didn't know, people they did know, and even strip searched themselves, but got nothing.

By way of an informant called Judas Dobber, the RBPPF found out about Jesus's farewell party, and immediately deployed their crack specialist group of highly trained Party Gate Crashers (PGC). In the wee hours of the morning, they struck. First, they sent in the Police Dog Squad who had a highly trained wolf, which huffed, puffed and finally blew down the doors. As the doors hit the ground, the PGC charged in; some went for the food, some went for the wine, and some went for the women. The wolf went for a mat and a lie-down. He was plum tuckered out.

When the PGC eventually got around to asking as to the whereabouts of Jesus, everyone looked nervously at the floor, shuffled their feet and mumbled they didn't even know him. A drunk called Peter denied knowing Jesus three times. This story is also touched upon in the Bible at Mark: 66-72.

When the rooster crowed each time Peter denied knowing Jesus, the PGC, thinking it was dawn, decided they had better get a wriggle on, hurry up, and find Jesus.

A couple of the PGC grabbed another drunk called Luke, tore off what few clothes he was still wearing, held him down and tortured him by tickling his testicles with the feather of a duck until he could take it no more and yelled, 'Jesus is probably outside sleeping or throwing up in the Garden of Gethsemane'.

Some of the PGC rushed outside towards the garden; others remained inside as it was a good party. One of them sticky-taped the feather back on the duck, and threw it outside so as it could go back to its pond. Those who rushed around to the garden to arrest Jesus suddenly started slipping on the path as Jesus had vomited all over it. Their rush came to an abrupt end when they fell into a big puddle of it. Their screaming and cursing alerted Jesus, who woke up and proceeded to bolt again, this time a somewhat more drunken bolt.

The PGC didn't bother chasing him, as they had a police policy of no chasing in dangerous conditions.

'No telling how much vomit is on his tracks,' one of them said.

They got themselves cleaned up and stayed at the party. Arresting Jesus was messy and they would catch him later. Jesus in the meantime had run into a cave, rolled a rock over its entrance and decided to stay well hidden until his dad answered his 'come save my arse' prayer.

The Chronicle of Heavenly Records reveal the RBPPF eventually gave up on their hunt for Jesus. They had scoured the land but couldn't locate him or his hiding spot. When the Head of the RBPPF interrogated Jesus's mother Mary, she confessed Jesus escaped to Heaven by way of a resurrection plan.

Instead he said, 'Wow, how about that? Went up to Heaven, you say. Well, if he's gone, there's no sense in wasting police resources looking for him anymore.'

He thanked Mary for being such a reliable witness and telling the truth, closed the investigation, and thereby ceased the search for Jesus. Mary thanked him for being such a kind interrogator, and for not using a feather.

The Chronicle of Heavenly Records also record that two days after the arrival of Jesus at his hideaway cave, Jesus heard a knock on the big rock sealing the cave entrance. By most accounts, he was shitting himself as he hesitantly rolled back the rock, and lo and behold, it was Easter Bunny greeting him. The Easter Bunny wished Jesus a Happy Easter and a Happy Resurrection, gave him a basket of Easter eggs and hopped away. Jesus appreciated the Easter eggs as he was hungry. Not long after the Easter Bunny incident, the tunnel from Heaven appeared and Jesus went back to his god daddy.

I shook my head and agreed with God – it was impossible for Jesus to run Heaven. He was too messed up.

Let Us Pray

Holy God and holy smoke
And bugger me, who would have thought
Your boy can not only walk on water
But he can also hallucinate
Imagine if he ran Heaven
He'd let all the bloody Catholics in
That'd be a sin
Amen

The Prophecies of Chapter Eleven

→ Baring your arse at police officers may be considered offensive in some countries. Do so at your own risk.

→ Likewise with the trafficking of narcotics. Check with your legal adviser first.

→ Be wary of men riding camels into your shed.

→ If you're going to inhale, show some respect and do it away from animals and children.

→ That goes for you priests as well; stop waving your stupid smoking canisters about the place.

→ *Away in a Manger* is not a Christmas carol written by religious people. It was written by three drug traffickers, one screaming woman, a newborn, and a man with a donkey. They were all stoned at the time.

→ Never judge a player on one bad game.

→ Before buying shares *only* beginning with the letter A, check with your financial planner.

→ Never take your own testicles to a party. Take someone else's.

→ If you're going to spend a few days in a cave, take a game and a few good books with you; some music may help as well.

→ If you see a wolf huffing, puffing, and trying to blow down your doors, shoot the mongrel. In the 21st century, doors are expensive to replace.

12

Every so often, I'd catch myself thinking of Earth. Did anyone miss me? Did Father look up Karen and her sisters? Half his luck if he did. I missed the agency girls and gambling. The agency girls never provided me a challenge like the lovely Golden Angel Jacquetta. I wondered if *Wind Between Ears* had mistaken a car for a buffalo and was now dead. Gone to a tee pee in Hell perhaps. I hoped so. *Speed* by now was probably bigger and stupider. I'm sure the 'Feel Sorry for Me Train' was clocking up many miles with Mother and the *Whinging Aunt from Whining Hill* at the helm. Toot toot to them, I say.

Meanwhile, the lifestyle of a dead Baptist is awesome. There are many things to do in Heaven, but only if you want to. You're dead; hence not much is expected from you. There are plenty of bars, clubs and sporting activities plus a myriad of other things. I ventured out one evening for some talent spotting. I was standing at a bar enjoying a drink and engaging in polite conversation with another Newbie when I saw a couple of flower sellers float in. My gaze followed them around the table areas. I was hoping they wouldn't come anywhere near me, as the words *nick off* can offend some people. Then I saw her, the lovely Golden Angel Jacquetta, shimmering and grooving on the dance floor to the song *Heaven for Everyone* by Queen.

My heart was racing. I had saliva dribbling out of the corners of my mouth; my wee-wee went all hard, so much so, Happy Face was all smiles. I started to hum, 'Tonight's the Night' as I warmed up my left calf muscle. My plan was to step forth, hit the dance floor and impress the lovely Golden Angel Jacquetta with my ability to waltz to heavy metal rock music all by myself, whilst holding my arms out wide and encouraging her to fall into them.

The Newbie with whom I had been chatting and drinking a moment before, attracted the attention of one of the flower sellers. I thought, if he buys me a flower, I'm gonna knock him out. He selected a deep red rose from the flowers on offer. I turned my back to the bar to protect my butt from his pointy bit, as I figured the worst. I'm in Heaven, I know; I'm dead, I know that too; hence I'm game enough to try anything, but I'm not going to try that. Much to my relief, the Newbie asked the flower seller to deliver the flower to someone else. But, my relief was short-lived; he pointed the flower seller in the direction of the lovely Golden Angel Jacquetta. My lovely Golden Angel Jacquetta.

Whoa now, Captain Cut-Me-Out. Not on my shift. I thought quickly. The flower seller handed the flower to the dancing Golden Angel Jacquetta and as she turned to acknowledge whoever had sent it, I stepped away from the bar so she could see me, and pointed to a vacant table. The Newbie glared at me as I floated past. I stopped in front of him, and thanked him for the flower. A nice touch on my behalf. Poor bastard didn't realise he was up against the master; I'd bought more women than he'd had hot dinners.

The lovely Golden Angel Jacquetta joined me at the table and we both commented on how well each other looked and discussed other nonsensical nonsense that two people discuss in a bar. We spent a number of hours in each other's company and just as I was about to ask her back to my place, she said she had to leave. If I had looked, I'm sure Happy Face would have had a look of total rejection on his face. I patted him gently, told him to be patient, and reminded him that Rome wasn't built in a day.

I'm sure I heard him say, 'See if we can buy her. I'm not getting any younger here.'

I did feel the relationship between us, (the lovely Golden Angel Jacquetta and me, I mean – *not* Happy Face and me), had raised itself a notch. Not a big notch, but a notch all the same. The relationship between Happy Face and me had always been one of those love-hate relationships. He just wants, wants, wants, all the time. He hates it when he doesn't get to come out to play.

The lovely Golden Angel Jacquetta was surprised when I told her I had discovered a way on Earth not to work. She was more surprised to find out I was a successful gambler. I, of course, didn't mention anything about the agencies. After we had been seeing each other for some time, the lovely Golden Angel Jacquetta began to drop little hints I should collect my thoughts and come up with an idea for contributing to the Betterment of Heaven. She didn't nag, merely encouraged. She didn't want to see a talent like mine go to waste in the Newbie realm. I did feel as if I should come up with a little something for the Betterment of Heaven, just to show my appreciation for the lovely Golden Angel Jacquetta. But where was my experience, just gambling and buying through the agency? Neither were suitable discussion topics for one so refined as her.

Later, I was reading a book on the psychology of the gambler when God floated over.

'What's going down?' he asked.

I answered, 'I've been mulling this idea around in my head for a week or so. It could benefit Heaven.'

God's eyes lit up like a couple of lighthouse beacons. 'Get the fuck outta here! You've had an idea. This I gotta to hear!'

I proceeded to explain to God my idea involved developing a product, namely gambling, so that people in Heaven could share the joy of winning, like I did on Earth.

'On Earth, I funded my lifestyle from it,' I said. 'Gambling was my Holy Grail. My gambling on Earth was based on knowledge so powerful that once harnessed, I didn't need to work anymore. It'd work up here as well.'

Not understanding what I was talking about, God asked, 'How can a Holy Grail of knowledge bring joy in Heaven?'

This is how I explained my Holy Grail plan to a sceptical God. I asked him to picture people rocking up to their places of work on Earth, walking up to their bosses, turning around, dropping their pants, bending over and pointing to their bare arses at them and saying, 'Look in the mirror, dickhead. Take a good look at yourself. I quit. I've decided to spend time with my family instead of with you numbskulls. I've found my Holy Grail, I'm filthy rich, screw you.'

God laughed and tried to picture it, for a short time at least. He stopped as he was seeing too many bare butts.

'That's the Holy Grail I'm talking about – the knowledge you need so you don't have to work anymore. Instead you have joy, the joy of winning,' I said. 'As we don't work in Heaven, nor have betting agencies, we can use what I know, my knowledge, my Holy Grail, to gamble on anything for fun. This fun would add to the Betterment of Heaven, would it not?'

I had tweaked his interest. God began to ask questions in rapid fire. I reminded him I was in the early stages of my thoughts. I had much work to do before I could even think of taking my idea to the Heavenly Spiritual Society for their approval. I had to map it out. The lovely Golden Angel Jacquetta was ecstatic for me when I told her of my plan.

My life in Heaven began to rotate between designing my Holy Grail project for God's Betterment of Heaven program and continuing to impress the lovely Golden Angel Jacquetta. I was busy at both.

One evening, over a meal of chargrilled lobster tail accompanied by a side dish of citrus and green salad from Leaping Lino's Lobster Cave restaurant, I told the lovely Golden Angel Jacquetta I was going to head off to Cloud View Resort for a couple of days' break. I needed a rest from designing my Holy Grail project. Much to my surprise, she asked if she could come along as well. I did think this might be good, as I am neither a monk nor a Catholic Priest. This little trip may result in another rising of the notch, a change for the better.

I informed the lovely Golden Angel Jacquetta that the apartment I had booked, only had one bedroom. She said those arrangements were fine. I smiled until she further told me I could sleep on a couch in the lounge room. This is the problem for us men getting into a new relationship. Women play this game with us where they think it's appropriate to have a certain amount of wait time between the initial date, and the getting it on and the getting it together bit. Try to throw the leg too early, and the woman thinks you're just after one thing, leave it too long and she thinks you can't get a 'hard on'. Damn tough being a bloke, you have to time it just right. No wonder I used an agency on Earth.

Cloud View Resort is a spectacular place with long, pale beaches east of Heaven Central. Prior to leaving, I called the resort to confirm my reservation. Upon arrival, I was bitterly disappointed to find the resort hadn't removed the couches from the lounge room as I'd requested. The resort had palm trees shading swimming pools, scuba diving in the ocean, para sailing, fishing, surfing – you name it, it was here to do if you wanted. Games of beach volleyball, touch football and beach cricket were played on the beach, where white-crested waves gently hit the soft sands. Further up, the waves pounded into the beach. That was Surfers' Heaven. People came to Cloud View Resort to relax, to recover from all the relaxing in Heaven.

Come morning I lazily sat outside the apartment while the lovely Golden Angel Jacquetta was still in bed. I gazed at the beach and had to think that my life in Heaven would be improved greatly, by my moving from the couch to the bed of magical times.

The lovely Golden Angel Jacquetta disturbed my thoughts as she came outside and asked, 'God wants to know two things: can we do dinner with him when we return, and where have you been sleeping?'

'I hope you answered yes to the first. But as to where I'm sleeping, did he mean last night or tonight?'

The lovely Golden Angel Jacquetta didn't respond as I thought, none of God's business where I sleep, the dirty old bugger.

Later I asked, 'Why does he want us over for dinner?'

'Who knows?' was the reply.

I assumed he wanted to discuss with us my Holy Grail design. He knew the lovely Golden Angel Jacquetta was encouraging with it. Alternatively, perhaps he was going to tell the lovely Golden Angel Jacquetta to hurry up and put out! Nah, I suspected the dinner had more to do with my Holy Grail. The quicker I got this job finished, the better off I was going to be. I suddenly burst out laughing.

'What's so funny?' asked my lovely Golden Angel who had now joined me outside.

'The irony of having dinner with God is what's funny,' I answered. 'So many people on Earth have tried to find him, but can't. For me it's easy; I know where he lives.'

Later, as I lay on the beach listening to the sounds of waves lapping onto the shoreline and feeling the gentle hands of the lovely Golden Angel Jacquetta rubbing suntan oil into my left calf muscle, I began to appreciate there was something therapeutic in finding your lazy button and chilling out. I wondered if I could *patent* lazy. Another idea. What a profitable business it would be – people would have to pay me for the right to be lazy.

I asked her ever so nicely to move slightly to the left, as she was blocking my view of a little game of beach volleyball playing out. I was appreciating the skill levels on display from both teams. When we returned from Cloud View Resort, we headed to my lovely Golden Angel Jacquetta's cloud, freshened up, and then went to the House of God. Joseph was sitting on the front deck playing with his donkey.

I announced our arrival by calling out, 'God, God, ohhhh God, damn, you're good; ohhh God, please stop and rest for a moment; ooooohhh good Heavens,'

My lovely Golden Angel Jacquetta immediately belted me on the arm and warned me to stop mimicking her. The couch in the lounge room wasn't used on night two. Mary greeted us as we entered and enquired as to why my right ear was swollen. I answered by mentioning I'd made just one little comment in front of my lovely Golden Angel Jacquetta concerning one little Brazilian woman in one little volleyball game, and she popped me.

Mary smiled and asked how our few days at Cloud View had gone. And, this is what my lovely Golden Angel Jacquetta, the lovely Golden Angel who had spent the last three days and two nights with me at the Cloud View Resort said, 'It was great, Mum, we had a lovely time.'

I nearly fainted. 'Whoa now, Captain Sunshine,' I exclaimed in one heck of a hurry.

Mary looked at Jacquetta, who shook her head and said she was waiting until later to tell me. My head spun. Jacquetta, my lovely Golden Angel had called Mary, 'Mum'. Get out of here. As I was trying to come to grips with the 'Mum' bit, the Big Kahuna appeared in his dressing grown and slippers. I thought the peace symbols on his dressing gown were a nice touch. He was God.

My lovely Golden Angel Jacquetta, the same lovely golden angel who for months had been entertaining me with her abundant knowledge of all things Heaven, said this to the God of all the Heaven, the earths, the stars, the moon, the universe, etc., 'Dad, it's nearly dinner time and you're still in your dressing gown.'

I stuttered, possibly aged way past thirty, lost ten kilos and said, 'Hold the phone just a darn minute here. Am I dreaming? Am I hearing things? What's with this Mum and Dad stuff?'

'Yeah, yeah, I know,' God answered. 'I've been deleting prayers on my MacPrayer computer and time got away from me. It was a good idea Travesty gave me about deleting prayers.' Then he added, 'He hasn't been told yet, has he?'

'No,' said Mary.

'We may as well do it now. I need to eat,' muttered God.

From memory, there was no fanfare, no great speech and no magnificent sermon from the Mount of Great Surprises. God simply informed me that Jacquetta, the lovely Golden Angel, was Mary's and his daughter. Jacquetta was born in Heaven soon after Mary arrived.

'Cheaper than paying child support,' laughed God.

For one of the few times in my life I was lost for words. I couldn't talk.

'You're aware of the Father, the Son and the Holy Ghost stuff people waffle about on Earth?' asked God.

I nodded.

'Partly true. I'm the Father, Jesus is the son and you can work out the rest, can't you?'

'You're the Holy Ghost?' I said, as I looked at my lovely Golden Angel Jacquetta.

'I sure am,' she answered. 'I was given the name Holy after one of my great-grandmothers from Mum's side and Ghost is our surname.'

'I don't get it,' I said.

'What's not to get?' said Mary. 'He's God Ghost, Jesus is Jesus Ghost and Jacquetta is Holy Ghost. Jacquetta is simply her nickname.'

'Holy Christ,' I muttered.

'He was a distant relative on Dad's side,' said my lovely Golden Angel Jacquetta. 'Jesus got his nickname Christ from him.'

'How come I didn't know?' I asked.

'You never asked!' she replied.

'I didn't realise I had to; who else in Heaven knows you're God's daughter?'

'Only a few people. I've kept it tight, as I didn't want every male hitting on me, especially the Newbies,' she said as she gave me a wink. 'But as from now, I've decided to give up my little secret.'

I looked at God, and blurted out, 'I slept on the couch! I did. A blue couch with yellow cushions on it. They had black buttons on them. I know that because I was looking at them all night. I didn't leave the couch. Honest.'

Mary wanted us to get ready for dinner as Jesus would soon be joining us. My lovely Golden Angel Jacquetta reassured me my shock was nothing compared to her family's shock when she told them she was dating me. Jesus arrived. He was happy, out of this world happy. Mary called out to Joseph and told him to put his donkey away and come inside. We adjourned to the dining room to be greeted by a table fit for – well, a God. Joseph scurried away to one of the bathrooms when Mary scolded him for not washing his hands. We spent the evening eating, talking and drinking. I do recall almost going into cardiac arrest as my lovely

Golden Angel Jacquetta informed everyone we were moving in together. It was news to me, but if one ever gets the opportunity to shack up with a daughter of God, one should. I felt a bounce of congratulations from Happy Face.

God looked at me and said, 'Better be separate rooms.'

Joseph piped up and said to God, 'Separate rooms never stopped you.'

Mary quickly interjected and asked who wanted dessert. Joseph declined and returned to the deck. The rest of us continued to joke, eat, talk, and drink until the rays of a new dawn started to creep across the Heavens. With that, my lovely Golden Angel Jacquetta and I said our farewells. I nearly tripped over Joseph's donkey as we were leaving. We floated back to her cloud and promptly fell into bed – her bed, our bed. We woke late.

I was drinking lots of coffee when God arrived.

He looked at me and said, 'It doesn't take you long, does it?'

After some idle chitchat, God asked me how my Holy Grail project was going. In my hung-over state, I couldn't say anything that made sense. I replied by saying there were things that I didn't know, but I should have known. And, there were some things that I did know but I had forgotten I knew. Had I not forgotten some things, it may have been much easier for me to understand other things. But then again, there were things that I already knew before I finally got to know them again. Now, I knew a little more about those things than I did before. But still, there were more things for me to know, once I worked out the other things.

For a moment, God and Jacquetta stood speechless. God suggested I had consumed excessive amounts of coffee and I should go back to bed. Great idea! I went away singing a little ditty:

> *Here come the Baptists*
> *Brave and tall*
> *God love us best of all*
> *When the time is right*
> *Our aim will be good and true*
> *As we flick the Catholics with doggie poo*

I believe that, as I left the room, God told Jacquetta she could have done so much better.

The next morning greeted me in a healthier state than I'd been in the day before. I felt good and floated off to the gym to continue the fine work on my sculptured left calf muscle. On entering the gym, I noticed one of the saints bending down and touching his toes.

He recognised me and said, 'Top of the morning to you, Travesty. You should try this exercise; it's good for your lower back.'

I responded, 'If God wanted me to bend over, mate, there'd be gold bars on the floor.'

I completed two raises on my left calf muscle and stopped. Time for breakfast and then time for God. Some people may put God first but not me; I have priorities.

'Hello dear, you look burnt out. A big gym session?' asked Jacquetta as I arrived.

'Huge session,' I answered. 'I'm feeling quite fatigued.'

I ate quickly and went off to see my main man in Heaven land. On the way, I noticed a couple of non-Baptists sitting in the 'Departure to Hell' area. They had tried to sneak into Heaven and had been nailed by the Guardian Angels.

They were crying. I stopped to console them. 'I guess you boys really messed up and backed the wrong horse. You've been fooled. You should have known all along, the Baptists rule! But look on the bright side.'

'What bright side?' one of them asked quickly, no doubt thinking he was about to be given a completely new lease in the afterlife.

I paused, 'Come to think of it, there isn't one,' and I floated off to the sound of much wailing and gnashing of teeth in the background.

Let Us Pray

....

Great leader in Heaven
Thank you for making my lovely Golden Angel Jacquetta
Go all weak for me
So as under her sheets I will sleep
Sometimes I will sleep
Amen

The Prophecies of Chapter Twelve

→ To have an idea or two isn't such a bad thing.
→ Before shooting your boss a brown-eye, make sure you've found your Holy Grail.
→ If you're invited to God's house for dinner, be prepared for a few surprises.
→ Beach time is very therapeutic. Do more of it.
→ For safety reasons, always watch female beach volleyball alone.
→ Find your lazy button every now and again and turn it on.
→ Ha ha, I know where God lives!

13

I arrived at the House of God to find Mary and Joseph having a barney. From what I could gather, Joseph wanted another donkey as his old one was wearing out.

'No way in Heaven am I going to allow you to have a second donkey to mess with!' shouted Mary. 'Why don't you play with your son instead? The kid needs one of his fathers.'

Joseph yelled back, 'Bugger Jesus. The last time I played with him he made me run around the place screaming, "A flood is coming! A flood is coming! Quickly build a boat." The Roman Boat People laughed at me.'

I excused myself by saying I had to see God, and ventured inside. 'Greetings, oh great one,' I uttered as I entered his cluttered-up office.

'And blessings to you or whatever,' responded God. 'What are those two carrying on about?'

'Something to do with you and Joseph not playing with Jesus,' I answered.

'That one again,' said God. 'The last bloody time I played with Jesus he made me dress up as a Roman governor and then threw rotten fruit at me, all the while screaming, "Pontius Pinecone, you're nothing but a poonce and a bum bandit. You dirty, rotten, freckle-tapping, heathen Roman Boat Person scum dog.'

'And Joseph wants a new donkey to play with as well,' I added.

'Joseph already has a donkey. Why does he need another to play with?' asked God.

'Because the one he's got now is tired and needs to rest,' I guessed.

'One donkey is more than enough for any man,' said God.

I nodded in agreement.

'And so this is the life of God,' he mumbled. 'Some Earth men are way smarter than I ever was.'

'How so?' I asked.

God replied, 'Because they wear a condom. They do that because they're way smarter than me. They should be God.'

'Right,' I said. 'I'd better start wearing one.'

God either didn't get my one-liner or he was deliberately ignoring me. He moved on.

'We have a problem, but a solution is at hand,' said God.

This statement has always bothered me. The 'we have a problem' statement. Automatically it means that everyone within earshot has a problem. I assured God I had no problem. He ignored me again.

'The *we* bit involves me?' I asked.

'Quite so,' replied God.

'How so?' I asked.

'No, not *how so*, you mean How Long,' said God.

'What the fuck?' I asked.

'You mean How Long, not how so?' repeated God.

'Nope, I mean how so, not how long. That's why I said how so,' I answered.

'No, you're confused,' said God. 'You see his name is How Long. How Long was not a question; it was a statement. How Long is a Chinese man; I don't know any How So's,' laughed God.

'For Pete's sake,' I said, 'you're meant to be God. Some may consider you such a disappointment.'

God stretched back in his chair, rested his feet on a corner of the desk, took a long draw on his cigar and said, 'I do love your idea of the Holy Grail Project. It's going to be a right regular show-stopper.'

'I'm still trying to pull the idea together; there's a lot in it,' I replied.

'I'm stoked you had an idea,' replied God.

'Me too,' I said. 'It felt good.'

God nodded and asked, 'How's it going, the *pulling* it together part?'

'OK, I guess. I'm not breaking into a sweat getting it completed,' I answered.

'Righto, back to our problem. Can you speed it up a bit, the Holy Grail thingie?' asked God.

'Why?'

'Just because, you never know,' answered God.

The Big Fella was keeping something from me. Then again, he was probably keeping lots from me. He was God. I mentioned my Workitis issue. God suggested I tackle my Holy Grail Project in thirty-minute periods, two or three times a week. At least he understood my work philosophy. Although, he did begin to regularly enquire as to my progress. His daughter too.

After much pestering from both, I finally said, 'OK, enough is enough; book me in to talk turkey with the Four Wise Guys who sit on the Board of Approvals for the Heavenly Spiritual Society.'

'Finally,' said Jacquetta as she ran her fingers through my flowing locks. 'Finally, we get to see your masterpiece, the great plan of your idea.'

Up until then, everything was honky dory. Jacquetta was smiling, laughing, ringing her friends and telling them I had a plan of my idea to present for approval. God was on his phone organising a meeting of the Heavenly Spiritual Society Board.

'They can see us now,' said God. 'It helps when you're God. I can jump the queue, just like the Boat People.'

Everyone was excited. Then God asked to see my plan.

'I don't have a plan to show you,' I said.

'What! You must,' responded God sounding surprised. 'Come on, cough up; where do you want me to sit to see your plan before you brief up the Wise Guys?'

'Sit where you want,' I replied. 'I don't have anything to show you.'

'Get outta here!' said God. 'How can you not have a plan to show me?'

Jacquetta told whomever she was talking too, she'd call them back later.

'You don't have a plan to show?' she asked, sounding perplexed.

'What's the deal with a plan to show? What kind of plan were you expecting?' I asked.

God looked at me and answered, 'Stuff like PowerPoint slides and notes on paper with graphs and buzz words. The Four Wise Guys love motivational buzz words in PowerPoint.'

'Oh please! That's the stuff of amateurs,' I said. 'The only people who use PowerPoint slides and notes in their presentations are those who haven't got a clue what they're talking about. Professionals such as my good self don't need pretty little slides to get a point across.'

God and Jacquetta both looked at me and said nothing.

'And what are buzz words? They're memory stoppers for people who forget what they're talking about. Now shall we go?'

'Oh bugger,' said God, 'I've got a bad feeling about this!'

The expression on my lovely Golden Angel Jacquetta's face asked, 'How's this going to work?'

'Oh ye of little faith!' I said. 'Do not fear, though I may walk through the valley of evil, I can still make shit up. I'm going to cuff it, you know, pull the presentation out of my backside so to speak. Now we must go.'

We entered the cloud belonging to the Heavenly Spiritual Society and I was ushered into the centre of the room. God made his way to the chairman's chair located near the Four Wise Guys. The Four Wise Guys appeared to be so old, I had a feeling their blood group may have been cancelled. They were the only ones in Heaven who didn't look thirty years of age. Their hair was long and white, as were their beards. They wore matching white sheets with the words, 'One of the Four Wise Guys' embossed on the front of them. Jacquetta sat in a chair at the side of the room. I exchanged pleasantries with the Four Wise Guys about the weather, which was a brief conversation as the weather in Heaven is always perfect.

'Enlighten us, Travesty,' prompted one of the Four Wise Guys. 'What idea do you bring to us to assist in making a perfect Heaven more so?'

'First off,' I said, 'I come with no slides and no notes, as I want to speak to you from my heart.'

One of the Four Wise Guys said, 'Damn, I was hoping to get some buzz words or some worldly advice to add to my collection.'

'OK, I'll give you some,' I replied. 'Never tell a one-night-stand your real name or where you live.'

He wrote it down, as did God.

'Here's another one. Peace Keepers are ultimately the ones with the superior fire power.'

He wrote that down as well. I took a deep breath and launched into my plan by explaining how I wanted to add to the Betterment of Heaven by creating more fun for everyone by showing them how to gamble.

The Four Wise Guys sighed. 'Heaven is full of fun already.'

'Fun is good,' I said. 'More fun is better.'

I felt I had lost the Four Wise Guys. Even God looked bored.

This is what I said to the Heavenly Spiritual Society, the Four Wise Guys and God: 'Heaven may be full of fun already, but not gambling fun. We should not disrespect Jesus by ignoring that his greatest gift to Earth was giving it gambling. Forget all the nonsense about his dying for everyone's sins. Jesus's greatest gift to the people on Earth was gambling.'

I immediately had everyone's attention. The Four Wise Guys looked at God, and God looked at Jacquetta, who looked at me as if to say, where is this going?

One of the Four Wise Guys asked, 'Jesus invented gambling, you say? Please explain.'

Another of the Four Wise Guys said, 'What? Jesus actually did something on Earth?'

The other two Wise Guys appeared to be without speech. God looked baffled.

Religious denominations have missed the true meaning of the 'Jesus in the cave' episode. Religion wants us to believe this period in religious history, now called Easter (after the bunny who delivers the eggs), is to celebrate the more morbid events concerning the death of Jesus. What rubbish! Good Friday should celebrate the strength, the power, the ability, and the agility of Jesus to be able to run through the night in a drunken, vomiting state and find a hiding place to escape the RBPPF. It just so happened the day was a *Friday*. Once Jesus was securely in a cave, he was able to sleep off his drunkenness from his farewell party. And that's always a *good* thing to do. You put the two together and you have Good Friday.

The next day was a Saturday. Jesus awoke in his cave with a massive hangover. In between sleeping and resting, Jesus waited for God to answer his prayers. Jesus was impatient; I'm not sure why. I know of people who have been waiting their entire lives for God to answer their prayers. While Jesus waited, he amused himself by throwing a pebble or two off the cave wall. It wasn't long before he progressed to throwing a handful of pebbles at the wall. Pebbles flew everywhere and Jesus had to duck and weave to get out of their way. Jesus discovered the more rounded pebbles bounced the furthest. As he continued with his game, Jesus pretended he was betting Roman Denarius (Boat People money) on which rounded pebble bounced the furthest. On this day, this Saturday, Jesus did not just invent a little pebble game. Jesus invented gambling!

Incredibly, Jesus has never received any recognition for inventing gambling. The day after Jesus's gambling invention is called Easter Sunday, when God finally saw Jesus's come-save-my-arse prayer. He immediately dispatched the Tunnel to Heaven and a very *relieved* Jesus arrived at the other end to be greeted by his other dad. Religion as usual gets everything arse about. Religious people believe that on Easter Sunday, Jesus was *resurrected*. Jesus was *not* resurrected on Easter Sunday. As I've mentioned, he was *relieved* on Easter Sunday to finally escape from his gambling den, and be in Heaven.

'I'll be buggered,' said God. 'We should all behold.'

'Behold what?' I asked.

'Nothing more,' said God, 'just behold. It's a religious saying.'

I argued my case with passion. I took no prisoners and I gave no quarter.

In summing up, I said, 'As on Earth, in Heaven we must carry on the tradition of gambling to honour Jesus for the abuse he suffered from the Roman Boat People.'

The Four Wise Guys mumbled amongst themselves for a while.

I heard one say, 'He's right. We should honour Jesus despite the fact he's as useless as tits on a bull.'

Yet another said, 'True. I suppose his idea will add to the betterment of Heaven.'

Another said, 'What'd I miss? I was having a snooze. Any new buzz words?'

The Fourth Wise Guy said, 'If we don't approve Travesty's idea, God might get pissed with us. Remember those rumours that were getting around ages ago involving God and sacrifices.'

Suffice to say, they approved my plan. God volunteered to be my Spiritual Overseer.

A few nights after my address to the Heavenly Spiritual Society, God and Mary arrived at Jacquetta's and my love cloud for dinner. Over a delicious, tender beef roast with succulent potatoes, peas, broccoli and pumpkin, topped with gravy and washed down with quantities of God's Own wine, God informed us how he had been flipping through the Bible the night before and having himself a good old laugh.

'As a man who believes in humour and fun, I read the Bible every so often. Of course, I gloss over the killing bits and the other murderous stuff supposedly done by God, or to appease God. Apart from that, the Bible has interesting stories made up by nomads who wandered the Earth tending sheep,' said God.

The Big Fella had Jacquetta and me in fits of laughter as he told us in Corinthians 14:34 it states: 'Women in church must not be allowed to speak; they must keep quiet and listen, they must be obedient.' God told us how Mary almost had a hernia when he read Corinthians 14:35 to her: 'If women want to know something they can ask their husbands when they get home.'

Mary was shaking her head and said, 'And don't forget it took those sexist pigs, some forty of them, a period of 1,400 to 1,800 years to write the Bible. What the Hell were they doing with their time?'

I tried to change the subject, but it was too late.

'I'll bet the Catholic religion gained its mistrust of women from the Bible,' said Jacquetta.

Here we go, I thought; I knew it.

Jacquetta elaborated. She had read Catholics don't allow women to be priests or hold any form of high office.

'It's because Catholic men are intimidated by women,' said Mary. 'There are no female Catholic priests and there'll never be a female Pope.'

Fair point I thought. Perhaps the Catholic Church was both sexist and discriminatory. But then again, if Catholic women aren't happy with their lot, they ought to protest against it. Sack the religion and join the Baptists. All sexes can preach in Baptist churches.

'The Catholic Church also discriminates against men,' I declared.

God, Mary, and Jacquetta looked at me as I asked, 'You ever seen a male nun?'

They now ignored me and left me out of their conversation for a while. But, I did think at the time, if Catholic men don't like women, I wonder what a Catholic boys' night out was like? How different from a Protestant boys' night would it be? What do Catholic blokes on a boys' night out do? Perhaps they sit around and show each other their willies?

I said, 'Perhaps the Catholic mistrust of women goes back to the days of Adam and Eve.'

Jacquetta looked perplexed and asked, 'What are you on about now?'

'The Bible states at Genesis 3, a serpent tricked Eve into eating a piece of fruit from the very tree God had forbidden them to eat from. Seeing as Eve ate first, it stands to reason the first person on Earth to create sin was a woman. Eve then conned Adam into eating some fruit from the same tree. She sinned twice. It went like this:

'Come on Adam, take the apple, man,' Eve said as she took her top off.

Adam replied, 'No Eve, we can't. God told us not to.'

Eve then opened up her bra and said, 'Come on, tiger, you know you want to. You know you want to taste the forbidden fruit; you know you have to. Go on – just a nibble, and then a bite.'

Adam weakened and did as Eve instructed. Ever since that fruitful afternoon, the Catholics have been blaming women for introducing sin.'

'I'll be buggered,' muttered God. 'I must have missed that bit.'

Mary couldn't believe it. She started to insist God send down a plague to stitch up the Catholics.

'So anyway, as I was saying,' said God, 'I was reading the Bible and chuckling away when it occurred to me, the word God gets mentioned a Hell of a lot.'

The Big Fella explained, as he was God, the onus was on him to correct the Bible in the parts that were wrong.

'The last Bible written turned out to be a massive seller and it's fiction. How much would a true version of the Bible sell for, a true version of God's word?'

'It would sell for a fortune,' said Jacquetta, 'especially if you autographed each copy.'

'I could be a celebrity,' said God.

'You'd get invited to lots of places,' I said. 'And not just into people's hearts either.'

'Yes, yes,' said God. 'Your stand-in God suggestion may be a good idea, especially when I leave for speaking circuit engagements.'

'Oh, how nice. I've always liked to travel,' said Mary.

'What would the true version of your Word contain?' I asked. 'I don't think you will be able to call it the Bible. There's probably a copyright out on the original.'

'I've given the question a great deal of thought since last night,' said God. 'Slept on it you could say. And this morning I woke up with the answer.'

'It's so exciting,' said Mary as she clapped her hands. 'That's why we wanted to have dinner with you tonight.'

'My Bible,' said God proudly, 'my true word will be about how to achieve your own personal Holy Grail by becoming a gambling

Baptist. No better idea have I heard to aid the Betterment of Heaven than the idea of attracting people to the Baptist religion by teaching them to gamble.'

'But, wasn't that my idea – the Holy Grail and gambling bit?' I said.

'Exactly, it was your idea,' said God. 'But your idea had nothing to do with Earth. Your gambling plan was for fun and for the Betterment of Heaven. I've merely added to your idea, expanded upon it. Now it's both our ideas, and I have made your plan larger.'

'How much larger?'

This is how God explained his *larger* bit to me. If a book was written on gambling and distributed on Earth to *only* the Baptists, the Baptists would get rich and soon be shooting their bosses brown-eyes.

I agreed.

'Imagine how people from the other religions would react if they saw the Baptists getting rich and not working anymore,' God said.

Jacquetta interjected and said, 'They'd want to know, what's making the Baptists rich, and then they'd want a part of the action.'

'Exactly, my dear,' replied God. 'Therefore, if Travesty's Holy Grail about gambling was only shared with the Baptists by way of my Bible, wouldn't the people from other religions want to become Baptists so they too could share in the spoils?'

The penny dropped for me. 'This would mean more people on Earth converting to the way of the Baptists, hence more people for Heaven.'

'Yes,' said Mary. 'But, just as important, if the Baptists were to become the dominant religion on Earth again, God would be the top-dog God again.'

'It's been a long time since I've had that title,' mused God. 'I miss it.'

'Fair enough,' I said. 'So when are you going to start writing?'

'Oh no,' answered God, 'You're going to write my Bible. We'll call it the 'True Word of Gambling'. Through your wisdom you will guide people to their Holy Grails, and in turn to their riches and the Baptist faith. And ultimately, I will be the head honcho again.'

I was flabbergasted.

I spat out, 'You're kidding me!'

'Nope, not kidding,' replied God.

'Mary, Jacquetta – I can't do this. It's too much responsibility for me. I am a man of very limited capabilities.'

'Well, he is God,' said Mary. 'He's been getting his own way for ever.'

'You better believe it, I'm God, Almighty God I am. I can kick arse when I have to because I'm God and I'm Almighty as well.'

'Yes dear, we all know; now please sit down again,' said Mary as she patted God's hand.

'I had a passion run once, and I got a son. He's the Son of God, the goddamn Son of God Almighty God. But, he can't kick arse like his daddy can. I've been kicking arse since the BC, long before he was born.'

'That's enough now,' said Mary sternly. 'Sit down and no more wine for you.'

'But I don't know anything about writing a Bible,' I pleaded.

'Neither did the other lot!' interjected Mary.

'Right, simple then, isn't it?' I replied sarcastically.

'That's the spirit, my boy,' said God.

'No, you're supposed to be the bloody spirit,' I replied.

'Isn't this so exciting?' said Jacquetta as she patted me on the head. 'You're going to recruit more Baptists by writing Daddy's Bible.'

I could see God's logic. It was a good idea, but to put it into practice would be difficult. That said, the Earth people were greedy; they'd flock to the Baptist religion once they saw the million dollar smiles.

* * *

Shortly thereafter, I committed myself to writing God's Bible.

'Good,' said God. 'Good. Equal rights for black gods. Why should them white honky gods have all the fun.'

'We're going home now,' said Mary. 'When he starts carrying on like this and the ends of his plaits drop into his wine, the old boy has had enough.'

Let Us Pray

Yo, Big Fella way up there in the air
Thanks for loving us Baptists best of all
I always knew that we were right
Ever since I heard the song
'Onward Baptist Soldiers Marching as to war
Let's look after ourselves and make the Happy Clappers poor'
Amen

The Prophecies of Chapter Thirteen

→ A plan is for people who don't know what they're doing.

→ Use the gift Jesus has given us. Gamble hard and gamble often.

→ Round stones bounce further.

→ Not one of the Ten Commandments states, 'Thou shalt not gamble.'

→ You can work some magic when God is on your team.

→ Never play dress-ups with Jesus.

→ Catholics should get on the Protestant gig – they love women.

→ End discrimination. The world needs more male nuns.

14

The initial problem I foresaw with writing a Bible was nobody anywhere had ever written one that's factual. Therefore, I had no blueprint to work from. Having said that, if I wrote a Bible from scratch, I could well end up becoming a literary giant.

People would point at me and whisper to their friends, 'That's him! He's the guy; he's the bloke who wrote God's Bible, the real one. He did it all by himself. He didn't need a bunch of others to assist; he's good!'

If my writing was deemed brilliant, I may have a doctorate bestowed upon me posthumously. I could be like some other up themselves, hey-look-at-me, full of their own self-importance type of people, who get a big thrill out of putting the acronym Dr in front of their names when they're not real doctors. These people have written a 100,000-word thesis on subjects like, 'Why does the river run dry in a drought?' or 'What reasons prevent a eunuch from getting a hard-on?' and for this senseless dribble, they are awarded a doctorate and the title Doctor. You *don't* have a medical licence, you numbskulls. You want to be a doctor – go to medical school. Get a real job! I decided I wouldn't accept, even posthumously, a doctorate.

God's instructions were basic, write a book on finding your Holy Grail through gambling. Put the Baptists and the winning feeling together, and more will follow the path. My lovely Golden Angel Jacquetta told me most of the writings in the Bible were plagiarised from other sources. She said most of the Bible text, in its original form came from the 'Epic of Gilgamesh', perhaps the oldest written word on Earth. The Epic of Gilgamesh was written in cuneiform script, and came from ancient Mesopotamia.

Cuneiform script is the earliest known form of written expression. The Epic of Gilgamesh was written around 2,000 BC and is older than any known reference in the Bible.

The similarities between the Epic of Gilgamesh and the Bible have not been lost on the scholars of ancient works. The flood story mentioned in the Bible at the Book of Genesis, is identical to the much older documented flood story told in the Epic of Gilgamesh. Jacquetta had explained many other themes, plot elements and characters in the Epic of Gilgamesh were plagiarised by the biblical authors. The story of Enkidu and Shamhat in the Epic of Gilgamesh is was very similar to the Adam and Eve story.

The 'Epic of Gilgamesh' was not the only source the biblical writers plagiarise from. The biblical story of Jesus is a collection of bits and pieces stolen from dozens of other mythical stories. The Greco-Roman deity Dionysus, worshipped from around 1500 BC – 1100 BC and therefore existing long before the biblical Jesus, is also reported as being the Son of God. He too was born of a virgin mother and was commonly depicted riding a donkey. Dionysus, similar to Jesus, healed the sick and turned water into wine. As per the biblical Jesus, Dionysus was said to have been killed and resurrected, and then became immortal.

These accounts were written long before the Bible characters existed. There are countless other examples of plagiarism throughout the Bible. Perhaps, I thought, the biblical authors of yesteryear worked on modern day university rules? Copying one person's work is plagiarism, but copying many people's work is research.

The main reason religious people don't want to accept the similarities between the Epic of Gilgamesh and the Bible is because their brains are wired to a belief system, underpinned by the Bible and the words of religious leaders, whom people blindly follow and trust. The process of causing normally sane people to believe in what is mostly *unbelievable* is not new. It's an old indoctrination method utilised by the early communist leaders on Earth. Hear it enough, read it enough, and do it enough and you will end up believing.

There is ample evidence to show the Bible itself had been re-written numerous times, and during those numerous re-writes, different religions and cultures had deleted parts of the original text and inserted their own pieces of text to suit their religion and beliefs. In short, groups of people, who disagreed with what the Roman Boat People university lecturers had written, went off and set up their own religion and rewrote the Bible to suit.

The Bible in its various forms has been the catalyst for more wars, more death, more suffering and more adversity in the human race than any other known instrument. I had to make sure God's True Word was a refreshing change from the sadness and gloomy stories of the much plagiarised and much altered Bible. It had to be an uplifting book, a book to make you happy and smile. Winning money achieves that for you. There is no better way to say, 'Thank you God', than when you're sitting down counting the *folding* stuff, you've won because of his book. I needed to ensure people throughout the world had the knowledge to bare their pimply arses at their bosses, and say, 'Screw you, I quit.'

Righto, now that I'd decided that, I was going to roll over and go back to sleep. I had the plan; that was enough for one day. No sense in burning myself out early. Later, my lovely Golden Angel called out breakfast was ready.

I stumbled out into the dining room and she greeted me with, 'Morning.'

I looked out the window and replied, 'Yes it is!'

'Smart Alec.'

I had barely sat down when God strolled through the front door and sat opposite me complaining how Mary was annoying him.

'It's not even 11:00am and she's giving me the shits already,' he said as he proceeded to move my breakfast plate that was in front of him, to a position in front of him.

Jacquetta shrugged her shoulders and off to the kitchen she trudged. God ate, Jacquetta cooked and I tried to read the *Heavenly Times,* the local newspaper. But God wanted a whinge, and a whinge he was going to have.

'She went into my office to clean up and found my magazines. She erupted like a volcano. Went right off her head, she did.'

'Got me beat as to why,' I said as I smiled from behind my paper. Breakfast arrived for me, again. This time I put down my paper and leaned over my plate of food in one of those 'I own this' stances.

'I'm going to have to hang out here for a while, if that's OK?' said God. 'I need time for the old girl to calm down.'

'Sure,' I said, 'I've been meaning to catch up with you. I've been thinking about a little something. How difficult do you think it would be to introduce gambling into schools on Earth as a part of the school curriculum?'

God almost fell off his chair. 'I can see the headlines now, God gets kids gambling.'

'Hear me out first.'

I told God that the problem with the education system on Earth, was it's useless and pointless as it teaches all the wrong stuff. Mark Twain, a highly regarded author on Earth, knew the same. He once said, 'I never let school interfere with my education'. Mark Twain did all right for himself.

In days well and truly gone by, nobody went to school. Without schools everyone got along, the sky didn't fall in. Like Twain, not one subject at school or university taught me anything about my preferred method of earning the golden dollar, gambling. I wrote an assignment for university once where I suggested that by gambling successfully, Third World countries could wipe out their national debt. Take a football game: two teams play; therefore, you have a fifty-percent chance of backing the winning team. If a Third World country stopped paying out most of the donated aid money they received on corruption, and instead, gambled it all on the winning team, their national debt would be neutralised. With no more debt to pay, the Gross Domestic Product of the country has to increase.

On the other side of the coin, if the team they've selected loses, so what? As a Third World country, it complains to the United Nations or the World Bank and a whole pile of taxpayers' money arrives on a big white horse to bail them out. If that fails, they can hop on a boat and go live in another country courtesy of *their* taxpayers. The lecturer was not amused. He didn't understand economics at all.

I've believed for many years, if schools taught gambling to children, the world would be a better place. Teaching gambling in primary school negates the need for high schools and universities. Sure, there'd be some initial job losses, but after a few generations, no one would remember. Children could utilise the internet at home to do their gambling homework, by way of online betting agencies. Teaching kids to gamble at an early age gives them a skill for life, a skill they can use anywhere, anytime, a global skill. Think of the security for the kids and the peace of mind for their parents, as they'd know their children were at home, safely gambling, instead of being out with nuff-nuffs, wearing hoodies, and stealing stuff from their local 7-Eleven.

Parents and their kids could gamble together; all-round wholesome family entertainment. Let's not forget if people were able to gamble from home, there'd be no need for any more social interaction with others. Gone would be the cafés and their overpriced coffee, fatty buns and biscuits – obesity crisis finished.

Instead, the kids of Generation Gambling would form strong relationships with online betting agencies. The smart kids could solve world poverty by teaching the starving how to gamble for food via social media like online poker websites.

'Well, bugger me,' said God, 'I hadn't thought of that. We could convert the young to the Baptist way in primary school. Kindergarten even! The only text book they would require would be my Bible.'

The following day I called Jesus and told him I was coming over for a chinwag about my Holy Grail project. Jesus, being the central figure in the New Testament, would know where to start.

I arrived. He said, 'Yo, bro, I'll get cooking on some crack. I mean I'll get cracking on some cooking and we can chew the fat over lunch.'

Lunch was lamb cutlets; they were delicious. One of the

benefits of having the Lord as my shepherd, is that he always manages to obtain the best cuts. I explained my plan for the Holy Grail to Jesus. Jesus advised me to research my subject fully to save the embarrassment of having a book published like the New Testament. Strangely enough, the biblical authors never asked to interview Jesus. They just sat down and made up the stories. Call me slow on the uptake, but if you're going to write stories with a main character, you should at least interview him; it's manners. They failed to mention his sand drawings too. Jesus told me I should concentrate my writing on strengths, not on any weaknesses. I knew exactly what he meant: 'Let the weak have Earth for the strong will have Heaven.'

This flies directly in the face of every Human Resources person in the world. For reasons beyond me, they seem to think the only way to improve yourself is to concentrate on your weaknesses. What rot! If you're about to get into a fire-fight with the enemy, and you're carrying a knife, a pistol containing ten bullets and an automatic machine gun with a belt of ammunition containing 400 rounds, where does your strength lie? Trust me; it lies with the automatic machine gun and the 400 rounds of ammo. That's your Goddamn strength, pull the trigger and introduce the bad guys to a world of hurt. Human Resources have also been giving the Earth the shits since they were invented.

The following morning I rose early. I had a Bible about gambling to write. I sat in front of a Mac computer in the study and scratched my head wondering where to start. Not on writing, but where do you start with a Mac PC? It's going to be easy to write God's true word, but to use a Mac computer – bloody Hell. I wondered if Macintosh and MacDonald's were related. I also wondered if eating a Macintosh is healthier for you than eating at MacDonald's. It's certainly easier to understand MacDonald's food. You open up the lid of the little box which holds your burger and you know what you're about to consume is nothing short of a massive intake of calories which constitutes a fat attack of mega proportions. Whereas when you opened up the lid of a Macintosh, you have no idea how to work it. It causes your frustration levels to rise. I decided the use of either a Macintosh or a Macdonald's was going to be bad for my health. I moved to a Windows-based computer.

Jacquetta came into the study after all of ten minutes and asked me what I was doing. I explained to her that I was commencing to write God's book.

'That's nice, dear,' she commented. 'What are you going to call it?'

'Good question,' I said. 'I have no idea.'

What was I going to call it? Bugger me, something more to think about.

'Do you want breakfast?' she asked.

'Sure thing,' said God as he appeared suddenly through our doorway. The Big Fella moves in mysterious ways and his ability to turn up at meal times is uncanny.

'How come you're not using the Mac?' asked God.

'I sacked the Mac,' I answered.

While Jacquetta was in the kitchen knocking up a feed for God and me, we discussed the task, especially what to call his new Bible. We bounced around a few possible title names. I suggested any title involving the words Holy Grail wouldn't be smart, as people would think the book was about some old relic. We couldn't use the title Bible either.

'Anything that looks, feels or smells like a Bible has a bad rap,' I said. 'A lot of people don't believe in it. Your book has to be believable as it is the true word of God,' I said.

'Well, let's put our thinking caps on and I'm sure you'll have another idea,' he replied.

Let Us Pray

....

God, this can't be right
A Bible you want me to write
The other one took so long
Jesus was dead and gone before it came along
A Bible of truth you say
Not full of crap like the other one
Amen

The Prophecies of Chapter Fourteen

→ To get to Heaven, you have to be of Baptist faith. To make money, you have to be of winning faith. Put the two together, and it's easy street for you.

→ I learnt nuffing in sckool as I never needled me too much of them that there edumacation stuff.

→ Governments who don't allow the teaching of gambling in schools hinder economic growth.

→ Nothing better prepares a young person for the future than a few winners at 10/1.

→ I simply do not understand Macintosh computers. They look neat. They look professional. But I do not understand how to use them.

15

Heaven was in party mode, and all around knew that it was so. The place was buzzing like a swarm of bees on a nectar patrol. A celebration, weeks in planning, had begun, but not because of the wedding in Cana, where Jesus turned water into wine by saying Abracadabra a few times. Neither did this celebration have anything to do with the possible sighting of an ark on top of Mount Ararat.

This celebration in Heaven was super special. Music was playing, champagne corks were popping and dancing and yahooing were the order of the day. It was the Big Kahuna's birthday, and he was having a blast. David asked God how old he was.

'Old enough to know enough, and young enough to do it all again,' responded God.

David laughed, but it wasn't a joke. How he ever beat up on Goliath is a still mystery to me. I saw Jesus in a party hat wandering around with his mother and the Three Wise Men.

The Master of Ceremonies for God's birthday bash was Ezekiel. He eventually summoned us to find a place at the enormous banquet table as it was time to eat. Jesus excused himself and stood in the corner sucking on a reefer. The lad has had a problem with banquets ever since the last one he attended on Earth. We ate, we drank and we had fun, because that's what you do at a party. God found me and suggested we take a walk to get some fresh air. He had a bottle of champagne and two glasses.

We walked and he talked and poured. He asked, 'How's my Bible going?'

'Good,' I answered. 'But to test it out before we give it to the Earth people and the folks in Heaven to mess with, we should introduce a betting agency in Heaven. Practise what we preach first.'

After more discussion and idea swapping, we floated back to party central and immersed ourselves in conversation, food and wine. God asked a few merry partygoers what they thought of having a betting agency in Heaven. They loved the idea. Only Judas didn't agree.

Judas scoffed, 'A betting agency? Ridiculous idea. Gamblers never win.'

Jesus yelled for Judas to shut his traitorous mouth.

In response, Judas commenced jumping up and down, yelling, 'The Romans are coming! The Boat People are coming!'

Jesus began to display the symptoms of an anxiety attack as he nervously looked around.

God was super happy. He was yelling, jumping, giving high-fives to everyone and screaming, 'Hallelujah, praise the Lord.'

Again, I reminded him, he was the Lord. 'Oh yes, of course, I am!'

I noticed God on the dance floor doing the moonwalk with another black guy, who was wearing a white glove on his right hand singing *Billie Jean*. Then, they broke into another song called *Beat It*. I've always had a problem with a black guy, wearing a white glove on his right hand, running around singing a song called *Beat It*. There's kids about for crying out loud. Behave.

'In our book, I want you to dedicate a whole chapter to yourself,' yelled God. 'Call it, The Book of Revelations.'

'Already been done,' I replied. 'It's in the other one.'

The quartet of Mathew, Mark, Luke and John took to the stage and entertained the crowd with juggling acts.

Jesus and Ezekiel made their way towards the stage. Joseph and his band, 'The Coat of Many Colours', who replaced the juggling idiots, became silent. Ezekiel walked to the stage and took the microphone. He asked for quiet and had nice things to say about God. He then asked Jesus to come up on stage and say a few words.

'Unaccustomed to public speaking as I am,' said Jesus with a wry smile, 'it would be wrong of me on such an auspicious occasion not to say a few words on behalf of one of my dads.'

'I hope this isn't going to be as boring as that bloody Sermon on the Mount speech,' yelled out Judas, who'd by now had had way too much wine.

A muffled laugh broke out across the room.

'Shut up, you backstabbing mongrel Roman Boat People lover,' Jesus retaliated with, clearly embarrassed by Judas's outburst.

'Come on,' taunted Judas, 'give us another *miracle*, why don't you! How long has it been?'

Jeremiah and Daniel, both veterans of the Babylonian wars, and a couple of Archangels were providing the security for God's birthday bash. They approached Judas and suggested he leave quietly or be fed to the lions.

Judas wisely left, but not before yelling out, 'I'm no fool, Jesus; come and try to walk across my swimming pool!'

Jesus ignored him and continued with his speech. 'It is important for me to say few words on my dad's behalf on his special day.'

'How many dads you got?' hollered out Job. Job's three friends, Eliphaz, Bilbad and Zophar, burst out laughing.

They were a bunch of larrikins, thick as thieves, but harmless enough. Jeremiah and Daniel appeared. The lads disappeared.

Jesus continued, 'Wow, big daddy of them all. Today we are gathered here to celebrate your birthday.'

God nodded.

'It's hard to believe you have been around so long, you old bugger,' said Jesus.

A laugh erupted amongst the partygoers. Jesus, thinking he was on a winner with the joke, tried another one.

Laughing, he said, 'Dad, you may not be over the hill yet, but you must have a great view.'

A small chuckle came across the room. Jesus moved nervously from foot to foot and asked God to join him on stage. Twenty-five Herald Angels appeared and brought with them a massive birthday cake. They placed it in front of God.

'One angel for each year,' said God, laughing while looking a tad embarrassed.

Jesus asked everyone to join him in singing *Happy Birthday* and we did. The beaming smile across the Big Kahuna's face told all in attendance he was certainly enjoying this moment. After we had sung *Happy Birthday*, Jesus asked God to blow out the candles, make a wish and cut the cake. I saw a tear in God eyes, and then more tears started to form until he had them flowing down his face. Emotion had the better of him.

As Jesus handed the microphone to God, he asked, 'What did you wish for, Dad?'

God shrugged his shoulders and replied, 'It didn't work; you're still here!'

We laughed hard.

'Anyway,' said God, 'I've decided I'm going to have a birthday every year.' He paused and said, 'Birthdays are good for you. Statistics show the people who have the most birthdays live the longest.'

The already warmed-up crowd was now laughing so much that drinks were being spilled.

'Thank you for the wonderful gifts,' said God. 'Please write your name on them. That way if I don't like your gift, I can give it back and you can get me something else.' God was in form all right. He raised his hands and we listened. 'Thank you for attending the party and helping me celebrate. Based on the evidence I've seen, I'm the oldest person in the universe. The great thing about growing old is you tend to get a little forgetful. But that's OK, as I can now hide my own Easter eggs.'

Too funny, he was knocking them dead.

God mentioned that you're never too old to recognise a good idea, and therefore he was going to print some money so as the Heavenites could get into the fun of gambling. He received a rapturous round of applause when he mentioned, with a bit of luck, he could again end up being the Big Chief of the most dominant religion on Earth.

God publicly thanked me for the wonderful idea I had put

forward to the Heavenly Spiritual Society, and my idea of setting up a betting agency in Heaven. I thought that was nice.

God asked me to join him on stage. Somewhat surprised, I hesitated slightly but a couple of Heavenites pushed me forward. I walked up the stairs and joined God. I stood beside him and he put his arm around me. If Mother could see me now, I thought. Without warning, God dropped a bombshell which almost made the clouds thunder. God announced to the assembled believers my gambling skills could predict the future. Therefore, he was *promoting* me to the position of 'Special Heavenly Adviser to God for Profits'. My name would no longer be, Travesty the Newbie. Instead, it would be the 'Profit T, Special Heavenly Adviser to God for Profits, an approved Heavenite'. The crowd was stunned and began to murmur to each other.

Most people did the 'Ohh ahh' thing, except for the person who said 'Holy Crap!' I immediately wondered how I would get that long title on a business card. When I was living on Earth, I noticed most people, according to their business cards, were managers, general managers, directors or a head of such and such department. Where were the workers, the doers and the people who made the stuff happen? I worked out long ago business cards with fancy titles were designed to match the ego sizes of stupid people, or to cover up for inadequacies such as incompetence. Having the words Special Heavenly Adviser to God for *Prophets*, instead of manager of something on my business card made me sound like a doer, a worker. That's way better than being a stupid person.

Hang on a minute. 'A Prophet!' I exclaimed, jumping for joy. 'I'm promoted to Prophet already?' I asked.

'Well, yes and no,' answered God.

'Explain, yes and no,' I asked.

'I'm making you a *Profit*, not a *Prophet*. It's a new position I've put on the Heavenly Organisation Chart. And, you are promoted to a Heavenite. Hence, from this moment on you will be known as the Profit T.'

An ex-warrior named Ishbosheth, who according to the Bible

at Samuel 2.23.8, is rumoured to have single-handedly killed 800 men in battle with his spear, complained loudly that my promotion wasn't right. He argued that my Betterment of Heaven plan had only been approved, not implemented, and as such, I could not be promoted to a Heavenite, let alone be made a Profit. To his credit, God did listen.

When Ishbosheth had finished complaining, God said two things. Firstly, God said Ishbosheth was partly correct. True, my Betterment of Heaven plan was not implemented, but it soon would be. Secondly, as he was God, he could do as he damn well pleased and if Ishbosheth didn't like the rules, he could direct himself to a perfectly good edge to jump over. Wow, brilliant, I thought; that's how to win people.

Ishbosheth quickly replied, 'Great idea you had, God, that Profit one, I love it.'

God explained my title was Profit as I made money from gambling by predicting the future or the outcome, hence Profit.

'I can't predict the future,' I protested.

'Rubbish,' replied God, 'you can predict the winner of a horse race before they run. That means you can predict the future.'

God now instructed me to go into an anointing room and to remove my sheet so some angels could anoint my naked body with the *promotion* oil.

'Give me the oil,' yelled Jacquetta. 'I'll do it at home!'

The look of bitter disappointment on the faces of the angels was there for all to see. The look of disappointment on my face ... I kept well hidden.

My wee-wee mumbled, 'For fuck's sake!'

Jacquetta got her wish, as she always does. People began to surge forward and came up on the stage to hug and congratulate me on my promotion. One of the Saints went to kiss me on the lips. Jacquetta was there in a flash and knocked him out.

'There'll be none of that on my watch!' she said.

'That's a big wrap that God has put on the Profit T!' I heard Matthew comment to Mark, Luke and John.

Peter said to Paul and Mary, 'Wow, there could be a song in this for us.'

'You idiot!' Mary responded. We're *not* that Peter, Paul and Mary, you bloody numbskull!'

We celebrated long and hard. My lovely Golden Angel was excited about my promotion. I sang to her on the way home: 'The Big Fella loves me, this I know, for his new Bible will tell me so.'

Yep, age shall not weary me, but too many champers will. As we entered our cloud, I suggested to Jacquetta that a man of my new stature should have a least three angels. She suggested I shut up and go to bed. This I did. I tossed and turned and just when I'd start to drift off, I'd wake up again. I eventually got out of bed. I had forgotten the oiling and now she was fast asleep.

The Chronicle of Heavenly Records states on this evening, the Profit T anointed himself with promotional oil, whilst alone. He did so enjoy it. During the anointment, the Chronicle of Heavenly Records also record angels as singing:

> *Hark, the herald angels sing*
> *Glory to the well-oiled him*
> *That guy, you know,*
> *The newly anointed Profit thing*
> *Or, they may have just been drunk.*

Let Us Pray

Whoa my main man in Heaven land
Time to get our heads together
A Bible we shall write
My words shall fill the pages
And some of yours as well
We'll put the record straight
We'll tell 'em what it's like
To be Baptist through and through
The Catholics won't like it one bit
They'll have a fit
The Happy Clappers will crack the shits
When they find out to church
We never go
Like they do
Amen

The Prophecies of Chapter Fifteen

→ I'm curious, where in Palestine did Noah find kangaroos, koalas and platypi for the Ark?

→ If you get the opportunity to stand on a stage with God, get photos otherwise no one will believe you.

→ The advantage of oiling yourself is that when you're finished, you don't have to talk to anyone.

→ Too much oil on you before bedtime will make you slip on the sheets.

→ Even in Heaven, you can't escape wankers.

→ The problem with women is that they promise to do so much to you, and then they go to sleep.

16

I awoke the following morning, still chuffed at getting a promotion but concerned as to what a Profit was supposed to do. I lay in bed thinking about it. I was the first Profit appointed in Heaven and, come to think of it, self-anointed in Heaven. God didn't have a position description for me, or a list of key performance indicators as the corporate knobs liked to call them. I was puzzled as to how I could adequately fill the role of a Special Heavenly Adviser to God for Profits, when the only money coming into Heaven was play money. What advice was I meant to give? There was no sense in advising on buying real estate by the beach; God owned it all and everything else up here. As I was getting up, I did think this Profit gig was going to be one cushy number for me.

Jacquetta popped her head into the bedroom when she heard my morning rustlings.

She said, 'I haven't done the oil anointing for your promotion as yet. We were both too tired last night.'

Working on the principle, 'so long as God knows the truth, it doesn't really matter what other people know', I replied, 'No we haven't', as I removed my pyjamas and layeth my body downeth uponeth the bedeth.

Yes, no doubt about it, I had died and gone to Heaven. Anointed and massaged with oil by an angel is truly one of life's great delights. The entry in the Chronicle of Heavenly Records on this morning of mornings was: 'The Golden Angel Jacquetta anointed the Profit T in promotional oil'. The Chronicle also recorded him as being *one* lucky bastard! Whilst this anointment was taking place, the angels sang:

Hark, it's us, the Herald Angels once again
Glory to the new born Profit guy
Don't disturb him now
He's busy doing his thing
The Profit T is getting all oiled up agin

When we got out of bed the following day, I sat down to concentrate on writing God's true word, all about gambling your Baptist way to happiness. I reflected on my understanding of betting techniques and the successful concepts and methodologies that I had developed during my Earthly life. I also consulted widely with my Spiritual Overseer, namely God.

One afternoon God and I were kicking back having a few cold ones, as you do. Sometimes I'd give him a tip on a horse running in a race on Earth. We would watch the race on Heaven Sky Network TV station. God would cheer the winner home or look despondent if it lost. On losing occasions, I reminded him you don't win all the time. Any idiot who says they win all the time should be treated as you would treat a meeting with a rabid dog – run away fast.

'You don't have to win all of the time or even most of the time to end up in front,' I told him, 'but if you bet in a business-like way, you will end up in front. By betting with this mind set you're not gambling, you are investing, investing in your Holy Grail.'

'This is the stuff that *has* to go in my new Bible,' said God.

You don't have to be smart to invest, but it does help if you're not stupid. Successful investors have been using the same fundamentals and principles since the beginning of time. It's not rocket science. Investing is a road much travelled; investing smart is a road less travelled.

God confirmed he was in the process of arranging for the betting agency to be established. He decided to call it the Heaven TAB, HTAB for short. As if reading my mind, God also mentioned he was organising to have money printed and distributed to all the Heavenites. There's a skill worth knowing – printing money. The money made in Heaven wouldn't have any value, as no one needed the folding stuff up here. The distribution of the money to Heavenites was set up with ease. The Three Wise Men stepped up to the plate and volunteered to take charge as they had intimate knowledge of setting up distribution networks.

At some stage during the conversation, God suggested that he might organise a competition to see who could win the most money, but only after I had written his new Bible. He figured if only he and I were betting as per my writings, we could wipe the floor clean with the others. So died any theories I may have had of a *benevolent* God.

I thought the competition was a good idea, a good test of what I had written. Over weeks and months, the writing of God's new Bible continued at a furious rate: thirty minute timeframes, three days a week. Whilst I was busy, so was God. He and his little team of questionable people began creating money from a printing press they'd pull together. To see this in action was amazing. You have to hand it to Baptist folks; they possessed many talents, and some were legal.

I went into the study early one morning and saw the Mac computer still sitting there doing nothing. I was sure it was mocking me. I became convinced it was gloating and saying to itself, 'Here comes dumb shit. He has no idea how to understand and use a Mac computer.'

I picked it up and threw it out a window. 'Who's dumb now, ya piece of garbage?'

I heard a scream, a loud blood-curdling scream. I looked out the window and saw Joseph on his knees, massaging the head of his donkey. He must have been floating by.

'Look at my donkey's head!' yelled Joseph, 'It's all flat. Where the Hell did the Mac come from?' he hollered.

'I dunno,' I answered. 'They've been falling all day. I'll look into it for you.'

Joseph and his flat-headed donkey hobbled away.

'What was that noise about?' enquired Jacquetta as she came into the study.

'Unless Mary lets Joseph get a new one, I don't think there'll be any more hee haw coming from Eeyore,' I answered.

I usually reserved three afternoons a week for discussions with God on my latest writings. God would read what I had written, ask questions, take notes and offer advice. During one meeting, God told me the newly appointed managers of HTAB were chomping at the bit to get cracking. They were two shady ex-bankers who had died because of the extreme stress placed on them by an investigation into their fraudulent activity during some Global Financial Crisis (GFC) on Earth. Fortunately for them, they had been baptised as Baptists. God believed they had the right credentials to manage other people's money. I didn't. I asked what a GFC was. God gave me a quick overview and said it was some big financial cock-up on Earth.

From God's quick overview of the GFC, I gleaned a few greedy people had shafted the working class people, again. Some things on Earth never change. This is where gambling is different. The gambling dollar is good for everyone as it keeps money flowing through the economies of the world. When some people have losing years, others have winning years and spend. Hence, money keeps flowing. Gambling money is not controlled by a select group of people as many people have seen the light and gamble. In other words, too many people are involved in gambling for anything *illegal* to happen, right? Whereas in the case of the GFC, the very people who should never control money, namely politicians, senior public servants and shady business people, kept the folding stuff for themselves. They didn't let the money flow. Due to this unequal distribution of money, good old Earth's financial system blew its poo-poo valve by way of a meltdown.

In the middle of the GFC, right when some people on Earth were struggling to put three feeds a day on the table for their families, bludging politicians gave themselves a massive pay rise courtesy of the taxpayers. Little wonder there wasn't enough money to go around. This is why the working-class people are the battlers of society. God's description of the GFC made me determined to ensure his new Bible was written to help the battlers. The people our governments ignore.

One morning, I could write no more. I had finally finished rambling. I had God's new Bible, his true word, the benefit of all my knowledge in the Sport of Kings to help those who sought their Holy Grail. The true word of God was complete. I told God and it blew him away.

He read the entire draft and hollered, 'Finally, something believable! A guide for people to find their Holy Grail based on facts and truths, how original.'

In the following days, the managers of HTAB got themselves organised and put out the sign, 'Open for Business'. God announced the competition details to select the best gambler in Heaven. No one had access to the details of God's true word, apart from him and me. The Big Kahuna was as happy as a baby bouncing in a cot that had just discovered that by standing up and screaming its lungs out, it could piss its parents right off.

God was rubbing his hands together. Yep, the Big Fella was ready to play; he was as keen as hot mustard on a hot dog. God and I entered the betting competition under the pseudonym of GodsOwn. God suspected no one would know who we were. I suspected they would. And play we did. We played hard and the Heavens shook as we brought the HTAB to its knees. The syndicate of GodsOwn took the lead early in the competition and never relinquished it. We invested our profits into good strong companies like the White Sheet Making Inc., Sammy's Sandal Manufacturers, HeavenNet and Cable Heaven. Most people lost because they bet haphazardly. Others lost because they got greedy. They gambled more than they should in an attempt to win more. There is no need for greed. Greed convinces the brain to imagine things that are hard to achieve, and hence greedy people lose.

GodsOwn continued to belt the living crapper out of HTAB throughout the Heavenly year that was. The Return on Investment (ROI) of 7,350% was another shining star. In other words, for every one dollar invested, GodsOwn achieved a return of $7,350.00.

Some of the money was realised from the profits of successful gambling, and some of the profits were realised from reinvesting. The old adage of never work for your money, let your money work for you is an excellent way to lead your life. By the year's end, GodsOwn had triumphed beyond my wildest dreams, the point proven many times, gambling is profitable, most profitable indeed. God's true word, his new Bible had earned its rightful place as being the guide for achieving your own personal Holy Grail.

Heaven was once again the scene of much celebration. The reason for this celebration was not because Noah had found his missing raven, nor was it because the Pope had decreed that it was OK for Catholic Priests to get it on with women. The reason for this celebration was because two weeks prior, I had formally handed my Betterment of Heaven plan to the Board of Approvals for the Heavenly Spiritual Society. Today, God's true word had been distributed to the people of Heaven. They loved it, apart from the HTAB managers. It was time to celebrate our success.

It was at this celebration God offered up one of the most profound and meaningful statements ever recorded in the Chronicle of Heaven. He said, 'If the Profit T becomes known for one thing and one thing only, let him be known for introducing gambling into Heaven.' I was proud.

Jonah, who always stank like a fish, sidled up beside me. According to Jonah 1.17 in the Bible, God sent a large fish to swallow Jonah whole. Poor Jonah spent three days and three nights inside the fish. Then bugger me at Jonah 2.10, it tells us God commanded the fish to spit him out. I know, some things are hard to digest, but I'm trying to give you an understanding of how much he stank. I accepted his congratulations and a bucket of squid. God saw what was happening, called me over and promptly gave the bucket to Joseph along with some instructions about rubbing his donkey with it to help inflate its head. Joseph immediately left.

I have no idea at what part of the festivities it happened, but the Big Fella dropped another bombshell. He told the assembled Brethren of Dead Baptists he would soon be going on a holiday.

Jesus piped up, 'Who the Hell has ever heard of God taking a holiday?'

I said to Jesus, 'I think you might be filling in for your dad while he's away.'

Jesus replied, 'Be buggered I will – far too much responsibility for me.'

I said, 'It'll be good for you to step up to the plate and take charge. Think of the experience, and it'll look good on your CV. Human Resources people love that shit.'

Jesus said, 'I tried that experience thing for a year once before. I ran my ministry where I had twelve other people working for me. Bloody pain in the arse it was. All they wanted to do was party. I had to do everything while they all sat around whingeing and bloody complaining; it gave me the shits.'

'You can't go on a holiday,' said Lazarus. 'Who would look after the place?'

'Running Heaven isn't all that hard,' answered God. 'Bugger me; dead people don't take much looking after.'

The general murmur from the crowd indicated all agreed with God.

'I'll take my Mac and my phone,' said God. 'Everything will be fine.'

Jacquetta raised her eyebrows at me. I shrugged my shoulders. Again, as on Earth, as in Heaven, women expect us men to be mind-readers. How was I to know that my lovely Golden Angel had borrowed her father's Mac? Yes, the very same Mac of 'out the window and donkey fame'.

'How long will you be gone on your holiday?' someone asked. 'Don't rightly know,' answered God. 'If I really enjoy the holiday, I might semi-retire.'

'Yea, yea, yea,' sayeth some Heavenly tongues.

Others yelled out, 'Semi-retire? That's a joke. You can't retire; you're God.'

'Sure, Heaven can look after itself for a while, but not forever. Who's going to look after Earth and the other planets and universes?' someone else asked.

This is what my gambling God, the God of all Baptists said, 'The Profit T can run the place. He will be my Stand-In-God.'

Complete and utter silence.

I was mid-stride to get another drink. I about turned and asked, 'What did he say?'

Others said, 'What did he say?'

Jesus looked at me with one of those stupid boy grins of his and said, 'You're it!'

Jacquetta said, 'Well, we never saw this one coming.'

I said loudly, 'I'm not it, and we have seen nothing coming because there is nothing coming.'

I looked at God and said, 'Whoa now Captain Suntan, you had better slow down and say again what you just said; we've quite clearly misunderstood you.'

And he did. God told us again: the Profit T would run Heaven while he was on his holiday.

I said, 'No, he can't.'

'Why not?' asked God.

I answered, 'Despite what your daughter may think of me, I am not a God! I've never done any God courses or training. Come to think of it, I've never done a Godly thing in my entire life. I'm not qualified. Even in bed I'm more beastly than Godly.'

God replied, 'Doesn't matter. I knew nothing about being a God first off either.'

'Why can't you leave it in the family, as per that Son of God stuff? Jesus can do it,' I said.

Judas yelled out, 'He wouldn't be any good at the job. The first sign of a Roman Boatie, Jesus would be straight on the phone to his dad pleading with him to come and save his sorry arse again.'

God looked at me and said, 'I am keeping it in the family. Everyone here is one big happy Baptist family.'

'I'm not happy,' I said, as I looked for some for assistance from my lovely Golden Angel. She offered none. She was preoccupied thinking about the new wardrobe of sheets she would have to get, to go with her role as partner of the Stand-In-God.

God said to me, 'You gave me the idea of having a Stand-In-God.'

Jesus said, 'Think of the experience. It'll look good on your CV. Human Resources people love that shit.'

'Fuck up, Jesus,' I snapped. 'I'm not in the mood for you right now.'

I pleaded with God, 'I didn't expect you to get on board with the idea. It was more of a suggestion. And there was no mention of me being the stand-in.'

'Your writing of my Word qualifies you for the job,' answered God.

I saw the nodding of the heads from the others and their mumbling of, 'Yeah, good point, God. Anyone who can write God's Word is surely qualified to be a Stand-In-God.'

'That still doesn't qualify me to be a Stand-In-God. I don't know what I have to do,' I fired back.

'Do what I do,' said God.

'You do nothing!' I replied.

'See how simple it is to be God.'

Dead set, I was on a flogging of floggings. Whenever God got a bee in his bonnet about something it was near impossible to change his mind. At times in my life, I'd known short spurts of pure brilliance intermingled with long periods of nothing. But this time, my brilliance had gone AWOL on me.

'I still don't know why Jesus can't do it,' I said.

'He doesn't want to because he's too busy,' answered God.

'Busy doing what?' I asked as I looked at Jesus.

God replied, 'He's working on his one-man play called "Walking on Water". He's already rehearsing.'

'But he's already done that one!' I yelled.

'Not recently, and not in Heaven,' said Jesus.

I looked at Jacquetta and said, 'Why can't you run Heaven for a while? You're God's daughter.'

Before she could answer, God interrupted and said, 'Nope, she can't. I've already asked her. Apparently, all of her spare time is taken up looking after you.'

I glared. She smiled.

'But God,' I protested, 'I was going to go on a resting sabbatical. I've written your true word, I need a spell.'

'No, you don't,' said God.

'I've got Workitis,' I said.

'Yeah, and I've got membership to John Boy's atheist club,' responded God.

Joshua yelled out, 'I can do it. I can be a Stand-In-God. Pick me, pick me.'

Joshua had become the leader of Israel after the death of Moses. The story I heard was Joshua, with a bit of God's help, supposedly captured many of the cities and towns of Canaan. To me, they sounded like good qualifications for the job.

I immediately said, 'Give the gig to Joshua. He brought down the walls of Jericho with his trumpet. Joshua also arranged for the huge hailstones to fall from the sky and crush the enemy at the battle of Gibeon. That has to be a good thing. It's a rare talent if you can pull that stuff off; give him the job.'

'I thought it was the Roman Boat People who broke the wall,' interjected Jesus.

'Nah, it was before their time,' said Joshua.

'The cursed Roman Boat People would have been somewhere,' mumbled Jesus. 'They always are, mongrel invaders. You never know when they're going to turn up on a beach near you.'

God said, 'Hang on, Joshua. You didn't do the walls falling down thing by yourself. I had to help.'

'But I could have done it all by myself,' replied Joshua.

'What rot,' said God. 'What baloney. You've never done anything by yourself, you nitwit. It was always me helping you.'

'People,' I said, 'let us focus on the issue at hand. Does it really matter who did what and who helped whom? The issue at hand is a Stand-In-God. Forget everything else. Joshua is well qualified for the job.'

My pleas fell upon deaf ears. No one was interested. Joshua and God continued to argue about who had brought the wall down, and then Joshua made a mistake. A big mistake. He told God he could prove he had brought down the wall of Jericho by going back to Earth, rebuilding the wall and having it fall again when he played his trumpet.

Unfortunately for Joshua, God said, 'OK, you can leave tomorrow.'

Whilst Joshua was spluttering and trying to back pedal, God looked at me and said, 'You're it. You're my Stand-In-God. Best you suck it up, princess.'

I'm not sure if I drank that evening because I was happy I had finished writing God's Bible, or because I was trying to drown my sorrows. I didn't want to be a Stand-In-God. I was a beast. Whatever the reason, I got drunk, legless, in fact. In the wee hours, my lovely Golden Angel attempted to take me home. My words were slurred and I was unsteady on my feet. I told her I was now a Stand-In-God, and therefore I would go home whenever I liked, and with whomever I liked. I'm not sure at what point it was exactly, that I realised I may have said the wrong thing. Perhaps it was straightaway, or perhaps it was later in the morning when I woke up inside a rubbish bin. I was upside down with a carrot shoved up my butt. I knew it was a carrot as when I removed it, it was orange in colour, with a green top. It was a large carrot, large to look at, and prior to removal, it had felt large.

After I got myself out of the rubbish bin, I floated rather erratically home and went inside. I acknowledged my lovely Golden Angel Jacquetta with a little nod of the head, and proceeded towards the bedroom. The evening was a learning experience for me. The lesson I learned was the wrath of a Golden Angel can be severe; being Stand-In-God counts for nothing.

The following day, we stood on the lush landing ground of the airport that belonged to the preferred airline of Heaven, 'On the Wings of a Snow White Dove', and bid farewell to Joshua. He appeared dejected and unhappy as he left for Earth, with his trumpet in hand. I appeared hung over and floated bow-legged.

'Good luck, Josh, me old mate,' God yelled. 'Have fun stacking stones.'

In a wave of the big bird's wings, Joshua had gone back to Earth to find a wall, an old and fallen down wall. I did hope he found it in a hurry; otherwise, he was going to be wandering around for a long time. Perhaps it was Joshua's trip that inspired the song, 'The Happy Wanderer'.

When God and Mary returned from their holiday, I handed God back his job. He was right; there really was nothing to do. I had long suspected it was purely a managerial job. Heaven ran itself. Some days I didn't even turn up. As soon as God settled back into his chair, he started gambling on HTAB again and working on a plan to see if it was possible to convert all the race-horses on Earth to being Baptist so they could get into Heaven.

Noted in the Chronicle of Heavenly Records around this time was that someone from Gamblers' Anonymous had rung God and asked him if he needed any help to overcome his gambling addiction.

God's response: 'I bet you fifty dollars I don't!'

Let Us Pray

....

Lordy, Lord, Lordy
Here's what I think
Earth people do far too much work
And have far too little play
In your new Bible
I'm going to show them the way
To gain pleasure from their work
By quitting and doing something else
It's much more fun
Especially, when you win a ton
Amen

The Prophecies of Chapter Sixteen

→ Never pass up the opportunity for a good oiling.

→ Money made in Heaven is not accepted as legal currency in any country on Earth.

→ In some countries, it may be against the law to print and distribute your own money. Once again, check with your legal adviser.

→ Never throw anything out of windows.

→ If you ever get to the position of being a Stand-In-God, don't fret. It's simple stuff.

→ Love God sure, but fear the carrot.

→ If you see a person building a wall, it could be Joshua. Stop and say hello.

→ If you see a person with a trumpet near a built wall, bugger off just in case it is Joshua.

17

There are days in your life when God should be ignored, totally. This day was to be one such day. In hindsight I should have run away and hidden, or jumped on a leaky boat and applied for asylum in another Heaven.

The day started well enough. My lovely Golden Angel Jacquetta and I floated towards the House of God for a spot of morning tea. We stopped and listened to Jesus and twelve of his long-haired mates singing praises about themselves. Birds were tweeting merrily in a couple of trees nearby. We listened to a few more Jesus songs before continuing to the House of God. God was sitting in his big wooden rocking chair on the deck, smoking his pipe when we arrived. Mary was sitting with him and Joseph was attending to his donkey. God's furrowed brow showed he was deep in thought. Mary and Jacquetta disappeared inside to talk girl stuff and make morning tea, but not before Mary patted God on the head and said, 'There, there. Profit T is here now. He'll help you, I'm sure.'

God grunted.

'Well now,' I said, 'what's bugging the big fella today?'

God stared at me as he took a long puff of his pipe, stopped rocking and said, 'We have a problem.'

See, here it is again. When people say *we* have a problem, it immediately implies you are somehow involved. Now I don't care if it's God or whoever, but every single time I've been told *we* have a problem, I never had one until after the person had finished saying *that* sentence. I enquired of God as to which part of the *we* bit he thought I belonged to. That was the signal for God to launch into a tirade of abuse directed at the people who caused the GFC. God pointed out to me the headlines in the *Heavenly*

Times. They told a tale of share market slides, high unemployment, low superannuation returns, ailing economies and other such harbingers of doom and gloom.

'I still can't see *we*,' I said after glancing over them.

'I may have found a way for *us* to solve the GFC problem,' God said.

Us as well as we! Now it's we and us! Not him and them, we and us.

'God, I don't have a problem. My life is cruising along wonderfully well,' I said as I emphasised how much I was enjoying my resting sabbatical after writing his Bible and filling in for him when he was on holiday.

I pointed to the front of my sheet that had the words, Special Heavenly Adviser to God for Profits, clearly embossed on it.

I added, 'In a roundabout way, that title says, I couldn't give a rat's butt about any GFC on Earth.'

God ignored me and proceeded to tell me the GFC on Earth was hurting people. People had lost trust in the world's financial systems and products. The financial regulations put in place to prevent financial declines like the GFC from occurring were either ignored or weren't sufficiently strong enough in the first place. Some of the banks required government taxpayer-funded bailouts.

The poor old taxpayer had to bail out the rich yet again, because the rich were greedy and always wanted to get richer. Bad government policy had added to the problem. A law should have been introduced declaring if a government loses taxpayers' money on dumb government policy decisions; then the dumb politicians who introduced the dumb policy in the first place, should be forced to pay for their mistakes out of their own personal money, instead of slugging the poor, struggling taxpayers.

God broke my train of thought by saying the battlers were hit hard. People put their retirement plans on hold as they incurred massive losses to their retirement funds. People were losing their jobs because of stalling economies or economies going backwards. Countries were going broke. The world was in turmoil, a global recession loomed large.

'So what?' I interrupted. 'We're in Heaven, not on Earth. Have a look around; no recession here.'

'We have to solve it,' replied God.

'Why?' I said defiantly. 'I've just said it's an Earth problem; let Earth solve it. I'm all right, Jack.'

God informed me the GFC was affecting everything including religion. 'Ministers and priests and whoever of religions were whinging and whining they weren't getting enough money in the Sunday collection plates to commence capital works programs,' he said.

'Hang on,' I said. 'The new capital works programs the churches are banging on about would be nothing more than building bigger churches designed to contained bigger auditoriums with coffee shops, car parks, and playgrounds for kids. This is so the wankers attending the stupid church can park their luxury cars in style, go inside, dump their kids, grab a coffee, sing a stupid song, say a prayer and then nick off and trample on the poor for another week.'

God replied, 'I'm hearing some churches have had to dip into their church funds to support the needy with food and clothing.'

'Imagine that! Religious organisations actually having to help the needy instead of helping themselves to more real estate, overseas trips and pay rises, courtesy of donations and government taxpayer handouts,' I said.

I settled back in my chair. I wasn't sure if God was listening to me or not. I pointed out that most of the money donated to religious groups, and, for that matter, charity organisations to assist the less fortunate, never gets to them. A raise of his eyebrows told me he was listening. Instead, the money was used to pay the salaries of staff associated with the charity or religious organisation. Employees of some charities fly Business Class on aircraft, courtesy of the money donated.

'Bloody Hell,' said God, 'I didn't know that was going on.'

'These scams would make the Three Wise Men proud,' I replied.

When I was living on Earth, I refused to donate any money to a charity or religious organisation unless it was non-profit. Executives of some charities earn high six-figure salaries, some seven-figure salaries. Those salaries come from people's donations and taxpayer government grants.

'My advice is to ignore the GFC,' I said.

'I can't do that. I'm God. I have to do something. It's becoming so bad that World Vision has a problem seeing a way out of it. Anyway, I have an idea for us.'

Here he goes again with this *us* stuff! God explained he believed Neville the Devil caused the financial turmoil engulfing Earth.

'It's trademark Devil stuff. Right up there with the Adam and Eve and the Serpent and Apple thing,' he announced.

Then God, the God of great concern, enlightened me as to the *we* and the *us*. He believed the only way to save Earth from further misery was to ramp up the distribution of his new Bible in pronto quick time to the Baptists on Earth. If they and others who joined the Baptists adopted its teachings, they would find their own personal Holy Grail and by doing so, would successfully gamble their way out of the GFC. Naturally, this would also assist him greatly in becoming the Top Dog on the block again. The people would see that he, a Baptist God, had helped save the world from the GFC, and in doing so, non-Baptists would flock to their nearest Baptist church to sign on.

I agreed. It all made sense to me. If things were as bad as God was portraying, our Baptist family on Earth needed to understand my teachings quickly. God gets the credit for saving the world; others see the benefits of belonging to the Baptists and join up. This equates to more numbers. God becomes the Head Honcho again.

'Good plan,' I said. 'I like it.'

My God, who now had a smile on his face, said this to me: 'I'm glad you like it. You have to go back to Earth and teach the Baptists about finding their Holy Grails and show them the path.'

'W-what did you say?' I asked.

He said it again.

'Pig's arse, I have to go back,' I said.

'Yes, you do.'

I believe at this stage of the conversation there was a long pause on my part, followed by, 'Whoa now, Captain Surprise, don't volunteer me. I didn't sign up for this. This is God shit. If you want someone to go back, you do it. I'm as happy as a piglet running around at a Muslim bar-b-que. I know I ain't going to get eaten. I can't say the same for the sheep or the goats.'

'I can't go back,' said God as he leaned forward and motioned for me to come closer.

I leaned closer and God whispered, 'Mary was *not* the only woman I sought solace and compassion and understanding from, if you know what I mean.'

'Get outta here!' I said. 'You randy old bugger!'

'Shush, shush, keep your voice down,' whispered God.

'Do you mean to say there could be more Sons of God or even Daughters of God getting around on Earth?' I asked.

'I don't rightly know,' answered God, 'but I do know there wouldn't be any animals of God getting around. I do have some standards – unlike others.'

'Well, bugger me, and let me catch my breath. You dirty old man you.'

'Leave the *old* bit out of it, will you? You have no idea what it was like to be up here for so long by yourself. I learned from the Mary episode. I never told the others my real name or where I lived. But my problem is, if I go back to Earth again, I may be recognised and I'll have to pay child support again for who knows how many. If the claims are backdated through the eons, I'm buggered.'

'How many others were there?' I asked.

'I never kept a tally,' answered God. 'I had a troubled youth. I had to seek solace and compassion and understanding regularly. My parents abandoned me, you know. Bugger me, I don't even know who they are. That shit's tough for a young god growing up.'

I had to try hard to hold the laughter in.

I said, 'Well, mate, you have to front up, accept responsibility and pay out if Jesus and Jacquetta have siblings, half-siblings.'

'No way,' replied God. 'Mary would kill me!'

That did it. I burst out laughing so loudly that Mary and Jacquetta heard me and came outside to see what was so funny.

God was onto it in a flash and said, 'Profit T thinks I'm joking when I say I'm going to send him to Earth to sort out the GFC.'

'No, you're not,' I said. 'I'm dead, so I can't go back.'

'I'll make you undead, and then I'll make you dead again when you come back. You can keep your other Heavenly abilities to float and I'll throw in the ability for you to work a few miracles,' said God. 'They helped make Jesus popular.'

'You can do that?'

'Yep.'

If I've said it once, I've said it a million times: God's skill set is simply breathtaking.

Jacquetta bought into the conversation and said, 'That'll be nice for you, dear; a trip back to Earth. You'll be able to catch up with your relatives.'

I fell off my chair in shock. I was lying on my back, thrashing my arms and legs, doing a dying-ant impression whilst yelling, 'No, no, not that. Please God, no. The toot-toots from their "Feel Sorry for me Train" would give me the utter bleeding shits. I couldn't take it. I'd go insane. You couldn't; you wouldn't.'

God and Mary were puzzled by my display. People believe you can pick your friends, but not your family. I'm smart, I can do both and I do it so damn well. I had Jacquetta, Mary and God in hysterics as I recounted some stories involving some of my annoying, whiny bum relatives.

God seemingly agreed with me as he said, 'There's nothing like burning a few bridges to stop the crazy ones from following you.'

Suddenly it dawned on me. I yelled, 'Holy crap! They've been baptised in a Baptist Church, the crazy ones. I'm screwed. One day they'll end up in Heaven. They could be my neighbours forever.'

The moment I opened my mouth I knew I had made a rod for my back. God latched on to this rod as quickly as a nimble-footed cat latches onto a dumb bird that lands in front of it. It didn't take long for God and me to reach a mutual agreement. If I returned to Earth to share the teachings about finding your Holy Grail by gambling with the Baptists and whoever else joined, he'd ensure the relatives of mine that used to annoy me would never get into Heaven. Besides, there is an ancient Heavenly rule banning trains because there were no railway tracks. Hence, the 'Feel Sorry for me Train' couldn't operate. Toot toot to that!

Whilst this frank exchange of views between God and me had been occurring, Jacquetta and Mary had gone back inside to get the pikelets and coffee for morning tea.

As they came back out, Jacquetta asked, 'Who won?'

'Who always wins?' I replied despondently as God lay back in his rocking chair, took a long draw on his pipe and said, 'I just love it when a plan comes together.'

'Let's drink to that and say Amen to whomever,' said God.

'I guess I must look at the positives from going back to Earth,' I said. 'My name could end up in lights.'

'Highly unlikely,' Jacquetta replied.

'Parks could be named after me,' I said.

'No chance in Heaven of that occurring,' Jacquetta replied.

'Statues of me could be erected,' I said.

'Nope,' Jacquetta replied.

'People will scream out my name wherever I go,' I said.

'Enough now, you're boring me. Be quiet,' Jacquetta said.

'Yes dear.'

In preparation for my journey to carry out my mission for God, I caught up with Jesus and asked for a few hints about teaching the masses, but he didn't have much of a clue. He told me he just made stuff up by telling stories and performing a few tricks to keep the crowd entertained. Not a great job, he admitted, but with his dad on his arse about getting one, he felt he had to do something. On the selection of his disciples, Jesus did point out with hindsight, twelve was probably *one* too many, and he emphasised to me the importance of appointing people who weren't smart.

'Surround yourself with dumb people. They'll make you look good,' he said.

God informed me I may have my job cut out for me trying to convert the people from other religions, especially the Catholics to the Baptist way.

'The other religions hate us Baptists, you know.'

'Why?' I asked.

God went inside and emerged a short time later with a small book about history on the Baptist religion I hadn't read or been told about. He suggested I have a read before I leave. Through this book I stumbled upon the reason why other religions don't like the Baptists.

Way back in time, the Roman Boat People were forever rounding up Christians and throwing them to the lions. This sport ranked high on the Boat People entertainment calendar. The Baptists eventually got smart, and when the Boat People came banging on their doors asking if any Christians lived there, the Baptists replied, 'Christians ya wanting, mate? Yeah mate, yeah. There's a bunch of them living in this street. Catholics they are. They breed like freaking flies mate 'cause they don't use contraception; there has to be millions of them, not flies, I mean Catholics. You go and get 'em from them houses over there, mate, and I'll see if I can round up some Happy Clappers for youse as well.'

History shows the RSPCA eventually put a stop to the lion and Christian feeding frenzy. But, the damage had been done. The world's oldest religion, the Baptists, the precursor of all the other religions, had to stand alone and unloved. All because our forefathers had dobbed the non-Baptists into the Boat People, who, in turn, fed them to the lions. But, I guess, the Baptists weren't the ones scarred by claw marks.

The day before I left for Earth, I arrived home to hear my Golden Angel Jacquetta in the shower. I went to a cupboard in the kitchen and took out the bottle, which still had some anointing oil left in it. I emptied the contents into another empty bottle and placed it on the table. My lovely Golden Angel Jacquetta greeted me as she came out of the shower.

I nodded towards the table. 'God has given me another bottle of anointing oil, smaller than the last.'

'Why?' asked Jacquetta.

'Something to do with it protecting me on my mission to Earth,' I answered.

'How strange!' she replied. 'I've never heard of that one before.'

The Chronicle of Heavenly Records do so record on this particular evening, the evening known as, 'The evening before he departed on his mission from God to save the Planet Earth,' the Profit T was anointed in oil by his lovely Golden Angel Jacquetta. The Chronicle also stated he did so love it, and whilst loving it, he sang:

All night long
She's gonna oil me
All night long
That's why I sing my song

Let Us Pray

....

Great giver of oil in the sky
Thanks for being wise
And making me thy Profit guy
Thy adviser on thy gambling
I shall be
Can I have many business cards
For all to see?
Amen

The Prophecies of Chapter Seventeen

→ Resting sabbaticals are good for the mind.

→ If anyone ever says to you, 'We have a problem,' block your ears and run.

→ It could *still* be against the law to feed Christians to the lions in certain countries. Check with your local RSPCA office before attempting.

→ When going away from home for some time, try to get one in the night before. It may be a long time between drinks.

→ Lose the fancy title on your business card; it impresses no one.

18

The day of my departure to Earth came far too early. I allowed my lovely Golden Angel Jacquetta to run her hands over my sculptured left calf muscle one last time. I was sure going to miss my free oilings. I had to pay for them when I was last on Earth.

God arrived. 'How do you feel?'

'I'm ready to rumble,' I answered.

'That's the spirit,' said God.

'Haven't we done this one already?'

The three of us floated to the airport where a crowd had gathered to farewell me. Music was playing, angels were singing beautifully and Newbies passed around drinks and meat pies. God went to a stage assembled for the occasion.

'Today,' said God as he spoke into the microphone, 'we are gathered to farewell the great Profit T, a man of vision and a whole pile of other things. So many things, he can't fit them on his business card.'

'Bloody Hell,' yelled out Isaiah, 'he won't fit in on Earth then. He needs to have at least manager on his business card.'

To the rousing applause of the crowd, God called me to the stage. God said, 'You leave today on your mission to save the Earth from the GFC. I, God of the Universe, do taketh this wine bottle and sayeth to you, taketh this wine bottle and go forth on your journey. Try not to get too pissed before you hit town.'

God looked around to see if anyone was laughing at his joke. No one was. Well, not until Jesus jumped up in front of the stage with a sign that read, 'laugh and applause'. Now the crowd laughed and clapped their hands – but not in a Happy Clapper way.

I took the bottle of wine from God and asked, 'Why do I need this wine?'

God replied, 'Have you seen the bar prices on the airline? Phew, it's highway robbery, mate, bloody private enterprise!'

'I wrote Psalm 23 for the wine drinkers,' yelled out David.

'What are you on about?' asked God.

David replied with a chuckle, 'Psalm 23 says in part; he maketh me lie down in green pastures. That's for the people who drink too much wine; it gives them the excuse they need to lie down.'

'That's not even funny,' yelled out Saul.

'You're an idiot,' yelled David. 'You're still trying to get over the fact that I killed ten times more Philistines than you. Go blow your nose and dry your eyes, ya big Nancy.'

'Whoever wrote the nonsense at 1 Samuel 18.8 that you killed more than me is a fool,' hollered Saul. 'I killed many more than you. I just didn't run around bragging about it.'

'That is so not true! And I also killed Goliath; beat that,' yelled David.

'Why don't you tell everyone you also went and killed two hundred Philistines so you could collect their foreskins for a bride price?' heckled Saul.

'I did not,' said David.

'According to what's written at 1 Samuel 18.25-27 you did so, you little foreskin grabber you. You're a bloody weirdo,' replied Saul.

God and I watched with amusement. Yep, there's some bad stuff going down in the old Bible. The very book that is supposed to subscribe to the theories of peace, happiness and love for one another, does nothing of the sort.

Ruth, the great grandmother of David said, 'Hey Profit Boy, seeing as you're going back to Earth for a while, I was wondering, did you get *one* last night?'

The assembled mass laughed and heckled until I said solemnly, 'With a face like mine, I get one whenever I like.' They went quiet.

Whilst we waited for my transport to arrive, Jesus walked up to me and said, 'Mate, I've got a piece of advice for you before you leave.'

On Earth, I had always been apprehensive about accepting advice from someone who was supposedly born of a virgin. Like how does that work? I didn't believe they could be trusted. But, this was different. This was Jesus, Son of God, brother of Jacquetta. Therefore, I listened.

Jesus said, 'Be afraid, be very afraid of the Boat People. They're no good, you know; they take everything a country has and give nothing back, and they take over the police and the government as well.'

I duly noted the sarcasm in his voice and ordered him a drink from one of the Newbies walking around with tray. I asked for a Bloody Mary. The significance of the joke was lost on him.

As we were idly chatting away, Jesus slipped a wad of notes into my hand, Earth money, and asked me to stop by Nimbin and pick him up some of the good stuff, the hooch, the Mary J, the happy grass.

I was stunned. I said, 'Jesus Christ!'

He said, 'Yes.'

I said, 'I can't do that.'

'Sure you can,' he replied. 'I've got me a plan to make hash cookies.'

Eventually, I agreed to his request, as in my head I was formulating a converting plan myself.

My Earth-bound transport arrived, looking well fed and well watered. God wished me good luck again and checked my hobile to make sure I had him on *speed* dial, in case I needed him in a hurry. My lovely Golden Angel Jacquetta hugged me and God kissed me. Or, maybe Jacquetta kissed me and God hugged me. I'm not sure; it was some time ago.

My wee-wee said, 'We'd better not be away for too long.'

I boarded the preferred airline for us Heavenites, On the *Wings of a Snow White Dove*, First Class of course. God may well love everybody equally, including the poor and the underprivileged; he may well frown upon the frivolous spending of the rich – but none of that means he wants me to fly Economy Class. Whilst flying downward and enjoying a nice red, I took time to ponder over some matters other than saving the Earth. If religion is based on a belief system, I wondered why atheists didn't have churches or hold church services. If they did, they could get in on the donation racket. It's a lucrative business. I wondered if churches had to declare to the Tax Office how much donation money they received. What did they actually do with all the donation money, apart from spending most of it on anything but its donated purpose? I knew the amount of donation money collected never matched the amount of money going out to assist the needy.

That's the problem with cash; there's no audit trail. A church or a charity could receive say $100,000 in donations during the course of one church service (Happy Clapper Churches with rich yuppies in the congregation) and give only $30,000 to the needy. That's a $70,000 shortfall. Online gambling is much safer. There's an audit trail, a digital footprint if you like, which makes it easy to see where the money has gone, when it was gambled, how much was bet and won. This means people who use online gambling sites are more likely to be more honest when compared to people who run churches and charities.

I was also giving some thought as to whether I should have a mobile ministry like Jesus did, or a static ministry from which to preach. Both had positives and negatives. Jesus was mobile, but then again, being out in the harsh sun and inclement weather might dull my complexion. Eventually, I decided to have both, which meant I would go one better than Jesus. If I was going to preach about the virtues of obtaining your own personal Holy Grail by way of gambling, I needed my own church, my very own monastery, as a base to work from. By god, I needed a *Monastery of Winning*! Of course I did! I wanted the name Profit T in lights. Having my own monastery would give me a place to put my sandals down. At times, I'd go mobile; I'd just pick the right days. I liked the name, Monastery of Winning. I quickly decided I had to find a monastery; I couldn't build one. That was too much like hard work.

Perhaps I could buy a Happy Clapper church. If the GFC was

going to be really bad, maybe some Happy Clapper churches would go into receivership. I'm guessing if the Happy Clappers couldn't afford to buy new cars every six months, and if they couldn't afford to eat out most nights of the week, their churches would be lacking donation money and be in financial strife. Imagine the uproar if the Happy Clappers couldn't afford to go to a café and order their usual 52.5 degree, half-strength, skim, chai, soy, decaf, skinny flat white, frothed cinnamon, spiced eggnog, raspberry-flavoured latte, with a marshmallow on top.

If the GFC continued long enough, Happy Clappers might have to give up buying the latest designer-label clothes to wear. Mind you, the latest designer clothes are made in exactly the same sweatshops of Asia and by the same children as the cheaper clothes. What a disaster it would be if Happy Clappers could no longer afford the expensive hand cream they needed to be able to keep clapping all the time.

My thoughts were interrupted by one of the flight attendants. The pilot wanted to know where to land as we were approaching Earth.

'Good question,' I said. 'Well picked up. We need a destination. Tell Fly Boy Nimbin, Australia will be our destination. I have a quick job to do for Jesus, and if I score for him, you guys can take it back on the return flight.'

'Imagine,' said the flight attendant, 'you're going to save Earth. What an honour. I think Jesus was on Earth once.'

'He was at that. But, he didn't save the place. He was lucky to have saved his own sorry arse,' I replied.

'Wow, he's so smart,' she said. 'To think, no one had ever heard of *sin* until Jesus starting telling people about it. You could say he invented it. I hear he also hid in a cave for three days.'

I replied, 'That's how he invented the caveman diet. He discovered by not eating food, you lose weight.'

'I bet his father is so proud of his bravery,' she answered.

'Yeah, but he's never saved anything! I'm braver,' I yelled as she floated up front to inform the pilot of the Nimbin landing, and no doubt the caveman diet.

I've heard it said Nimbin is a small town, full of tree huggers. We landed on the outskirts of Nimbin, New South Wales. In the 1970s, Nimbin was the quintessential utopian paradise heaving with idealistic hippies. Long before the rest of world caught on to climate change and global warming, the hippies were already saving water by not showering or bathing or having a decent hair-cut. Though, they did use copious of water on their dope crops. The hippies of Nimbin attempted to make life work by living in communes. A commune was the 1970s' expression for multiple occupancy, and multiple occupancy was the 1970s' expression for group sex, narcotics, weird music and strange dancing. A great gig, if you can get it.

The poor souls who lived this way did so as they needed some-where to congregate and discuss the virtues of growing alterna-tive medicines like marijuana. Many hippies attempted to prove how good marijuana was by becoming guinea pigs for their own products. Some thought marijuana improved their vision, as they could see many colours and strange sights when they were stoned. A few hippies believed their product kept them alive and feeling free, whereas many other people believed if the govern-ment stopped giving the hippies social welfare payments, they wouldn't be alive for long, nor feeling free. Some hippies, the smart ones, thought their product was so good they went entre-preneurial and sold it.

The hippies of Nimbin were very much into the working from home philosophy. Yep, they discovered how to grow little plants right in their own backyards, and other people's backyards, and in the country, almost anywhere really. The work from home philosophy became popular in Nimbin, and it wasn't long before many people went to live in Nimbin so they, too, could work from home. The area surrounding Nimbin was as pretty as a pic-ture. There were lots of rolling hills and mountains, and plenty of rainforests intermingled with a few plantations. It was very scenic. When I disembarked, the weather was hot; the flies were everywhere, but there wasn't a hippie in sight. Where are all the hippies? I shook a couple of trees, none fell out. I headed into town. Well-heeled tourists looked at me dressed in my sheet and sandals. Some nodded their heads as I walked past; others hid their children. In the main street, I saw a sign outside a shop called 'Hemp Embassy'. Just the shop I needed. How easy was this? I'll get Jesus his good gear and I'm out of here. I swaggered into the Hemp Embassy looking as hippified as I could.

I asked loudly, 'Got any dope for sale, yeah, hey, but? I want the good stuff for the son of my main man in Heaven land, not lawn clipping rubbish.'

The eyes of the dude behind the counter nearly fell out.

'Like, hey bro,' I said, 'I wanna let me hair down with some of the, you know, the Happy Grass, the Mary J, the Big Smoke, the Reefer, the beefer the better. You know man, the shit that makes you want to love everything, everybody, and where's your mama live?'

A group of Japanese tourists at the counter started to move away slowly, while smiling and nodding at me. I noticed one of them had left a camera on the bench. I picked it up and asked if they wanted to take *my* photo. The group of tourists kept on nodding and smiling at me as they made their way towards the door.

I quickened my pace towards them whilst saying, 'Come on, take my photo, man! You know you want to; you can't help yourself.'

They started to run to the door as I yelled, 'How do you like it?'

They hit the street outside and ran as fast as their little, white legs would carry them.

I went back to the counter, laughing, as the dude behind it appeared to go into cardiac arrest.

'Bag it up man and I'm outta here,' I said.

In a quivering voice the dude said, 'Jesus Christ, mate.'

I replied, 'Great, that's the man. He must have called ahead. What's the cost?'

I was quickly informed the Nimbin Hemp Embassy doesn't do the cannabis thing. In fact, the shop sells everything to do with hemp, except the cannabis itself. I was trying to point out the bleeding obvious to this guy, like how it was false advertising to call the shop the 'Hemp Embassy' and *not* do cannabis sales when I was reliably informed that hemp doesn't have enough THC (active ingredient in marijuana) to get you high. Hemp is not the same as marijuana.

I'll be buggered, I didn't know that.

My hobile rang. I looked at the caller ID and answered the call. The one thing I'd learned in life is this: if God calls, take the call and don't put him on hold. It pisses him off.

'Yo God, my main man in Heaven land,' I answered.

'How was the trip down?' he asked.

I told him it was OK but Nimbin was nothing like I expected it be. No hippies, no cannabis and the place was full of flies. The guy behind the counter started to go Japanese on me, and he too moved very slowly towards the door.

My eyes followed him and just as he almost reached it, I yelled, 'Yeah, I'm going to get God on your arse, boy. You don't want to mess with his skill set. He can lob hailstones at your head and he might do that pillar of salt shit again. You'd better look out.'

And, as per the Japanese tourists before, off ran the dude from the Nimbin Hemp Embassy in the township of Nimbin. God must have heard what was going on as he said, 'Not again! Jesus and his bloody cookies! Last time he made those damn things at home we ended up having Joseph walking around for a couple days showing off his donkey to everyone.'

'I'm going to get out of here. For some strange reason the townspeople don't understand me,' I said.

'That's how it goes sometimes,' replied God.

'Jesus had the same problem when he was down there.'

I left the inappropriately named Hemp Embassy empty-handed and returned to the Big White Dove. As I was about to board, a strange-looking person emerged from the trees and enquired of me if I was interested in buying some A-grade, Happy Big Reefer Grass. I looked at him and observed he looked like a hippie. His long matted hair, beard and the ornamental things such as peace symbols, love symbols and earrings hanging off him gave him the appearance of a hippie. I noted his flower-power shirt, unbuttoned to his waist, his flared purple pants and his bare and dirty feet.

Wild Flower Child said, 'Man, my stuff is really good. I've been in the bush over back and I could swear I've been looking at a giant freaking bird for some time. And then along you come as if you're going to ride outta here on it like Jesse James in a cowboy movie.'

We did the deal as he was still prattling on about how good his stuff was.

'A raven,' I said. 'If you see a raven, can you let Noah know?'

'Sure man, sure. Noah. Right, man; he lives nearby, does he?'

'Not really but if he turns up in a big boat sometime, you had better pull on a raincoat and some floaties.'

'Yeah, man, sure, OK and right on. Like wow, you going to ride that white bird? Man, that's grouse. You got a business card I can have?'

I gave him one. He looked at it for a moment and read aloud, 'The Profit T, Special Heavenly Adviser for Profits. Fuck me man, I'm not interested in your card unless you have the word manager or something like that on it.'

I left the only hippie in Nimbin. I was pleased with myself. My faith in the hippie movement was restored, and I did manage to score the baking mix for Jesus.

On leaving Nimbin, we flew in an easterly direction over the thick rainforests towards the beaches and the ocean of the East Coast of Australia. I wanted to scout around the area of Byron Bay to see if it would be suitable for a monastery location and outdoor sermons.

I knew Byron Bay had sparkling beaches and the region was full of natural wonders. I also knew the natural credentials of Byron Bay were impeccable. You can see humpback whales cruise past the headland, storms that create rainbows on the mountains across the bay and hang-gliders riding the thermals above the lighthouse. I knew all of this because I was reading the tourist brochure. I put it down. If the place had a beach, there would be beach volleyball. I bid farewell to the crew of On the Wings of a Snow White Dove, but not before informing them the baking mix was for Jesus.

'And tell him I want some of his biscuits when made.'

The smell of the ocean and the lovely weather of Byron Bay convinced me to find a beach, trot out the Heavenly body, grab some rays and watch a volleyball game or two before climate change raised the sea levels so much that everybody on Earth drowned. First, I decided I needed to wet the whistle. I found a pub on the main beach of Byron Bay.

I was standing by myself, bending the elbow with a glass or two at the bar when a young woman walked up, stood near me and asked the barman for a chardonnay. The lady looked at me and quite clearly liked what she saw as she smiled. I told the barman I'd pay for her drink. She thanked me and started up a polite conversation. I mentioned I'd just arrived from Nimbin. She nodded and remarked it explained a few things. She asked my name and I told her I was called the Profit T. I asked her name and she said that it was Irrelevant. I told her Irrelevant was a nice name, mysterious yet ubiquitous. Irrelevant asked me what I did for a living.

I answered, 'I've been sent from Heaven by God to save the people of planet Earth.'

I thought Irrelevant was impressed because she stood for a moment, motionless, staring straight at me. She was speechless, mouth agape.

Finally, she said, 'You're an idiot. You're a freaking, fully fledged, loony-tune nutter,' and promptly walked off.

A thought crossed my mind, two thoughts actually. The first thought was this woman didn't buy me a drink in return, and that's not on as it was her turn to shout a round. Secondly, God taught me the sweetest thing you'll ever taste is revenge.

'Interesting,' I yelled. 'Both your thighs rub together when you walk. I'm not sure I've ever seen that before. You are a big girl, aren't you?'

Irrelevant proceeded to hurl abuse at me. She questioned my parentage and the inner workings of my brain. She said I looked like the sort of bloke my relatives would love to kill. I had heard enough. I snapped. I didn't want her to be airing the family's dirty laundry.

I yelled for all in the bar to hear, 'She's piked out on her shout. It was her buy and she's doing a runner.'

Chaos erupted around me. People screamed in terror. Mothers grabbed their children, some of whom were drinking at the little kiddies' bar. Gallant fathers rushed to assist the hotel security people as they moved swiftly, and forcibly crash-tackled Irrelevant to the ground. Two bouncers held her in a headlock while others proceeded to beat her with snooker cues and chairs. Irrelevant was screaming and trying to plead her innocence, but no one was buying it.

People put ice cubes inside her clothes whilst yelling, 'How do like that, Devil woman?' Other people tried to give her a wedgie, but her butt was so big they couldn't pull her undies up. The Head of Hotel Security arrived with a shotgun and told Irrelevant to leave the premises immediately, and never to darken the hotel again. This she did, ably assisted by the people who threw her out the door. The barman shouted me a beer and said, 'Well spotted, mate.'

'You just never can tell these days,' I replied.

'You can say that again,' he said.

So I did.

After a couple more freebies, I left the pub and hit the beach. I was lucky enough to find a pair of budgie smugglers in the men's change room. I assumed they were hanging up for general public use. I did look quite the part of something, of what I'm not sure. I chilled out on the beach of white sand and soaked up the rays while listening to the sound of waves crashing onto the shoreline. To my front was the wonderful ocean, to my left was a pleasant game of beach volleyball and to my right were other people enjoying the beach. Behind me was the pub. I knew this place wasn't Heaven, but as I dug my feet into the cool sand, I thought it could well be pretty close to it.

I stretched out, thinking Byron Bay could work as a place to base my monastery. It had everything: pubs, restaurants, beaches, betting agencies and internet access for online gambling. Byron Bay was also a melting pot of surf culture, alternative philosophies and hedonistic indulgence. To me this meant one thing: more hippies, but here they were sophisticated ones. Many people holiday in the area. This was not lost on me. Holidaying Baptists would be able to spread the word of my monastery and my teachings when they got back to their home turf. Yes, Byron Bay had potential. It was also the ideal location for preaching in the outdoors. There was certainly a lot of water to do the Frolic.

Whilst deep in thought and listening to the breaking of waves collapsing onto the sand, I heard the sound of beating tom toms. I sat up and noticed a small group of people walking along the beach chanting something about finding Jesus.

I jumped up and hollered, 'I know where he's at! I know where he lives!'

Someone from the group yelled back, 'If he's in your heart, come and join us. We will praise him together.'

'It's got nothing to do with the heart; he doesn't live there,' I yelled back. 'He's in Heaven; he's got his own place.'

'He's all around us,' a woman yelled back.

'Rubbish,' I replied. 'That's the air. Jesus is in Heaven, I'm telling you.'

'Praise the Lord,' somebody with flowers in her hair hollered.

'You can forget about that,' I retorted. 'He's not into religion anymore.'

'We know he went to Heaven, but his spirit is all around us,' she answered.

'I'm still running with the air thing,' I replied.

Religious people, since the dawn of religion, have taken something simple and confused it. If Jesus was in our hearts, that would be a good thing, as he could give us early warning of heart disease. But, he's not in our hearts.

'He went to live with God for a while and now he's back with us,' some other fruit loop hollered.

'Granted,' I said, 'Jesus went to live with God but it wasn't for a while. Right now, he's probably busy in his kitchen knocking up some cookies. Truth be known, he doesn't like you lot anyway.'

'No-o way,' they responded. 'He loves us all from our Pentecostal Church.'

'We're all about campaigning for more money for Boat People,' said a person who appeared to be the head fruit loop.

'Don't tell Jesus,' I hollered.

'He'd support us,' replied the head fruit loop.

'Highly unlikely,' I said as I shook my head. 'You lot aren't going to Heaven, you know.'

They ignored me and moved on. I thought that was a nice gesture on their part. I lay back down on the sand and briefly wondered where it all went so wrong.

I wondered how people who practised the art of religion in line with the teachings of Happy Clappers, recognised each other. There are many Happy Clapper churches on Earth. How did you know who belonged to which church? Perhaps, as with the Freemasons, Happy Clappers have a secret ritual to identify who is who? Maybe a secret clap to identify their respective Happy Clapper church members. Perhaps they all had the clap, and the jumping around stuff they do isn't dancing; it has more to do with an itch. Perhaps Happy Clappers identify themselves by the way they start up their BMWs or other flashy cars, or by how they wear their designer-labelled clothes. I know there'll be no Hallelujah Brother when they're staring at the furnace and a dude with horns on his head wanders past and says, 'Come on then. No time to mess about; in you go!'

I was deep in thought when two young kids ran past me and one of them accidentally kicked sand over me. I told them both of them to nick off and behave themselves or I'd hurl them into the ocean. They ran off screaming to their mother.

'Like I care,' I yelled after them. 'Run off to your mummy, you little snot gobblers.'

I lay back down. Out of the corner of my eye, I saw one of the kids point towards me. Then I saw her. Holy crap! Emerging from the group like a baby elephant, she was coming towards me at a great pace. It was her again, thunder thighs, the woman from the pub, Irrelevant, whom I'd accused of not *shouting* a round. Very quickly, I put my on white sheet and sandals and went to run away with the speed of a thousand startled gazelles.

Herein was the problem I immediately noticed. You may want to learn from my mistake. When one has only been exercising one's left calf muscle, one finds one's running ability and one's running style becomes somewhat hindered and erratic. I could only run in a circle. I heard the crazy cow grunting, as she got closer to me. My biggest concern was that if she got hold of me, I was eunuch material for sure. I was screaming blue murder and getting dizzy when I noticed that my circle running had kicked up a lot of sand and must be blurring her vision of me. I had a flash of brilliance. All my dedicated years of training were about to pay off. I did some quick mental arithmetic and worked out that if I used one leg, perhaps I could still get away from lard arse, albeit at the speed of only five hundred startled gazelles. I went for broke and commenced hopping on my left leg. I bolted into the rain forests surrounding Byron Bay and hid out for a while. There would be no Monastery of Winning or outdoor preaching for me in Byron Bay. I eventually sneaked out of the forest, and booked into a motel, locked the door and put a call into the Big Fella upstairs.

His PA answered. I know this as she said, 'Good afternoon, God's PA. How can I help you?'

I replied, 'Hello, are you God's PA?'

She replied, 'Yes, how did you know?'

'A lucky guess,' I responded. 'I never thought I would ever say this, but I need to talk to God. Can you go and get him for me?'

'Everyone needs to talk to God,' she replied. 'But I can't disturb him right now as he's busy.'

I laughed and said, 'God is never busy; tell him it's the Profit T.'

I could tell by the way she said, 'Oh no, not the Profit T!' she'd heard of me.

'OK, then, have it your way,' I said. 'Tell him it's not the Profit T; just get him all the same.'

'Hey Profit, good to hear from you, how goes it?' came the unmistakable voice of power.

I filled the Big Kahuna in on what had happened. I had to take the hobile away from my ear because he was laughing so loud.

'Running around in circles; how funny!'

'It's not funny when the she-Devil is on my arse,' I replied.

'Why didn't you just float away?' God asked.

I had forgotten about that.

I quickly changed the subject. I asked him about the PA thing he had going. I found out God was vetting his phone calls as he was getting more than the usual numbers of people in Indian call centres phoning him. He suspected Joshua had been handing out his number. We chatted some more before I signed off. I was tired. My left leg was in pain from too much hopping. It and the rest of me needed to sleep. Before bedding down, I called my lovely Golden Angel Jacquetta. A little something I needed to do each night; otherwise I couldn't sleep.

Let Us Pray

Oh Great Thunder in the sky
Thanks for giving me the speed
To escape the crazy one
A eunuch Jacquetta doesn't need
Not after being with a Profit like me
Amen

The Prophecies of Chapter Eighteen

→ In some countries, it's probably against the law to kill men for their foreskins, no matter what the reason. Check with your legal adviser first.

→ Hippies offered the world so much; unfortunately most of it was illegal.

→ The Hemp Embassy in Nimbin does not sell the Mary J. I know. The bastards tricked me as well.

→ Keep track of whose shout it is in the pub.

→ Budgie smugglers give you wedgies.

→ Ban kids from beaches.

→ When in a panic, think clearly and hop.

→ Exercise both calf muscles equally.

19

The next day I awoke feeling refreshed and more importantly, safe. My left leg was a bit sore but otherwise good. I opened the motel door slowly and cautiously. I was still feeling a tad nervous after my little escape from 10-ton Tessie. I had to be sure she wasn't hiding around the corner and ready to pounce on me to part me from my family jewels.

I peeked around the partially opened door and couldn't see her. As much as I would love to hang out here, I was unsure if I had put enough distance between old thunder thighs and me. I answered a call from God. He was calling to see which horse I fancied in the third race in Melbourne that afternoon.

'Now there's an idea,' I said.

I told him I was going to check out Melbourne as the city holds the Spring Racing Carnival, which includes the richest horse race in Australasia, the Melbourne Cup.

'I'm going to have a mobile monastery as well. I hear the Rolling Stones made a fortune from touring.'

'Good idea. It worked for Jesus, for a while,' God said.

'Send down the Big White Dove,' I requested.

The Wings of a Snow White Dove duly arrived and we headed southward towards the bustling city of Melbourne. Melbourne is the capital city of the State of Victoria. It sits on the Yarra River and around the shores of Port Phillip Bay. Lauded for its sense of style and elegance, Melbourne boasts glamorous festivals, events, Australia's best shopping, a lively passion for eating and drinking, and a flourishing interest in the arts. Restored and preserved nineteenth century architecture, built following the discovery of gold, provides a heady reminder of a prosperous age, while beautifully tended parks and gardens present a therapeutic respite from the pace of city life. As we flew into Melbourne, I looked down on the place where fortunes have been won and lost since the gold boom of the 1800s and thought, yep that's me, the fortune bit especially. I then dispensed with the tourist brochure.

We flew over Port Phillip Bay for a couple of minutes while the Big White Dove jettisoned some fuel (dove talk for *poo*) prior to landing. Whilst this was occurring, I pondered on where we should land in Melbourne. Once again, I hadn't given it much thought. I really missed my lovely Golden Angel Jacquetta in times like this. Since hooking up with her, I've never had to make a decision. Even before I've thought about making a decision, she's made it for me. Brilliant. Sometimes when I've already made a decision, she makes another one.

We flew over Melbourne repeatedly and I couldn't see a suitable monastery anywhere. Where are all the Baptist monasteries? I could see some monasteries for the followers of Buddhism and the like, but no Baptist monasteries. I also saw a monastery for the community of Cistercian monks. That will never do, I thought, sounds like they preach in a toilet. I also saw monasteries for the Marist Brothers. The Marist Brothers, also known as 'Little Brothers of Mary', are Catholic religious institutes that know nothing. Mary didn't have any brothers; instead she had two husbands. In addition, she's not a Catholic, she's a Baptist like God, and I can tell you, neither of them are impressed with the shenanigans the Catholics get up to.

My observations from above were making me realise the sheer scale of all the different religions on Earth. I had forgotten about them in Heaven. In Melbourne there were countless religions represented. I could see buildings for the followers of Islam, Hinduism, Buddhism and the Christian religions of the Protestants and Catholics. I had no idea how many variants of those two there were. If I were to search long enough, I was sure I could find followers of Judaism, Taoism and perhaps even followers of the religion for philosophers, Confucianism. There is also a religion in Melbourne called *AFLism*. AFLism is so popular, its followers fill large stadiums when their gods are on display.

I suddenly had the idea to take over a Baptist Church. This was a Boat People trick Jesus had told me about. The worshippers may think at first it was strange to see the Big White Dove landing in their church grounds. But, if I were to announce on landing that I was from Heaven and on a mission from God to save the world, they'd understand.

'Tell Fly Boy to find me a Baptist Church, any Baptist Church,' I instructed.

On our approach to one such church, the Flight Captain played some Heavenly music to announce our arrival. I made a mental note to suggest to God to look at an alternative to this god-awful noise. I was getting sick and tired of the noise of bloody harps and trumpets. As we landed, the people inside the church rushed out to see what the commotion was about.

Someone yelled, 'What the Hell!'

Other people appeared as if they were about to panic.

I alighted from the Big White Dove and said, 'I'm from Heaven and I am on a mission from God to save the world.'

'Phew, that's OK then,' I heard someone say. 'I thought for a moment that something really strange was going on.'

'Well, that's a load off my mind. I was wondering why a Big White Dove was here. Thanks for clearing that one up,' someone else said.

Somebody yelled, 'Are you God from Heaven?'

'Not a full-blown God as such,' I answered. 'I am the one who goes before him. God's the boss, but he doesn't like to work too much these days. I am a Stand-In-God for the real deal. I am a great Profit. I go by the name of the Profit T. The Profit T, I shall be called.'

'So we should call you the Prophet T?' someone else asked.

'Yes,' I answered, 'something like that. But let's try Profit T.' I spelled it for them.

'Amazing,' one woman said. 'We were just praying to God to ask for forgiveness for our sins, and you suddenly turn up.'

'You're forgiven,' I said, with a wave of the hand.

'Just like that?' she asked, 'You can do that?'

'Sure, just like that. I forgive myself all the time. Besides, it's not as if God gives a hoot what you do,' I answered.

A man pushed through the small gathering and whispered in my ear that he had broken one of the Ten Commandments by coveting his neighbour's wife, by way of a knee trembler one afternoon in her bathroom. He too asked me for forgiveness.

'Was it good for you, the knee trembler?' I asked.

'It sure was,' he said.

'Good, you're forgiven as well,' I said, as I fondly thought of my lovely Golden Angel Jacquetta and me in the shower.

'Beauty,' he yelled into my ear. 'Are you going to be around for a while?'

'I could be, why?' I answered.

'I might go back there and see her again, if you know what I mean. Can I see you afterwards for some more forgiveness?' he asked excitedly.

'What the heck,' I said loudly, 'everyone is forgiven for whatever you've done in the past and for whatever you do in the future. Call it one of those *ongoing* forever forgiveness things. It saves you praying and asking all the time.'

With that, my newfound knee trembler friend ran off, just as the flap of a set of wings alerted us all to the departure of the great bird from above, the Big White Dove.

'I've never seen anything like it,' commented a man, looking upwards. He introduced himself as the Baptist minister of the church. He was tall and his follicles were most challenged. So much so, his baldhead glistened in the sunlight. He introduced himself as Gordon.

'I'm sure it's unique to Heaven,' I answered. 'God may well have the Wings of a Snow White Dove patented, I'm not sure. By the way, do you wear sunscreen on your head?'

'No,' replied Gordon. 'You should,' I said.

My words of advice were met with joy and immediate admiration. Good old Gordon threw his arms around me and said, 'Sunscreen on my head. What a great idea. Please come inside our humble abode.'

On entering, I had a quick glance at the walls to see if there were any photographs depicting people who had been expelled from Baptist Churches. I was in luck. Only pictures of Jesus were on display.

'Those pictures don't look anything like him, you know? I said to Gordon.

I heard some members of the congregation behind me mumble that I should know as I was from Heaven and probably knew Jesus.

'Please sit,' said Gordon. 'Allow me to grace you with some refreshments and rub your feet with oil. You have travelled a long way.'

'Gordon,' I said, 'can I call you call Gordy? Yes, I have travelled far. I believe I may have more acquired more frequent flyer points than Superman.'

I sat and the minister knelt before me, took off my sandals and anointed my feet in oil. I leaned back and thought that my oilings from my lovely Golden Angel were far better.

Gordy asked, 'When I have finished, Oh Great Profit T from the sky, could you please lead this congregation in song? As you're from Heaven, perhaps we could sing something godly.'

Shortly afterwards, and to the shock of the congregation, I floated slowly above them and then positioned myself over the church pulpit. I saw the look of awe and amazement on their faces and heard a few *what the's*. I did some loops and a couple of figure-eights. By the time I had finished, the congregation was eating out of my hand. I perused the church song list and threw it to one side. There were only hymns on the list.

'I will teach you a godly song,' I said.

The sea of stunned faces stared up at me and they soon began screaming in delight, like little children receiving a lolly bag.

'Holy crap, how good is this? A godly song!' I heard.

It didn't take me long to teach them the words. Soon we were all singing with great gusto:

Onwards Baptist soldiers
Sneaking up behind the Catholics
Scaring them half to death
Telling 'em God hates them all
And the Baptists rule
Boom Boom
'Cause our boy's no fool
He can walk across swimming pools
I couldn't be a Mick
I don't think they're that quick
They hail Mary, when everyone else hails a cab
The Baptists rule
Boom Boom
We're not fools
Not like them Happy Clappers tools
They can't clap in tune, they can't dance and they can't sing
They can't do any blessed thing
The Baptists rule
Boom Boom
Find us a nunnery among the gum trees
And we'll stay all night
'Cause the vow of silence that they take
Is a blessing for the married guys
Yeah, the Baptist rule ...

The congregation went absolutely off their nut. They were laughing and cheering so much some of them ended up rolling on the floor.

'You're good,' someone yelled out. 'Can you perform miracles as well?'

'Of course,' I answered.

They wheeled in before me a man on a stretcher and Minister Gordy said, 'Great Profit T, this man is bedridden. He is sick with disease. He's been sick with disease all of his life.'

I replied, 'If I had a disease all my life, I'd be pretty damn sick of it too!'

The congregation went bananas. They were cheering, laughing and screaming out my name, but not the way my lovely Golden Angel Jacquetta does.

Someone hollered, 'Oh Profit, thy one-liners are brilliant. You are indeed a very funny Profit.'

'Hey you, sick of disease you. You bloody lazy layabout, get off the stretcher, stand up and run around the block. Go on, off you go, before I kick your arse,' I commanded.

And this he did. The congregation were beside themselves with amazement. Silence reigned as the merry band of Baptists assembled before me tried to understand how I got lazy bones to stand up and run.

'It's a miracle, a freaking miracle.'

'You mean to say all he had to do was get off the stretcher? My goodness, this Profit bloke is really really good.'

'Come on, Great Profit T, give us another one,' I heard from the back of the room.

'Sure, why not.'

They brought a homeless man before me they had abducted from outside a nearby shopping centre as he kept annoying people for money to buy food. He looked up at me with pleading eyes, which seemed to be begging for help.

He said, 'I am without food. I have not eaten for three days. Please feed me.'

I looked down upon this poor, wretched, starving creature, weak from no food and said, 'Mate, I admire your willpower. Your diet is going so well. Stick at it.'

He started to cry.

The person who had been previously sick with disease came back into the church doing cartwheels and bouncing around as if he had an itchy bottom from worms. He was breathing hard and sweating profusely as he displayed his appreciation for my healing by kneeling in front of me.

'Oh Great Profit T, you Profit of delight, thanks for putting me right. My name is Fred and if not for you, I could be dead. How can I ever repay you?'

I looked at Fred momentarily and said, 'I have an opening for a personal valet, a hygienist, a foot masseur and a personal body guard to protect me from any 10-ton Tessies. Interested?'

'No, not really,' answered Fred.

'Do you want to go for another run, a long one.'

'No!' answered Fred. 'I can start immediately.'

I whispered to Gordy, 'Are you guys licensed here?' He sounded shocked as he answered, 'No!'

I said, 'Bugger, but no biggie.'

'Bring forth to me one glass of water,' I instructed my newly appointed servant. When Fred returned, I took the glass of water and did hold it in my right hand, and then I took my left hand and waved it all about. I did this whilst standing on one leg with my sheet raised to knee height, so as to show the congregation that not only was I a great Profit, but if they looked closely enough, they would also be able to see the intricate details of my sculptured left calf muscle.

After I finished working my miracle, lo and behold, the water had become wine. The congregation could see that it was a red wine, as red was its colour. A Shiraz from the Yarra Valley, a 1985 vintage, I believe.

The congregation shook their heads in amazement and muttered amongst themselves, 'This guy is brilliant and he's good as well.'

'How the Hell did he do that?'

They also applauded loudly.

I cleared my throat and said, 'I float before you as a representative of Heaven and, therefore, a representative of God. The Big Kahuna, Oh he who can do no wrong (if he does, nobody is going to pick him up on it) and the God of all things universal. He has directed me to save the planet from the worsening GFC.'

'Any chance of a drink, mate?' some bloke yelled out. He must have been thirsty as he was shaking badly.

'Fred, bring me many glasses of water. And please, no more interruptions; I'm not used to them,' I said.

The homeless person, named Charlie, sitting in a pew all alone, because he smelled so bad, said aloud, 'I've lost all my money because of the GFC. What are the chances of a sandwich, a big one?'

I smiled politely and said, 'No, you are too advanced on your diet. Let's not spoil it now.'

The congregation was in a jovial mood as Fred dispensed the water-come-wine to all. Charlie commented that he could be jovial as well if he had something to eat. I ignored him as I explained to the bubbling group of assembled Baptists, God had figured out all by himself that the GFC was the result of Neville the Devil. Neville had tapped into some people who felt the need for greed, and the rest was history as they say. I went into some detail to explain God's plan to save the world by having me teach the people how to gamble their way out of the GFC. I detected their sudden keenness when I mentioned once you've achieved your own personal Holy Grail by gambling, you can go and give your boss a brown-eye, and never work again.

I also told them their Bibles were old and had never been updated or amended to reflect the truth, therefore they should put them in the bin. As I was handing out copies of the true word of God, I heard people muttering as to how they had never understood what they had read in the old Bible in the first place.

'Bloody print was too small in mine,' said one old dear.

'The pages in mine are like tissue paper,' said a woman who ripped out another page as she sneezed.

A couple of other people mumbled that they hadn't even read the Bible.

'There were too many big words for me,' said Fred.

'I hope in your new book there's no animal cruelty like in the old Bible,' said a parishioner called Alex.

'The old Bible is full of animal sacrifices.'

Alex was an animal liberationist who wanted to free all animals from the zoos and let them return to the wild. I didn't necessarily agree with everything she said. I remembered on weekends in my previous life on Earth how I loved visiting the zoo. Many young kids would turn up with their parents who always bought them an ice cream or two. On hot days I would walk around the zoo, identify an ice-cream eating kid, and when their parents' eyes were diverted, I would lick the kid's ice-cream and run off. I stopped doing this after zoo security caught up with me. But my point is, if it weren't for the animals in captivity, I would have had to buy my own ice-creams. But, I did agree with her on the issue of animal sacrifices. The old Bible had too many stories of people thanking God by killing some poor animal. Surely if you wanted to thank God for something, it was better to write him a letter. No need to kill anything.

Gordy stated he only really read the Bible to identify the erotic stories. He had the entire congregation in fits of laughter as he told us that at Ezekiel 23 there is a great story about two sisters who must have been the original nymphomaniacs. Ezekiel 23:20 states: 'She lusted after her lovers, whose genitals were like those of donkeys and whose emission was like that of horses'. I wondered then as I wonder now, how can a man walk upright if his genitals are like those of a donkey?

'The old Bible discriminates as well,' said another. 'It tells us at Deuteronomy 23: 1: "If a man's testicles have been crushed or his penis cut off, he can't fully belong to the Lord's people".'

I cringed at the thought of something like that happening to any male. Besides, you shouldn't discriminate against a bloke just because he's got a couple of flat balls or no pecker. The poor bastard has enough worries; let him be.

Questions rained down upon me about Heaven and God. The congregation was excited when I told them God only loved the Baptists and the rest could bugger off. I informed my *flock of flockers* that since God had specially chosen me to save the world, and as I had specially chosen this church to stop at, they had to help me. I told them I was to train them up in accordance with God's true word; then we would make a shed load of money and show it to all the other heathen religions.

Their Baptist brains slowly assimilated what I had just said, and finally there was much cheering, yelling, hooraying, back-slapping and kissing. Men kissing women and women kissing men. Though, I did pause briefly to observe one or two women kissing women.

'I think I could help save people if I had a bowl of soup,' pleaded Charlie.

'My main man from hungry land, Charlie,' I said, 'according to some people, God loves everyone. But, that's him, not me. I don't have to love everyone. Now stop moaning, be quiet and please stop your stomach from making that awful racket.'

Over time and through many sermons I came to explain more on the inner workings of Heaven to my newly adopted Bloody Baptist brothers and sisters. The congregation loved my ramblings on gambling from God's true word, especially Gordy, who insisted I use his church as my monastery to preach the wonderment of gambling. We christened it the *Monastery of Winning*. My name was in lights.

Throughout my teachings, we had plenty of fun. We would tell jokes, drink and toast the Big Fella. We would sing his praises and sometimes we would send Fred out to get pizzas and when he came back, we would all laugh at him as I had performed another miracle and made plenty of pizzas from some old bread. Poor Fred! Once Charlie tried to steal a piece of pizza when he thought no one was watching. But, I nailed him right in the nick of time and saved him. He walked away a shattered man. Ungrateful bastard, I thought.

'Are you going to try and convert the Catholics to the ways of the Bloody Baptists as well?' I was asked.

'I'll try,' I answered.

'There is no way in this world I'm going to share a monastery with a bloody Catholic,' said Hannah, a flaming redhead.

'They don't like women, sexist pigs they are,' she yelled out. 'They think we women are stupid!'

'Yes, yes, I know the history,' I said. 'I'll work hard at trying to convert them and correct their attitude towards women.'

Fred said, 'I heard that Catholic Priests don't root either.'

'Well, not women anyway,' replied Hannah to the hoots and jeers and laughter of the rest of the congregation.

To avert the discussion heading further downhill, I brought us all back on track by leaping into a fire-and-brimstone speech. I told my flock of flockers that we stood on the brink of religious history and we were going to change the world. I told them we couldn't fail God because if we did, he'd be one super pissed-off God with a marvellous skill set to put to use. He didn't get mad these days, he got even, and I'd have to tell him it was your fault, not mine.

I heard Charlie mumbling he was feeling faint from lack of food, and he began to collapse in front of us. I looked at this smelly brute of a man, all rags and bones, and I took pity upon him.

I asked, 'Do you have the faith, Charlie?'

Barely audible, Charlie replied, 'If I can get a feed, I'll have the faith in anything.'

'Will you stop hanging around shopping centres and annoying people who are busy trying to fill their trolleys with all sorts of food?' I asked.

'Yes,' my weakened friend replied.

'Eat then, my boy,' I said. 'Eat to your heart's content. And then bathe. You freaking stink.'

'It's another bloody miracle,' Charlie hollered as he ran into the kitchenette and began gobbling mouthfuls of food. 'The more I eat, the more faith I'm getting.'

And all around saw that it was so.

'Did you see that? The Profit T just fed the starving guy and saved his life. Gave him faith too. It's another miracle all right. I'm going to hang out with him for a while.'

It came to pass that this chosen church, which housed God's Chosen Ones, began to learn one of the greatest lessons ever taught. In the name of God and for the sake of humanity, I began teaching them how to gamble so they could venture forth and assist me in saving the world.

Let Us Pray

Hey God,
I'm the man I've got a plan
I'll take the Baptist people to riches beyond their wildest dreams
We will all buy BMWs and caviar
We will honk our horns outside Happy Clapper land
And when they come a-running
They'll see us doing burnouts in their car parks, swearing,
Picking our noses, giving them a brown-eye and stuff like that
Then we will throw our fish eggs on the ground, right in front of them
That'll piss them off
Amen

The Prophecies of Chapter Nineteen

→ If you can perform miracles, family and friends will sponge off you a lot.

→ If your genitals are like those of a donkey, be careful how you sit.

→ If one gets one's feet anointed in oil, tread warily and watch your step afterwards.

→ If you have the ability to turn water into wine, you will find that you are invited to lots of parties.

→ Religious sermons based on how to make money are much better than sermons, based on giving money.

→ Take it upon yourself to find a Catholic Priest and take him out for a night on the town. Show him what he's missing.

→ The trouble with homeless people is they have nowhere to go.

20

Minister Gordon stood down from his preaching duties as I had more or less taken over the reins and was in charge of his little Baptist domain. To be honest, the parishioners preferred my sermons over his. The break was good for Gordy; it gave him new hobbies to concentrate on. He sought me out one fine summer's afternoon and found me chilling in the warm outdoors and perusing the form guide. He brought with him two glasses of water. I did the usual and soon we were kicking back and drinking a very pleasant and refreshing Sauvignon Blanc from the Mornington Peninsula region of southern Victoria.

As we drank, he talked. Gordy felt he had wasted many years of his life making a living by scaring people half to death about the Devil. He now wanted to put things right by making an honest living, whilst at the same time earning some of the folding stuff for the church, without the use of a collection plate. Despite me telling him that making an honest living is hard work, Gordy was still Hell bent on having a crack at his entrepreneurial fling. The business he settled on was one which involved the selling of cheap alcohol and cigarettes to the poor and underprivileged. I liked the concept. The government does nothing to help *keep* low income earners in alcohol and cigarettes. It is true they do the opposite. They make both products more expensive by raising taxes. Good on Gordy for helping out.

I told Gordy his plan was a no-brainer and would be a success, as for many years I had believed governments had discriminated against the poor and underprivileged.

Gordy had been expressing a keen interest in the science behind a good wine; I suggested he pursue this interest and produce a good cheap wine to counter the more expensive cha-teau collapsible cardboard brands available.

Spurred on by my encouragement, Gordy informed me the wine I had chosen for consumption on such a warm afternoon was a bright wine with the intense aromas of fruit. The wine also contained a gentle herbal edge with a crisp and delicate palate, while a clean acid finish with floral nuances balanced the fruity sweetness. I told Gordy to shut up as nobody likes a wine tosser. I gave Gordy the benefit of my abundant knowledge of the science behind a good wine.

I said, 'A wine has to have the aroma of fruit, does it not? Wine comes from grapes. Grapes are fruit, get it? How hard is this to understand? You don't have to have a PhD in the biochemistry from walking on grapes to understand. As for the gentle herbal edge and the floral nuances, who the bloody Hell cares! If the wine tastes all right, drink, say nothing, just consume. If the wine doesn't taste all right, throw the bottle out and crack another one. That's the science behind a good wine. No wine-tosser training required.'

Gordy thanked me for my ideas, and left to input them into his business plan.

From our conversation would grow a business which would flourish beyond Gordy's wildest dreams. You see, Gordy thought smart and he cornered the cheap wine market. He circumnavigated the science behind making wine and the monastery began producing its own wine on the church premises. Naturally I was involved. I wandered around waving my hands over bottles of water and empty jugs and the like. Our advertising banner out front of the monastery proclaimed:

*Allow us to help you make your social welfare money go further –
drop in for a free consultation.*

Our wines were labelled, Almost Made in Heaven, Feel Close to God and Jesus's Jungle Juice. The labels meant nothing. It was all the same wine. During the cooler months we sold red wine, and during the warmer months we sold white wine. Gordy didn't want to complicate his business model. As our wine market grew, some good-hearted parishioners dug out and built a large room underneath the monastery. Gordy placed large wooden wine barrels in this room, and whenever the wine levels got low, a hose would be inserted and the barrels filled with water. I'd arrive and do the usual and hey presto, the water became wine.

Gordy was also putting in the effort in his other business line, the provision of cheap cigarettes. At regular intervals, under the cover of darkness, Gordy arranged for a large truck to arrive into the monastery grounds. A Good Samaritan who worked at a cigarette factory donated the cigarettes, for a small fee. By having the cigarettes coming directly from the factory, Gordy was able to cut out the intermediary and more importantly the taxman. Gordy paid the driver night rates, and always cash. The power of some people's compassion to help others less fortunate never ceased to make me happy. If ever a person deserved to have an award presented from the government, it was Gordy. His tireless work for the poor and underprivileged was an example to everyone.

During all this, I was still teaching my Baptist brethren the power of the punt. They were keen to practise what they knew. They were just as keen to travel the world and convert others to the way of the Baptists. At times, I had to remind them that converting others is like building a betting bank. You have to lay the foundation first, build upon it, and build slowly and surely.

Charlie caught Gordy's infectious enthusiasm and he too decided to have a crack at being an entrepreneur. He was grateful to the church for allowing him to eat, and he decided to repay it by opening up a little food stall in the same annex of the church that sold the cheap wine and cigarettes. All the foods were sold fresh. They had come straight out of local rubbish bins the night before. It wasn't long before I came to admire Charlie for his dedication to the recycling cause. Charlie called his little food stall venture, 'Surprise'.

I needed to select the best of my flock to form the inner circle of the Monastery of Winning. They would become known as the 'Punting Buddies of Oh Ye Faithful'. I had decided Jesus had done the disciple thing to death. The Punting Buddies of Ye Faithful had to be enterprising people. I needed people who were committed, fully committed, to teaching others about the power of love: the love of gambling. They would be my executive management team, so to speak. I ended up appointing Gordy as *Head* of the Punting Buddies of Oh Ye Faithful.

After making my decision on whom to appoint, I gathered my selected group together to inform them they were members of my inner sanctum, the Punting Buddies of Oh Ye Faithful. This group consisted of Fred (my valet, come servant, come foot rubber), Charlie (I needed to keep an eye on him) and Big Slamming Kick-Arse Steve (he could really get a point across). On top of big Slamming Kick-Arse Steve, I selected two women. This made him happy. One was a journalist called Paige Turner and the other was the fiery Hannah. The Punting Buddies of Oh Ye Faithful were finalised by the appointment of Hung Lowe, who was very good at martialling the arts. I believed Hung Lowe would be of great use to me, especially if I ever had to preach the good word of gambling in an art gallery full of art snobs. You know the ones I mean: they sip champagne while pretending to understand the finer details of brush strokes upon a canvas made by an artist who had passed away long ago.

On paper, I believed we were a stronger group than Team Jesus. 'Bring on the Roman Boat People,' said Charlie. 'I'll eat the bastards, I will. That'll put a damper on their sea trips.'

I reminded Charlie the Roman Boat People were long gone, and had been replaced by others. I was able to get God to organise some business cards for us. The group was impressed when I issued them, embossed with the wording, 'The Punting Buddies of Ye Faithful – Never Fear We Are Here & Sometimes Near'. I was asked if I would get the word manager written somewhere on their cards to impressed other people on Earth. I said, 'No.'

The most important role for these people was to not only look after me, but to study and become subject-matter experts in the true Word of God. They had to understand gambling inside out. I also suggested to the Punting Buddies of Oh Ye Faithful they should all dress like me, white sheet and sandals. It distinguished us from others.

One of the first orders of business for the new group was to organise a large heated swimming pool to be built at the monastery. My sermons were attracting many people from various backgrounds and religions who were all in search of their own Holy Grail. Some had not been baptised. Others had been baptised, but not in accordance with the sacred ritual of the Baptist baptism. These people all had to follow the same frolicking ritual that had been adopted by John Boy and Jesus in the Jordan River. Off with their clothes and into the swimming pool the new people would jump, to emerge after doing the Frolic as Baptists. A simple process, yet so effective. At times, to help the new arrivals feel more comfortable in their skin, some already baptised Baptists would take off their clothes and jump in the pool as well. From a Baptist point-of-view, I believe we single-handedly kept the practice of skinny-dipping alive. For the elderly, I decreed that a shallow bath would suffice for the Frolic. Often I'd be invited to witness such Frolics at old-age homes. I always declined and instead sent Charlie on my behalf. This act had the desired effect; it turned him off his food for a few days.

The decor of the monastery was changing rapidly. How can you preach the virtues of gambling and hope to attract like-minded people when pictures of Jesus and other church things surround you? Hence, the inside of the monastery was renovated to look more like a betting agency and gambling den. Racing form guides were placed on tables with betting slips. Televisions were strategically placed on walls so patrons could view the races and the latest betting odds. A betting agency was installed and its operators were trained in taking and placing phone bets. Internet betting was also introduced. We replaced all the pictures of Jesus with photos of racehorses. More renovations saw the monastery expanded to include a casino. The people who ran this business-arm of the monastery were called the 'Sacred Order of the Betting Baptists'.

The days passed quickly between my weekly sermons. At one sermon I announced, much to the shock and horror of my Brethren of Bloody Breathing Baptists, I still had much work to do, which involved travel.

'The time will shortly be upon us,' I informed the faithful, 'when I will have to leave the Monastery of Winning to convert the pagan heathens of the other religions to the Baptist way.'

I was honoured by the reaction from my flock. Sobs and tears ebbed from their disheartened faces.

I soothed them with my soft words. 'Toughen up, you bloody princesses; I'm not going to be gone forever. Get a grip of yourselves, you big Nancy girls. Grab a tissue and dry your eyes; the whole lot of you are an embarrassment to the Baptist religion.'

They felt better when I mentioned that in the future, some would follow and do my work for me, as I knew that once my work was done, I'd be returning to Heaven and my lovely Golden Angel Jacquetta. Once the Devil and his GFC were beaten, and the Baptists had the necessary foundation in place to rule the other religions, I would be going home.

I decided to try to convert the Catholics first. The Catholics are the largest of all Christian dominations, in numbers, due to their successful 'breed like rabbits' program. This is a direct result of their belief in not using contraception. Amongst them exists pretend Catholics. Pretend Catholics would have us believe they're Catholic, even though behind closed doors they use contraception or the men have had a vasectomy. I mean to say, either you're on the team or you're not on the team. You can't do things piecemeal and be partially on the team.

I made the call.

He answered his phone, 'Pope Giorgio Von Stickenhoffen XXVI, head honcho of the Catholics.'

I replied, 'Profit T the first, Stand-In-God and God's Special Heavenly Adviser for Profits, Boss Cocky of the Punting Buddies of Oh Ye Faithful. You're number twenty six; I'm number one.'

'Bloody Hell,' said the Pope. 'How do you get all that on a business card?'

I ignored his comment and informed him I was coming to visit. The Pope sounded rather excited about meeting me. Despite his many decades of praying, I was the first contact he had ever had with anyone from Heaven. He invited me come by on a Sunday. We could do Mass and the good-old Sunday roast afterwards.

'Popey,' I said, 'please note for the record that I would rather be chased through the African jungle by one hundred homosexual gorillas, and take the risk of tripping over a log, falling face down on the ground with my butt pointing in an upwards direction, than do Sunday Mass. Thanks all the same.'

'I know what you're saying,' replied the Pope. 'I find Sunday Mass annoying. On the odd occasion I have to wander amongst the faithful, all they want to do is try to touch me. I have no idea where their hands have been, especially those Italians. They're the forefathers of the Roman Boat People you know.'

Just as I was about to say, I'll see you shortly, the Pope said, 'If you arrive just prior to Sunday Mass, I'll have an excuse to get out of it.'

'Fred,' I said, 'pack light, we leave very early in the morning for the

Vatican. We have to get there before Sunday Mass.'

Later that evening, I called Heaven, booked our flight, spoke briefly to God and called my lovely Golden Angel Jacquetta. The Big White Dove from above arrived in the morning. Fred and I said our goodbyes to the Punting Buddies of Oh Ye Faithful and the rest of my flock of flockers. The pilot gave me a parcel from Jesus. I smelled it. Ahh good, the smell of freshly baked marijuana cookies. Off we fly, first class for me and economy class for Fred. En route, I texted the Pope to let him know we were Vatican bound. I asked him to ensure St Peter's Square was clear so we could land safely.

The Pontiff texted me back with, 'Safe trip and may God bless you.'

How strange, I thought, God doesn't bless anyone. The flight to the Vatican was so fast that I barely had time to consume my first-class meal while Fred appeared to have plenty of time to eat his economy class sandwich. It wasn't very big and didn't appear to have much in it. We commenced a low pass over St Peter's Square. I noticed the Papal Swiss Guard kicking people off the landing strip. The people in the square were all looking up at us, curiosity written over their little faces. That was until the Wings of a Snow White Dove decided to jettison some fuel before commencing our descent. I watched the curiosity on their faces turn to disgust.

Let Us Pray

God Almighty, man of steel
Hang on, that's another bloke
God Almighty, my main man in Heaven Land
You may be the light
But John Boy and Jesus were right
This skinny dipping stuff gives us some sights
And at times a couple of frights
Like I'm no fool, I've seen some ghastly tools
But overall
Frolicking and skinny dipping and hanging free
Works for me
Amen

The Prophecies of Chapter Twenty

→ When frolicking in the bath with elderly people, be careful about stepping on their bits.

→ In some countries, it is against the law to take off your clothes. Check with your legal adviser first.

→ The reason the Pope waves from the balcony of the Papal Palace is because he has a phobia about people.

→ When the dove is above, don't look up. Stand under something.

→ Don't be a pretend Catholic. It's not right.

21

We landed to much fanfare and a little abuse. It may have been the poo thing. The Pope stood high up on the balcony in St Peter's Basilica witnessing our arrival.

I heard the shepherd of the world's largest flock yell, 'Hey, you lot down there, shut up and bugger off. Leave the dove alone. Go home and wash. You're dirty and covered in poo.'

Simon from the Pontifical Commission for the State of Vatican City was present to meet Fred and me as we alighted from the Big White Dove. I had a feeling Simon was important as he was being escorted by a couple of Swiss Guards.

'Welcome, oh Great Profit T.'

Fred introduced himself by saying he was one of the Chosen Ones, a Baptist, a member of the Punting Buddies of Oh Ye Faithful, and asked Simon if he would like one of his business cards. Simon looked at Fred for a brief moment and then ignored him.

I introduced myself by saying, 'I'm the Profit T. I talk to God.'

'But Profit T, I speak to God all the time,' replied Simon.

'I'm sure you do, Simon,' I replied, 'but the difference is, he answers me.'

That buggered Simon.

One of the Swiss Guards puffed out his chest, and asked me to prove I was really from Heaven.

'Anyone can say they're from Heaven,' he said.

I replied, 'Good point.'

I floated up to the top of his head and proceeded to do a short, but effective, Irish jig on the top of it. He was immediately convinced I was from Heaven. People who witnessed the event were convinced as well. While Fred was gathering our one bag, I made some meaningful, polite conversation with the Swiss Guards.

'I love your uniforms,' I said. 'Very colourful, they are. You wouldn't be out of place in the ballet, would you?'

Both guards looked at each other sheepishly and mumbled something about when they went to ballet practice, they went straight from work. No need to change.

I asked, 'So tell me, how many wars have you boys fought in?'

They shifted nervously from one foot to the other and finally one of them said, 'Well, none really.'

'But can you fight, if you had to?' I asked.

The other Swiss Guard answered, 'We're not sure. But I know one of the other guards won a fight he had by two hundred metres.'

'Interesting,' I said, 'but tell me, if you had to fight, you wouldn't go off to war wearing those fancy clothes, would you? I mean to say, you don't wear pantyhose to battle, do you? They might get all torn and dirty.'

'I think we have other uniforms for battle, don't we?' one guard asked the other.

He shrugged his shoulders as if to imply he wasn't sure.

'Do you carry a gun?' I asked.

They looked horrified and said, 'No way! Guns are too noisy for us, with all that bang-bang stuff. But we have Swiss Army knives somewhere.'

'Right, right,' I said. 'What is it you guys actually do?'

'We are here to protect the Pope from the Catholics,' they both said.

Before I could respond, Fred had appeared with our bag and Simon said he would escort us to meet the Pope. I could tell he was in complete awe of us. I wasn't so sure about the Swiss Guards.

Through the masses we went.

Just as I heard a flap of wings behind me, I yelled, 'I wouldn't do that looking-up thing again'.

'Right, right,' some muttered. 'Top advice that! Thanks for the warning.'

I stopped briefly and addressed the crowd by saying, 'Hey you lot, do you want to hear a good joke?'

'Sure, OK,' some said.

'Being Catholic, we don't have much to laugh at,' said another.

I asked, 'Do you know why Adam had it so good?'

'No,' they replied.

'Because he never had a mother-in-law,' I answered.

Some burst out laughing while others stood idly by, waiting for someone to explain the joke.

'Go on, give us another one,' I was asked.

'OK,' I replied. 'How's this? I'm going to have an audience with the Pope to convince him that he and all the Catholics in the world should convert to being Baptists!'

They laughed long and hard on this day in St. Peter's Square.

'Sometimes, Fred,' I said with a wink, 'the best jokes are when you tell the truth.'

'While I think of it,' I hollered out to the crowd, 'did you know Adam and Eve never got married?'

The crowd became very silent and still as they digested this morsel of information.

As I followed Simon, I overheard them murmuring, 'He's right. This Profit guy is right. Adam and Eve never did marry.'

'They never married!' scoffed a woman in front of the crowd. 'Well, isn't that just so typical? One rule for some and another rule for others. God help us.'

No, I thought, as Simon led us to the Pope's residence in the Papal Apartments, I don't think that'll happen somehow.

A journalist from the L'Osservatore Romano, the Vatican newspaper, was lurking in an ambush position behind a bush and jumped out and took my photograph while saying, 'Welcome to The Vatican, Great Profit. Can I have an interview?'

'Sure,' I answered.

The journalist asked, 'What does it feels like to be in the wonderful Vatican City?'

'I've been waiting a long time to come to the Vatican. This is the home of the Catholic religion, the Catholic faithful. You people never cease to amaze me. You're into everything: secret societies, crime and, who knows, perhaps each other.'

The journalist left without asking me another question. 'Must have been something I said,' I mentioned to Fred.

Simon had fallen over in shock. Fred was trying to pick him up. I helped by suggesting Fred put down our bag and then assist Simon. This he did. Simon stood up and dusted himself off.

'How did you know we're into all that the stuff?' Simon asked while looking around nervously.

'Everyone knows,' I replied. 'It's not as if it's a secret.'

Simon was stunned.

'You Catholics and all the crap you carry on with at times is ridiculous,' I said to Simon. 'You have no secrets. We Baptists are smarter than you give us credit for.'

'And we're the only religion God loves,' chimed in Fred.

Simon began to show the traits of a man completely puzzled. 'There will be time for this conversation later,' I said. 'I want to talk to the Pope. Let's move it. I'm running out of time here. I've got some horse races I need to listen to later.'

'Wow, this place is flash,' commented Fred, as we walked towards the Papal Palace.

'It took a lot of church donation money to build it,' said Simon proudly.

'And a lot more to maintain it as well, I bet,' I replied.

The Papal Palace was located off St Peter's Square. It was here the leader of the Catholic faith conducted his business and met with foreign representatives. I'd read that the Vatican is a state within a country and, as such, has its own post office, commissary, bank, railway station, electrical generating plant, radio station, television centre and publishing house. I wondered if the television centre broadcasts Sky racing.

As we arrived at the main steps of the Papal Palace, official-looking Vatican people came out and surrounded us. Some were dressed in black, others were dressed in red, a number were dressed in white, and some were dressed in red and black. No wonder the Catholic religion is so confusing; they can't even co-ordinate their clothing. Simon escorted us through the sea of people. Some of them were trying to touch me. The Swiss Guards attacked them with their water pistols. The crowd backed off. Simon led us past the government offices, the chapels, the Vatican museums and the Vatican library. All of these areas were contained in one massive building. We briefly stopped at the library so Simon could show off the size of it.

'Good Lord,' I said, 'there appears to be more information in this library about God and Jesus than in the Old and New Testaments combined. How can that be?'

Simon informed me that the Vatican library contained a lot of interesting history on the formation of the Catholic Church. The library also held all of the documentation relating to the customs, traditions and rituals of the Catholic Church. There were so many, they had to be written down so people could remember what to do.

'Why do you have so many customs and traditions and rituals?' I asked. 'Jesus didn't have any! Only the Frolic.'

'It's because of our history,' answered Simon.

'Does your history tell the story about you Micks stealing ideas from the Baptists?' Fred asked.

Simon said, 'Strangely, it does. I'll give you a brief history of the Catholic Church if you wish.'

This is what Simon from the Pontifical Commission for the State of Vatican City told us about the history of the Catholic Church, the same church that stole its early ideas of religion from the Baptists. A Roman guy called Octavius Cornelius Gnaeus Cattletick founded the Catholic religion. The Roman Mafia nicknamed him 'The Mick' for short; then it was shortened to 'Micks'. Octavius made the decision to start a religion once he heard how popular Jesus had become, especially with the women. Octavius's problem was that he had always been a shy and reserved person. He lived as a recluse. He blamed all of his women issues on being raised by his two mummies. By starting his own religion like Jesus, and becoming popular, Octavius figured he might be able to get a date to take to the Romans versus Barbarians sporting event. The Romans always won this game as they carried the weapons, whilst the Barbarians carried chains, the ones they were bound in. Everyone went to these games and if you were single and without a date, you were scoffed at, called funny names and made to sit by yourself.

When sitting alone, cheeky children would run past yelling out things like, 'Come on darling, blow us a kiss now, ya big girl. Ya haven't got a date because you're ugly.'

Upon investigation as to why Jesus had become so popular, Octavius discovered it was because Jesus had cornered the market early with the one God who lived in Heaven who had a son, yada, yada, yada. Not to be outdone, Octavius copied what he thought the women liked about the Baptist religion and added in his own little specialities, including rituals and dressing up in frocks. He believed women admired the more feminine look in men. Octavius also attempted to go one better than Jesus did. He called his religion, Catholic, meaning universal. He believed this would show women he was a global thinker, as he also believed women loved men who portrayed a worldly image.

Octavius sat back and waited to be rushed at by women all wanting to participate in horizontal folk dancing with him. As soon as the good folks of the Judean provinces heard what Octavius was up to, they went ballistic and began to label him a cheat and a copycat dirty rat. Some folks said he was so precious, he was not only a mama's boy, worst of all, he was a mummies' boy. Octavius became most upset when he began receiving hate mail from women.

A woman in Philistia wrote an article about him for the local newspaper. In it, she implied Octavius would remain a *virgin* until the day he died because he had a massive nose, which took up most of his face. The article went on to say Octavius was born ugly, got worse as he got older, and he would die ugly. The article further stated no woman in her right mind could even use drunkenness as an excuse to have sex with Octavius. Even prostitutes ran from his face.

This same story was picked up by a number of other Middle Eastern media outlets who, as happens with the media, embellished the story by adding to it. The comment of 'any man would be happy if his wife had breasts the size of Octavius's nose' was the one Octavius found most hurtful. It's fair to say Octavius wasn't painted in the best light, and he was greatly offended and upset by what he read and heard. Octavius the recluse became Octavius the even more reclusive. Early Catholic doctrine informs us Octavius decided to fight the copycat and cheating allegations. He set about introducing even more rituals, customs and traditions into the Catholic religion to ensure his religion was not only different from the religion of Jesus, but also different from any other known religion. Octavius went so far as to introduce funny hats for the leaders of the Catholic religion to wear. Octavius also introduced rods and smoking canisters for his priests. The rods were for the priests as most were old and needed walking sticks.

Given the pasting Octavius had copped previously from the Middle Eastern media, one of Octavius's mothers suggested he should look further afield for a date. She suggested Asia, as she herself had grown quite fond of Asian women. She showed Octavius some of her magazines. History shows Octavius took this mother's advice and began to advertise himself not only throughout Asia, but also throughout all of the countries that the Roman Boat People now controlled.

Poor Octavius never did get a date. He changed the name of his church from the Catholic Church to the Roman Catholic Church and only allowed Romans to join.

'Wow,' I said, 'all that donation money wasted on advertising and still no date. Did he ever get one? And a date as well?'

'Octavius died a virgin,' answered Simon. 'On his deathbed he decreed that all who followed him into the Priesthood of the Roman Catholic Church had to die as virgins, to suffer like he did. Hence, no shagging for us, ever.'

'To think,' said Fred, 'if he hadn't had a big nose, the whole Catholic religion could have been so different.'

'Tell me,' asked Simon, 'this whole shagging thing, is it any good?'

I looked at poor Simon, bit my bottom lip and said, 'Naw, it's overrated, mate.'

We moved through the building and headed in the direction of the Pope. Simon informed us that the building we were now in was so big that no one knew what to call it.

'Whatever do you mean?' I asked.

Simon answered, 'Some people called this the Apostolic Palace, some called it the Sacred Palace, and now some refer to the building as the Papal Palace and others refer to this building as the Palace of the Vatican or the Residence of the Pope.'

Simon escorted us to a room on the third floor. Two Swiss Guards were standing outside a closed door with a couple of spears. Simon spoke to one of them as he opened the door silently. The guard immediately put his hands on his head and in doing so dropped his spear.

Simon said, 'I get them every time with that Simon-said game.'

I smiled at the other guard and commenced polite conversation by commenting on the tights he was wearing and his shiny spear.

'Very nice get up,' I said. 'You look most rough and tough and fearsome.'

This guard smiled back at me and suggested when he got off shift we hook up for coffee. I stopped smiling and suggested we couldn't. The doors opened fully and on entering the room, I saw three people. Two of them were clearing a large wooden table while the third person was looking at Fred and me. He was smiling. Not again, I thought. Where's the old guy? Imagine our surprise when Simon introduced the smiling guy as Pope Giorgio Von Stickenhoffen XXVI, the Head of the Catholics and the Chief Mick of all the other Micks. He smiled at Fred and me through his gold-studded teeth.

For a Profit and a Fred, who were both expecting the Pope to be dressed in white robes similar to ours, but much fancier, wearing a hat and looking really old, we were somewhat taken aback. The Pope looked no more than forty years of age. He was dressed in the latest Italian Gucci fashion, which gave him a kind of nautical look. He may have had a yacht moored nearby. His long hair was pushed back and tied into a ponytail, and he stood about my height at six foot. I soon realised the other two people were servants.

This was confirmed when the Pope motioned to Simon and the servants to leave us alone with a simple wave of the hand and, 'Simon, you and the servants can bugger off now.'

One of the servants bowed and the other curtsied as they were leaving. The Pope yelled, 'Bloody cross-dressers, how did you get a job here?'

As soon as they had left and the doors had been shut by the Swiss Guards, the Pope walked towards me with his hand outstretched, shook my hand and said, 'Welcome to my little home. I'm not one for formalities. Please call me Giorgio. I insist.'

As we shook hands, I noticed how Giorgio touched his nose with the index finger of his opposite hand, wiggled his ears up and down, and winked at me three times whilst standing on one leg and whispering, 'Cock-a-doodle-do.'

'Stone the flaming crows!' I said in a shock-horror kind of way. 'You're a Freemason! I know the signs. A bloody Freemason, how can that be?'

Giorgio shrugged his shoulders and said, 'I like women. That celibacy rubbish might work for those who are as ugly as our founding father, but it doesn't work for me. I root at the drop of a hat. Please if you have a hat, don't drop it. I'm feeling very tired today.'

'I thought Catholics didn't accept Freemasonry,' I said.

'So they would have you believe,' replied Giorgio. 'I did pray to God first and asked his permission to become a Freemason.'

'God gave you his permission to get laid?' I asked.

'I'm not sure,' said Giorgio. 'I took his silence, his non-answer to my prayers as being *yes*. It's not as if he came back to me and said no.'

I was lost for words. Fred had commenced to deep breathe into a paper bag to settle his nerves. I was lost for more words when Giorgio informed us most of the hierarchy of the Catholic Church were Freemasons for the same reason as he. Simon was the exception as he was an ex-Swiss guard.

The Freemasonry and womanising is kept secret because if the other Catholics found out, some might try to have them excommunicated from the church. If this happened, the Catholic hierarchy, including the Pope, would have to get regular jobs. Giorgio motioned for Fred and me to occupy a couple of chairs near a large sofa. I took the paper bag from Fred and commenced to deep breathe. Looking like a Roman Emperor from days gone by, Giorgio stretched out on his sofa, propped himself up on a couple of cushions and double-clicked his fingers. Almost immediately, the two servants who'd been waved away previously reappeared with refreshments. One of the servants poured me a glass of wine from a carafe, while the other servant began feeding the Pope some grapes. I handed my glass back to the servant and took the carafe.

I said, 'You're younger than I thought. You're a Freemason, you dress like a yuppie and you shag women. Definitely not what I expected.'

The Pope smiled and said, 'Wait a moment!' He got up and went into a room that ran off his office. A short time later, he reappeared in his Pope clothes and wearing a mask, which made him look much older.

'It's all about appearances,' he said. 'I need to live a life outside of being a Pope. I feel the need to express myself and my feelings more fully, as I am a new-age, tender type of person. I cannot express anything being the Pope. My staff direct me here and there, and instruct me to say this prayer in the mornings and meet this person and so on. They own my life. I don't fit into the Catholic religion, you know.'

I could only shake my head in more astonishment and say, 'You've done very well for the son of a farmer.'

'Yes, I have,' replied the Pope. 'When I was a young man I had to live on a farm. This meant I lived in shit, I worked in shit, I got paid shit and to be honest the whole thing gave me the shits. Then I got smart. Being the Pope, all I have to do is *talk* shit. It's much easier and I don't smell.'

Whilst we chatted, Giorgio began to twirl his rosary beads

that came with his Pope outfit. I asked him for a look at his beads. He handed them to me and I threw them out an open window.

'Men don't play with beads,' I said. 'It's bad for our image.'

Giorgio agreed and confirmed my suspicion that the beads did come with his uniform. He went back into the other room and reappeared a short time later all Guccied up again and smelling of Armani aftershave. I told my new friend Giorgio it was enlightening to see that at least some of the Catholics were into Freemasonry. I reminded him that many years prior, long before his reign as the Pope, the Vatican had issued Papal Bulls banning Catholics from becoming Freemasons.

'Did we?' Giorgio asked. 'I really should read more. I'll have to fix that.'

Giorgio called out to a woman named Rosabella. When she appeared, Giorgio introduced her as his girlfriend. I found out later she was on the Vatican payroll as his Personal Assistant. It had something to do with dodging taxes. Giorgio asked Rosabella if she could chase up some administration person and have a Papal Decree issued instructing all Papal Bulls be brought back to the Vatican cattle holding pens.

'I'll have them all sent to the meat works,' he said. 'I can't have Papal Bulls running around; it's dangerous.'

I was going to point out to him the bleeding obvious, but decided against it. I wanted to see how many Catholics had a Papal Bull. Giorgio explained the Catholic hierarchy had a Freemason Lodge meeting that very evening. He had organised it to welcome his visitors from Heaven. The three of us talked well into the afternoon. Giorgio enquired as to the purpose of our visit. I informed Giorgio that, as he had discovered, there's more to the world than the Catholic religion, and God had sent me with a message for all Catholics. As he was Head Catholic, it was up to him to pass my message on.

'Well, now, that does sound exciting,' said Giorgio. Then he abruptly said, 'You can tell me over dinner tonight at our Freemasons' meeting.'

Giorgio had an antioxidant facial-scrub appointment he didn't want to miss. He suggested Fred and I go to our rooms and relax prior to the evening festivities.

Giorgio clapped his hands twice and the servants appeared. A servant showed us to our rooms and informed us he would knock on our doors in a couple of hours to escort us to pre-dinner drinks. I made a couple of calls to the monastery and to Heaven. On a call to God, I asked him what protocol I should follow at a Freemason function.

'Isn't that where they ride billy goats or sheep or something?' he asked.

'Doubtful at a Vatican Freemason function,' I answered. 'Could be the go at a New Zealand Freemason function.'

In short, God didn't know. He suggested that I play it by ear and roll with it. We chatted some more before I hit the sack and punched out some z's. The Catholics can be so bloody tiresome at times.

Let Us Pray

Big Fella, way out there in the blue
Have I got a surprise or two for you
Good God I'm shocked
The Catholics, holy crap
Where do I begin
The chief Mick's a Stonecutter
A bloody Mason he is I'm telling you, it's no joke
According to him, it's not a sin
To love women again
Amen

The Prophecies of Chapter Twenty-one

→ There's something odd about security guards who dress up in colourful clothes.

→ More people would be attracted to St Peter's Square if they had a pizza shop and a bar.

→ A Papal Bull is not a moo-moo type of bull. It is a particular type of letter, patent or charter issued by the Pope of the Catholic Church.

→ The Pope has a big place. Go visit sometime; he won't mind.

22

I was awake when one of the servants, accompanied by Fred, knocked on my door to announce it was time for pre-dinner drinks. On entering the room set aside for drinks, I noticed a large bar area at one end, bar stools near it and a couple of pictures, supposedly of Jesus, hanging off the walls. They looked nothing like him. I couldn't help but notice the number of almost dressed beautiful women serving drinks. In the middle a large group of men in frocks gathered around the Pope. I knew it was the Pope as he was wearing one of those tall funny hats I'd seen him wear on television. There was much yelling and cursing going on around him.

We've all seen some sights in our day, but nothing prepared me for this sight. Giorgio was tossing coins up in the air, two coins to be exact. He was running a two-up gambling ring. This traditional Australian gambling game involves a designated Spinner who throws two coins into the air. Players gamble on whether the coins will fall with both (obverse) heads up, or (reverse) tails up. The game is often played on Anzac Day in pubs and clubs throughout Australia and is a part of the Australian culture and tradition and marks a shared experience with the Diggers (soldiers) through the ages. People were screaming out heads or tails. They groaned or uttered sounds of delight depending on the toss of the coins. To attract Giorgio's attention, I floated upwards and over everyone's head.

'Evening Giorgio,' I said.

Everyone immediately stopped what they were doing and looked upwards. I could tell they weren't sure what they were witnessing. They knew I had arrived, but when you arrive above their heads, they do take instant notice.

'Good evening to you as well,' replied Giorgio. 'That's a neat trick. I wish I could do that. What an attention grabber. Come down here and let me introduce you to the boys. We're all still in our working clothes. I had some Pope stuff to do at short notice.'

'Two-up, I see,' I said.

'An Australian priest showed me this game; I love it,' replied Giorgio. When he dies I'm going to make him a saint, canonise him, or is that shoot him out of a cannon? I always get the two mixed up.'

'Two-up can be a good little money earner if you get a run,' I said,

'And let's be honest, money is how God says thanks.'

They laughed.

'How the Hell do you do that floating thing?' a Cardinal asked me.

'It's a Heaven trick,' I answered. 'Don't try it at home, it can be dangerous to the untrained.'

Giorgio introduced Fred and me to this amazing array of people who filled various positions within the Vatican. Whilst all the Patriarchs, Major Archbishops, Cardinals, Primates, Metropolitans, Normal Archbishops, Diocesan Bishops and Deacons may have been stunned to meet a floating Profit, I was equally stunned to see so many leaders of the one religion. If these people were all on the Catholic payroll, it's easy to understand why the Catholic religion is big on donation money. Jesus didn't have this many people. Only the twelve and none of them were paid. The position of Primate interested me most of all. What the Hell did he do? He didn't look like a monkey; perhaps he dressed up later. The entertainment, maybe. Giorgio's religious friends introduced themselves in the same Freemason way Giorgio had earlier in the day.

One of the Bishops said, 'So God is real, wow. Who would have figured that!'

'Hell yeah,' replied Fred. 'He's up in Heaven as well.'

'Unbelievable,' said another. 'After all these years we find out he's real.'

'Good God!' remarked a surprised Deacon.

'He's not bad,' I replied.

Many questions followed, what does he look like? What does he do all day, and so on? Fortunately the dinner gong saved me from answering most of them. Fred and I were escorted into another large dining room containing long rectangular tables placed to form a large square. I was seated beside Giorgio. Fred was seated on the other side of me. We felt quite chuffed to be the honoured guests. Everyone else sat where they wanted. I remembered what Jesus had told me about one of his dinners, the last one, so I asked a Cardinal to watch my back in case any Romans showed up.

He replied, 'But Profit T, most of us here are Romans.'

'Bloody Hell!' I said. 'Fred, you watch my back.'

Ingrained in the centre of each rectangular table was the universal symbol of Freemasonry, the square and the compass. Lying on the top of our table, directly in front of the Pope, was the Masonic gavel. The gavel was the emblem of authority used by the Master of the Freemason Lodge to show his executive power. Or perhaps he has it because if you were to argue with him, you'd get whacked.

Dinner arrived on silver platters. The wine poured from golden carafes into equally golden goblets. Once all the guests had a plate of food and a goblet of wine in front of them, the Pope banged his gavel on the table and asked for silence so he could say grace. Here we go, I thought; grace was a prime example of why perfectly good warm food goes cold. Grace was a time-wasting mechanism introduced by people who stupidly believed by giving thanks for food, it would help them get to Heaven. Guess what, God doesn't give a hoot about grace. He doesn't even say it; no one in Heaven does. But, as the honoured guest, I showed respect and said nothing. We bowed our heads as Pope Giorgio Von Stickenhoffen XXVI, the big boss cocky of the Catholic Church, a Freemason, a gambler, a drinker and a man with a girlfriend, prepared to say grace.

He prayed:

Our Heavenly Father
Whom we've just found out, really does live in Heaven
Thank you for the food and wine upon this table
Thank you for getting the Catholic faithful
To donate so much money
Without their generosity
We couldn't maintain the lifestyle
We have become accustomed to
Can you find it in your heart
To get them to part with some more
I've got my eye on some expensive art
Amen

I have to admit, it was one of the better graces I've heard.

'A toast to the Catholic and the Freemason faithful,' hollered one of the Patriarchs.

As soon as we had slammed the toast down, they broke into song called, *Give us more of your money*. This number was followed by, *We're not Greedy, Just Needy*. Fred and I had no idea of the lyrics. We just banged our cutlery on the table in tune. In between songs we laughed, we ate and we drank. Song after song sung with great passion, *Don't be Tight, Open up Your Purse Tonight* was one of my favourites. As the evening progressed people would break into spontaneous singing whenever they felt like it. I heard, *I'm With You Tonight for your Cash, not a Rash*. The Catholic Freemasons sang loud and long. When I heard them sing, *I Wanna Rip you off Today*, followed by *If you Wanna Shock, look under my Frock*, I had tears running down my face from laughter.

In amongst all of the jocularity and entertainment, I asked the Archbishop of wherever, why Freemasonry? There has to more to it than just the women bit.

'We chose Freemasonry,' he answered, 'because Freemasonry is a male only association. This means we can have our gambling and drinking and socialising, but our girlfriends or wives haven't got a bloody clue what we get up to. Women are only allowed to be in the bar area and in the kitchen, both of which are outside this Great Hall of Fine Dining.'

'This is where we conduct our secret men's business,' one of the Cardinals added.

A Patriarch chimed in and said, 'Another reason we decided to join the Freemasons is because we discovered in Freemasonry, one just has to assent to a belief in a Supreme Being, who is really the great architect of the universe. Freemasonry doesn't shovel all the other religious waffle down your throat.'

'Yes,' I nodded, 'I somewhat agree, although I wouldn't hang my hat on the great architect of the universe bit. From what I understand, not a great deal of architectural thought went into the planning phase of the universe.'

A Metropolitan, who looked nothing like a city, joined in the conversation by adding, 'Another game changer for us was when we researched all of the other religions and we discovered Free-masons only had to meet once a month. All of the other religious have to meet a lot more regularly.'

'We need a full month to get over a night like this,' remarked Giorgio.

'Fair enough, but why do you still pretend to be Catholics?' I asked.

Giorgio answered, 'To get our hands on the donation money. This wonderful entertainment and lifestyle of ours is expensive. It has to be funded from somewhere. The drinking, gambling and socialising doesn't come cheap, you know. The Catholics have more money than the Freemasons; actually we have more money than anyone; hence it pays to have a foot in both camps.'

These boys were good. They had put a lot of thought into what was essentially nothing more than good old-fashioned graft and corruption, mixed with a lot of fun. Giorgio added, with some regret, it was becoming harder and harder to keep up the pre-tence. He feared they were going to be caught out eventually.

I looked at Giorgio, the leader of the Catholic faith, and with a big smile I said, 'I am here to help you. Let me explain how. Assemble all the party dudes.'

On this evening, as opposed to other evenings, I had the great pleasure of informing Pope Giorgio and his Catholic Freemasons, their Catholic doctrine wasn't worth a damn thing. It was plagiarised, and what wasn't, was invented by a bloke with a big nose who couldn't get laid.

'Which bits aren't true?' asked a Patriarch.

'All of it,' I answered. I went on to inform them they didn't have to continue with their masquerade any longer.

'Your drinking, gambling, womanising and partying is what God does, minus the womanising, as he's hooked up to Mary. The only difference between him and you guys is he doesn't hide any of it.'

The comments came thick and fast.

'I want to be like God,' I heard somebody say.

'I am still trying to comprehend that God is really true.'

'Does this Profit guy mean we can date a woman in public like other men do?'

I continued to inform my astonished dinner friends about God, Heaven and the ways of the Baptists. At one stage, I made the point of telling them about me shacking up with God's daughter. They couldn't believe it.

'God has a daughter?'

'I didn't know that, bloody Hell. You're living with her in a cloud?'

'I'll have a glass of whatever he's drinking.'

'Hey Profit bloke, has God got any more daughters?'

The moment I said only the Baptists, practising or non-practising, gain entry into Heaven, there was silence. Some looked at me with their mouths wide open. The silence was broken by more mutterings.

'Well, he must be right; he's from Heaven. He would know.'

'I hardly think a person from Heaven would lie.'

'What's a Baptist?'

'This conversation is going way too fast for me. I'm still trying to understand the daughter bit.'

'I believe him because he can float.'

'The Catholic religion isn't true. Thank bloody Hell; the pay was lousy.'

'God doesn't go to church; wow, who would have thought?'

'Did the Profit T answer the question from before? Does God have any other daughters?'

'No, he doesn't.'

'Lucky bastard, aren't you?'

'Yes.'

'I want to go to Heaven. See if he tells us which direction it is.'

Giorgio couldn't speak. His lips were moving, but no words escaped from his mouth. I patted him on his head to reassure him all was fine. Questions, questions and more questions were raining down upon me from every direction. Finally, Giorgio found his voice and his gavel.

With a bang he said, 'Hold your horses, you lot.' He looked at me and asked, 'Why do you have to be a Baptist to get to Heaven?'

I started from the beginning, the beginning of time. I told them everything. They were amused when I told them about God's little accident, which resulted in the formation of the universe. They were impressed with God's period of Accidental Evolution and subsequent Natural Selection of the Baptists.

They were gobsmacked when I explained how this came about because John the Baptist baptised Jesus in the River Jordan. I emphasised how this act of Baptism, was known as the Frolic, and once you've frolicked, you're a member of the Baptist religion, which is the first religion to have a belief in the one God who lived in Heaven, had a son, yada, yada, yada.

They agreed with me when I told them God had decreed in the Chronicle of Heaven that as the Baptist religion was the first true religion created, and subsequently preached by his boy Jesus, it was only fair to admit only Baptists, practising or not, into Heaven. I painstakingly explained my contribution to the Betterment of Heaven program was writing the true Word of God. I spoke of God's concern for the world because of the GFC. He was so concerned, he sent me down, his only begotten Profit, to save the world by showing its people how to achieve their own personal Holy Grail by instructing them how to gamble their way out of it, in accordance with God's true word. I also mentioned while I was on Earth, I had to try and covert the people of world, no matter what their religion, to the ways of the Bloody Baptists so that God could become Top Dog again.

I took a breather and let Fred talk about the Monastery of Winning and the inner sanctum, the Punting Buddies of Oh Ye Faithful.

'Imagine,' I heard someone say, 'a book by God about winning on the race horses. How good is this Baptist gig?'

Everyone was impressed when I said God may well have approved his true word, but I had written it. Fred and I spent a lot of time answering various questions. Not so much on God and Heaven, but more to do with how to win at gambling, although some did want to know if Heaven had a licence, and if it was easy to pick up good-looking women. I spoke of the long term plans God had for the people on Earth, for example the *Gambling in Schools* program to give the kids an international skill for life.

When I had finished speaking there was no silence, only noisy chatter as the astonished group of Catholic Freemasons began to realise by converting to the ways of the Baptists, they had a lot to gain, and nothing to lose. They could even wear yuppie clothes in public, instead of frocks and girlie blouses. Giorgio, the Pope Master come Freemason gavel holder, had a worried look on his face.

'Problemo, my main man in Catholic town?' I asked.

Giorgio said, 'There's no doubt about it, the Baptists have more fun than we Catholics. But, I'm sure some of us would still want to keep our monthly Freemasons' meetings going. It's a male-bonding socialising thing.'

'Bloody oath,' said one of the Primates as he peeled a banana, 'that has to stay.'

'It can. The Baptist faith is a tolerant religion. You can be a Baptist and a Freemason,' I replied.

The Pope enquired about whether he would lose all his titles when he converted to the Baptist way. I informed him he would not.

'Keep all the titles you want. Hell man, you can add new ones if you want. Fill up your business card with titles. It's not as if anyone is going to be impressed or will take any notice.'

After pausing and thinking about it for a moment, I said, 'Instead of being the Head of the Roman Catholic Church, why don't I make you the head of a sub-church of the Baptists. We can call it the Church of the *Bapfreeholics*. It'll be for people who want to be Baptists, Freemasons and Catholics, all in one'.

'Get the fuck outta here,' said Giorgio as he slapped me on the back. 'Can you do that for me?'

'Yeah, of course I can. I'm a good man,' I answered. The Pope's eyes immediately lit up and sparkled like a couple of diamonds lying in the dirt.

'What do I have to do to convert to being a Baptist?' he asked.

I explained the Frolic once again, in more detail. I believe this was the decisive factor for them, the turning point. I hardly had the words out of my mouth when some of the party started taking off their clothes while someone held a cigarette lighter under a fire sprinkler. It wasn't long before the fire sprinklers mounted on the ceilings started spraying water.

'Can we let in the waitresses?' someone yelled.

'Let 'em in,' I said. 'The Baptists don't discriminate against women; we love them.'

'They love women. You hear that – they love women. My God, it's good to Frolic and be a Bapfreeholic!'

Fred and I ended up as wet as a couple of shags on a rock. It didn't bother us as we thought, when in the Vatican, why not. We too pulled off our clothes and joined in the Frolic. You never can get too much of this Baptist stuff.

When the fire sprinklers in the Vatican go off, the Rome Fire Brigade is notified by way of an alarm. This was confirmed when the doors of the Great Dining Hall came crashing down and I saw bewildered firefighters looking for a fire but instead, only seeing naked and semi-naked men and women being sprayed with water and dancing. When they were told of what we were doing and the reasons for it, they peeled off their uniforms and started doing the Frolic with the rest of us.

Word quickly spread throughout the Vatican there was no fire; instead, the Pope and his merry band were doing the Frolic with some bloke whom God had sent down from Heaven. More and more of the Catholic clergy came to join us. When they found out the Pope was doing the Frolic to become a Bapfreeholic, some were a tad hesitant to get involved. That was until they found out if they became Bapfreeholics, they could get it on with the women in public.

Most immediately ran back to their rooms and grabbed their mistresses and they too joined us. It wasn't long before the rooms in the Papal Palace were overflowing with people doing the Frolic underneath water flowing from fire sprinklers. The naked firefighters solved the people problem by manoeuvring their fire trucks and fire hoses in such a way they were able to spray water all over St. Peter's Square. I loved the idea. I led a bunch of people outside to do the Frolic in the great outdoors.

St. Peter's Square filled quickly as more and more people began to pour into it. A woman yelled out the Holy See was becoming flooded with water and people. I had a look around and I couldn't see what she was on about.

The Swiss Guard with whom I had declined coffee earlier, came up beside me, gave me a wink and took off his brightly coloured uniform and joined in the Frolic. He looked down and witnessed my manhood.

He immediately moved away, shocked, muttering, 'Have a look at the size of that? It's a weapon.'

Happy Face wanted to scare him one more time, so he let his head fall gently on the ground, whilst I was frolicking upright.'

The Swiss Guard ran. So much for bravery.

Eventually, I said good night to Fred and Giorgio, who were both now frolicking outside, grabbed my clothes from the dining room and wandered off to my room. I phoned Jacquetta and hit the sack. I was one frolicked-out Profit.

The next morning, Giorgio was a wreck as he limped in for breakfast. He wasn't used to frolicking. He told me that prior to him going to bed in the wee hours of the morning, he had ordered the release of more Papal Bulls. As we spoke, the Papal Bulls were pounding across the world and delivering messages informing the Catholics that he, the Pope, had recently found out the Catholic religion was a crock of crap and therefore all Catholics were to immediately lose their Bibles and convert to the ways of the Bloody Baptists by participating in the Frolic. All priests were told to release any women from their closets and return all stolen art and treasures back to their rightful owners. The Pope was now to be known as the *Head of the Bapfreeholics*.

I called Headman Gordy and asked him to despatch Big Slamming Steve and Hung Lowe to the Vatican in pronto time. I wanted them to teach the finer points of gambling to Giorgio and his head honchos. Then, they would be able to spread the good word of gambling by way of pilgrimage, missionary work, the internet and more Papal Bulls.

I also suggested to Giorgio that as the Catholics had no need for churches any more, to perhaps turn them into casinos and betting shops. Another Papal Bull was saved from the meat works and let loose. I heard later that the Vatican ensured it took thirty percent of all house takings by way of donation. That's not being greedy, that's smart business. The rest went back into the business and to the needy. Giorgio was to mention many years later it was a good idea I had given him.

'Helping the needy, who would have thought?' he said.

The Vatican eventually cleaned out their archives and gave them to Dan Brown.

Let Us Pray

....

Hey Big Dude in the sky
I've got the Catholics in the groove
They're really happy to make the move
To the Baptist way
Onwards to the Mormons next
Then home I'll come for a rest I need to see your daughter
After all, I'm not a Catholic Priest
Amen

The Prophecies of Chapter Twenty-Two

→ Just because the Swiss Guard have never been in a scrap before, does not mean they can't fight. Maybe they work on the principle that their uniforms would scare the enemy.

→ Earth is a dangerous place. Not only do you have to look out for the pooing dove from above, but you also have to keep an eye out for all the Papal Bulls running around.

→ To be canonised as a saint in the Catholic Church does not mean you are shot out of a canon.

→ Where do the Catholics get all this saint stuff from? Jesus was never a saint. God was never a saint. My school reports clearly indicate I was never a saint.

→ There is not a shred of evidence existing anywhere to suggest life is to be taken seriously.

→ If you get the opportunity to party with some Bapfreeholics, go for it. It's a lot of fun.

23

Big Slamming Steve and Hung Lowe arrived aboard the Big White Dove and wasted no time in settling into their task of teaching the art of gambling to the Bapfreeholics. They also brought me up-to-date on the activities of my flock of flockers and the Punting Buddies of Oh Ye Faithful. Gordy was busy with his businesses, although he needed me back in Melbourne soon to conduct some hand waving over some water. Others were spreading the good news about how to combat the GFC by way of the Gamble and the Frolic. The Catholics may well make use of the Papal Bulls for sending out messages to their faithful, but we Baptists are much smarter – we use a telephone and email.

Charlie's recycling efforts were also going well and his little food stall *Surprise* had been mentioned in a *Best Eats* magazine. I know, the human race continues to amaze me as well.

Fred and I farewelled our Bapfreeholic friends, promised to write and pop back again real soon. Fred was a little disappointed when he found out Big Slamming Steve and Hung Lowe had travelled First Class, so for this trip I let him sit in First Class with me if he promised not to talk. Fred and I, with the cookies, kicked back and relaxed as we travelled to Salt Lake City, Utah, and the headquarters of the Mormon faithful.

At any one time, the Mormon Church has up to 50,000 missionaries across the world running around knocking on people's doors and squawking about whatever it is they squawk about. What I wanted was those 50,000 people running amuck across the world squawking about the virtues of the Baptists, gambling and saving the world.

The religious beliefs of the Mormons are somewhat difficult

to grasp. Despite the fact Jesus was causing all sorts of hysteria on Earth during the period 5 BC–33 AD, the Mormons didn't get into the religion game until the spring of 1820. Joseph Smith Jr. was reported to have gone into the woods near his home in Palmyra, New York, and offered up a simple prayer to God. True to form, God never answered him. Even if God did answer prayers, he would have looked down at Joseph Smith Jr. and said, 'Why would you go into the woods to pray? How stupid is that?'

It was safer to pray in your home. In the woods, there are bears, snakes and all sorts of other bad shit. Since I was a kid, I'd heard the warnings about teddy bear picnics in the woods. Take the hint: if you go into the woods, especially on a bear picnic day, you'd better beware.

Stay with me here on the Mormons, this bit is good. Three years after Smithy had been in the woods to pray, he alleged that an angel called Moroni popped up and told him to go and dig up some golden tablets and translate the Egyptian hieroglyphics written on them. The dig spot was in upstate New York. I kid you not. Why the bloody Hell would an angel tell you to go and dig for Egyptian artefacts in upstate New York? Egypt, yes, but upstate New York, I think not. Upon deciphering the golden tablets, Smithy gave them back to the Angel Moroni. No one else saw them or has ever seen them. I know, I'd like to see a bit more evidence as well. So 'ho hum' to that. I think Smithy was in the woods looking for magic mushrooms and found a couple. But he sold his religion to others, who too may have had a few magic mushrooms.

I made a few notes on the Mormons. I wanted someone in authority to explain to me how the Mormon Church can state that Smithy, and all the other past Presidents of the Mormon Church, including the current President of the Mormon faithful, can be Prophets of God. God has no prophets that aren't of the Baptist faith. He has a Profit; that's me. When I last spoke to God he said he'd never heard of an angel called Moroni. He thinks the Italians might have pasta called Moroni; perhaps that's confused the Mormons.

After we had landed and alighted from the Big White Dove, we had a stroll around the main part of town and took a quick peek at the Mormon temple. Bloody Hell, it was huge. I cannot fathom why religious organisations had to spend so much money on fancy buildings in order to pray, sing and whatever else it was they do in their god's name. The practising of religious beliefs has become entertainment for lazy people, and therefore it was this practice that had contributed to the global obesity crisis. People drove their cars to a church and sat on their bottoms for an hour. If the ministers and preachers of religion were fair dinkum, they'd do their spruiking in the outdoors like Jesus did and combine it with a cardio class. Preach halfway up a mountain and make the people walk up to you.

Fred and I booked ourselves into a self-contained unit. This was important as I needed a kitchen with an oven. Much to his disgust, I woke Fred early the following morning. I told him after such a busy time at the Vatican, it was time to reward ourselves with some fun. It was a beautiful Friday morning as we ventured forth. I had read once that most of the people who lived in Salt Lake City were Mormon. That means when you knock on someone's door in Salt Lake City, there would be more than a fifty percent chance a Mormon will open that door. To prove my hunch, Fred and I went door knocking.

When the door opened, I would say, 'Hi, I've been sent from Heaven by God, who has a son called Jesus, to save the people of Earth by teaching them how to gamble their way out of the Global Financial Crisis. I've just bet my friend here $50 you're a Mormon. How am I looking?'

As these wonderful people slammed their doors in our faces, we would yell, 'How do you like it, you annoying bastards? How do you like it when people knock on your doors, you bloody knob heads? And stop congesting our roads with your stupid push bikes.'

Then we would run away laughing like a couple of school kids. Eventually we both tired of having so much fun and retreated to our self-contained unit to warm up some cookies. Like the

Catholics, I wanted to hit Mormons at the top. The game plan would be pretty much the same. Get the Mormon hierarchy on side first, introduce them to the Frolic and the rest would follow. I was working on the premise that any person who believed the yarn about Smithy and Egyptian artefacts in upstate New York was a fool who would believe anything. As such, it shouldn't take me long to convert the Mormons, and then back to Heaven and into the bed of magical times I would go.

I explained to Fred I wanted him to wander throughout Salt Lake City and hand out the freshly warmed hash cookies for free. I also instructed Fred to pop into a number of fast food places and give the staff some cookies as well. When they were as high as kites, walk into their kitchens and drop a cookie or two into their vats of artery hardeners. As for me, I would go and visit the President of the Mormon Church and chew the fat with him for a while. On the way, I was going to drop in on a lawyer to have a legal document or two drawn up and photocopied many times. I took numerous cookies with me.

After the lawyer visit, I arrived at the Mormon Temple and walked in. I was dressed in my finery: white sheet and sandals. More by good luck than by good management, I was to find that I had timed my visit perfectly. Not only was the President in residence, but so too were his two Counsellors. These three people constitute the First Presidency of the Mormon Church. The First Presidency is assisted by the Twelve Apostles. You read correctly, Twelve Apostles. They copied this one from the Baptists. These imposter Twelve Apostles would have us believe that they were the special witnesses of Jesus Christ. Yet none of the twelve were around in the days of Jesus.

As I walked inside the temple, I was challenged by a security guard who informed me there were no public tours of the inside of the temple and I would have to leave.

I said, 'But I'm a Profit from God.'

He said, 'OK then, another one of you. They're all meeting on the fourth floor. Is that a bag of cookies you have?'

I ascended to the fourth floor in a floating manner. The

security person witnessed me doing this and burst out laughing (children, never eat your cookies in one mouthful). After walking in and out of a few empty meeting rooms, I found them. I knocked on the door ever so politely and went straight in. To say the President, his two Councillors and the Twelve Apostles were somewhat shocked to see my sudden intrusion into their little meeting would be an understatement. When I told them that I was a Profit from God, they were more shocked.

The President said, 'You can't be as I have that title.'

I showed him my business card. To further prove the point, I floated above the heads of all the President's men, including the President. I gave them a ballet twirl on the point of my toes.

'A Swiss Guard showed me that one,' I said. 'But more importantly, my little, annoying, door-knocking, nummie-nuts type of people, what gives here? What sort of a racket have you boys been running since 1820? Would you like a cookie?'

One of the Apostles looked at me as I sat down and said I looked familiar. I asked him if he had answered any doors yesterday morning. 'All right, El Presidente,' I said as I eyeballed him. 'You are not a President and God has never heard of you, so you can't be a Prophet.'

He looked down at the table.

'Technically speaking,' I continued, 'the first Presidency consisted of George Washington and his advisers back in 1732. This was long before your old boss went off into the woods looking for mushrooms. So let's cut the crap; let's get to the crux of matter. What's going on?'

While El Presidente thought how best to answer me, I enquired as to which of the Twelve Apostles was Judas. Their blank stares indicated they didn't understand the joke, or perhaps the cookies were starting to kick in. Later, when I enquired about Donny and Marie and they laughed their heads off, I knew the cookies were kicking in.

One of the Apostles told me to compliment my wife on how good the cookies tasted.

I said, 'Jesus prepared them in Heaven.'

Hayden Bradford | *Travesty*   **279**

The Apostle said, 'What? Why was his wife out of the kitchen?'

And, they all started laughing again. As the Mormons got more and more stoned out of their minds they loosened up. The two Councillors ended up admitting to the President of the Mormon Church that they didn't know anything about being councillors. They were both howling with laughter as they told him they had fudged their résumés when they had applied for their jobs. The President said it was OK, as he didn't know anything about being a President. He just made shit up as he went along and besides, he never read résumés. The Twelve Apostles admitted to naming themselves after some rock formations in southern Victoria, Australia. In reality, all they ever wanted to do was to become a backing band for Donny and Marie.

We laughed and backslapped each other, they ate more cookies and eventually I told them I was also a part-time marriage celebrant in Heaven. I filled out all their names on a marriage certificate and gave them a copy. The marriage certificate stated in the fine print that as they had all partaken in the eating of the sacred cookies made in Heaven, and therefore, in the eyes of the Profit T, the Stand-In-God for the real God, they were now married to each other.

Instant silence.

'Well, bugger me,' said the President, 'how did this happen?'

One of counsellors said, 'It's going to be tough explaining this polygamy thing to the wife. There are some things she just doesn't get.'

'Fear not,' I said. 'I know how you can all get out of this awkward marriage.'

Two of the apostles, who I'd noticed were now holding hands, suggested that there was no great need to find a get-out clause in a hurry. I explained to my new-found cookie-eating friends that in the eyes of the Stand-In-God, all they had to do, to make their marriage contract null and void, was to sign a document called the *Let's Make the Marriage Null and Void* contract. The President, the two Counsellors, and ten of the Apostles immediately signed up. The other two hand-holding apostles abstained. They wanted to wait until the following morning.

I took them through the fine print of the *Let's Make the Marriage Null and Void* contract. It clearly stated they were to relinquish their Mormon beliefs for Baptist beliefs, and they were to be baptised in the traditional Baptist way.

'Well, bugger me,' said the President and chief manager of Mormons, 'I have to remember to read the fine print. But a contract is a contract and it has to be honoured.'

Not long after this momentous event, I sat opposite the chief Mormon as he signed the official orders instructing his followers to convert to the ways of the Baptists by participating in the Frolic. He also instructed the Mormon missionaries to return home so they could be taught God's true word before venturing out once again in the missionary position. El Presidente did express some concern about getting the word to everyone as some of the Mormon missionaries were located in hard to reach places of the world. I suggested he communicate with them by way of the Papal Bull and gave him Giorgio's phone number.

We heard much laughter coming from outside the temple so we went down to investigate. Fred had been hard at work. Outside the Mormon temple, people were frolicking together in swimming pools, under fountains, under taps and under hoses. Happiness was everywhere. We walked further up the street and in doing so, we passed a couple of fast food restaurants where people had painted graffiti on the windows. *Baptists rule, Long live the Profit T, God is a Baptist* and *The Government Sucks* screamed out at us. I wasn't sure who wrote the last one.

'My goodness,' commented the President, 'I've never seen people so happy.'

I replied, 'That's because these people know they don't have to go and knock on other people's doors anymore. We have a strict *No Knocking* on people's door policy in the Baptists.'

The President, his two Councillors and the Twelve Apostles commenced to remove their clothes and began to head in the direction of the Great Salt Lake to get some serious frolicking underway. The two handholding apostles couldn't wait. I found Fred and called God. I informed the Big Kahuna that he needed to send the Big White Dove from above to pick up a couple of the Punting Buddies of Oh Ye *Faithful in Melbourne*. The return flight would be back to the Monastery of Winning for Fred and me. We needed time for the Papal Bulls to deliver all their messages and for the missionaries' work to kick in. As we waited for the flight, I thought, why not? We found a swimming pool nearby, stripped off our gear and joined in doing the Frolic.

There really are times in your life when you feel as if the good old good luck fairy has kissed you on the bum. As Fred and I stood in a vacant field, completely refreshed after our late afternoon Frolic and waiting for On the Wings of a Snow White Dove to land, I felt this was one such time. The *Monastery of Winning* was up and running.

The Punting Buddies of Oh Ye Faithful were well established and working well. The congregation of the monastery, my merry band of the *Flock of Flockers*, continued to increase their numbers with gathering speed. The *Bapfreeholics* were converted and as yet, no one had been hurt by the Papal Bulls spreading the true word of God. The Mormons would soon be converting everyone they could find.

The Big White Dove from above came into sight. I noticed it was flying lopsided. Perhaps one wing was more tired than the other wing. The flight from Heaven to Melbourne, then on to Salt Lake City, was one of those long haul jobs. I had already decided that as the late afternoon was turning into early evening, we would stay in Salt Lake City overnight and fly out the following morning. The Big White Dove would get a rest.

The Big White Dove landed and as Charlie and Paige disembarked, I commented to Fred, 'Now that explains why the dove was flying lopsided, Charlie been eating far too much again.'

Paige, Fred, Charlie and I spent the evening partying and frolicking with a bunch of ex-Mormons on the banks of the Great Salt Lake. The following morning Fred and I departed for the greener pastures of the *Monastery of Winning*. Paige and Charlie were left in charge of teaching the new syllabus of gambling.

Let Us Pray

....

Hey God, yo God, I say
I've done my bit
50,000 ex-Mormons will soon be running amuck
Donny and Marie who sing like shit
Might write a song
Preaching your word
To tell the world
Gambling's good for your godly soul
Amen

The Prophecies of Chapter Twenty-three

→ What is it with the Christian religion and bears and woods?
→ Bears crap in the woods, be careful.
→ Bears live in the woods, be careful.
→ When in the woods, be very careful of stepping on a bear whilst it's having a crap.
→ Come to think of it, why go into the woods in the first place?
→ In some countries, it may be against the law to mess with legal documents. Check with your legal adviser first.
→ The same applies to the making, distribution and consumption of marijuana cookies.

24

It was great to be back in the Monastery of Winning. Judging by the number of people in the monastery at any one given time drinking, gambling and cursing, Minister Gordy and the Punting Buddies of Oh Ye Faithful had been working hard. Charlie's restaurant was being run exceptionally well by some of the congregation whilst Charlie was doing his missionary work.

A few days after our return to the Monastery of Winning, I heard on the television a new rock band had been discovered in Salt Lake City. My ears pricked up as the TV presenter said that the name of the band was the Twelve Apostles. Get out of here I thought. Donny and Marie were going to front the band. The band had written a new song and dedicated it to all the Happy Clappers in the world. Then, there they were, on stage, about to do their song, *The Sounds of Real Silence*. And, that's exactly what it was. They stood on the stage for four minutes, played no music and said nothing. Then they walked off. The whole production was very well choreographed, I thought. Exactly what Happy Clappers should do.

I was to spend another couple of months with my budding Baptists. I assisted where I could, although I did slowly start to withdraw from such activities as I knew soon I would be heading back to Heaven. The Earth people had been shown the light and given the very tools they needed via God's Bible, his true word, to achieve their own personal Holy Grail and thereby gamble their way out of the GFC. Enough people had been trained in the ways of the Baptists and in the art of gambling to train all the other religions. Whilst all this was happening, the Gambling in Schools program had commenced. It turned out to be a huge success.

Initially it was newsworthy as more and more people were dropping their pants, bending over and pointing their bare arses at their bosses, saying, 'Look in the mirror, I quit. I've found my Holy Grail and now I'm filthy rich.' But, after a month or so, it wasn't newsworthy. It was happening all the time.

I watched the financial markets on Earth with great interest. When I witnessed the bear market start turning into a bull market I knew that it was now safe to go back into the woods as the Papal Bulls had done their job and run over all the bears. I also knew my work on Earth was drawing to a close. One morning I watched a young kid come into the monastery, go to one of the many computers and place his bets online for the day's racing. I asked him how old he was.

He replied, 'How old do I look?'

I answered, 'You look seven.'

He smiled, 'Wanna bet?'

The big doom and gloom cloud that had hung over the Earth like a manure fog was gradually disappearing. I could see the beginnings of a new world, one that would be dominated by the Chosen Ones, the Baptists, the preferred religion of God, the only religion accepted in Heaven.

My leaving was to happen soon after an evening when all of the *Punting Buddies of Oh Ye Faithful* were in the *Monastery of Winning* together. It wasn't often we were together these days. Not with all the tasking and teaching going on around the world. It was fun to have the old gang back together again. I spent some time with them doing a few miracles. I showed Gordy how to turn water into wine. We laughed, we drank and we did the Frolic in the pool. I think when I performed my last miracle for them they knew I was heading back to Heaven. I pulled a free pizza voucher out my arse and gave it to Charlie.

That night I called Jacquetta and told her I was coming home. I then called the Big Fella and let him know as well. A few days later, I stood in front of the Big White Dove to say my farewells and it began to rain. For the last time, we tore off our clothes and did the Frolic together. A short time later, I left planet Earth and commenced to fly back to Heaven, but not before we'd made a small diversion. We went looking for Joshua. When we found him, we landed and I suggested he give up his quest.

'You're not going to find the walls of Jericho. Jump aboard and let's go home.'

I think he was glad we had stopped.

I called God and asked him to do me a small favour. As we approached Heaven, a number of Guardian Angels escorted us. We arrived on the landing strip to much noise and celebration. The Heavenites knew what had been achieved. Even the wise old souls from the Board of Approvals for Heavenly Spiritual Society were present to greet me. They were very excited as they were expecting more dead Baptists at any moment.

God picked me up, put me on his shoulders and carried me around. He was very happy to have saved his little accidental creation called Earth, though he'd had some help from Earth people. God was also visualising his Top Dog award.

Jesus was happy for a couple of reasons. He was messing around eating some of his cookies and seeing that Earth had been saved, he knew his old man wouldn't be putting the heavies on him about a Second Coming. Mary, Joseph and his donkey were there to greet me as well. After God had put me back down, we chatted for a while. I thought it was the polite thing to do as so many Heavenites had come out to greet me. One of them actually suggested I should write a book about my adventure on Earth. When Jacquetta thought I was having too much fun, she suggested we leave. I was somewhat hesitant until she whispered a few things into my ear.

As we were leaving, God yelled out, 'Don't forget the night racing that's on tonight. I've got a couple of good things going, if you're interested.'

'No, he's not,' yelled back Jacquetta.

We floated into our cloud and I had to admit, it was great to be back home. I sat on the couch and let Jacquetta run her fingers through my hair. She produced a bottle of anointing oil and was somewhat confused. It had arrived this morning from her dad.

'There wasn't a note with it either,' she said. 'What's it for?'

I answered casually, 'It's my re-entry to Heaven anointing oil. Apparently it's meant to help me readjust to Heaven after being away for so long.'

She replied, 'I've never heard of that before. We'd better do it straight away.'

Yes, I do so love it when a plan comes together.

Let Us Pray

....

Dear Heavenly Father
Not now man
I just got home
Beneath the sheets I do sneak
You can work out the rest, can't you
Bother me in a week
Amen

Why I Wrote 'Travesty'

Time for some honest words. Words I feel are necessary. Words which are true and serious.

I wrote this story because my head needed to laugh. Man oh man, did it need to laugh. You see, the *strangest* thing happened to me. The wiring and circuits carrying the pink – cheeked chemicals of happiness inside my head stopped flowing, as the neurons in my brain ceased communicating with my neurotransmitters. This caused parts of my brain to become overactive or under responsive. All of this occurred rather suddenly and dramatically. As I said, the strangest thing.

The year which sometimes sneaks into my dreams and haunts me is 2009. It was some year, especially for me. I'd had the blues before; who hasn't? They were no biggie. They would come and go, but this time they didn't go. This time they stayed and bubbled in my blood, and scorched parts of my brain, messing with it in ways I can't explain.

Later I would learn there was a name for what was happening to me. I had a full-blown disease called *depression*, major depression I was told. She's a nasty piece of work. Whoever she touches ends up in a 'world of hurt'. I have a name for my depression. I call her the *fuck-up fairy*. When she visits, I'm all fucked up for a while. On such visits, the normality of the ebb and flow of my life ceases.

But the good news is, I was told, there are medicines to repair my burnt-out brain. Medicines to make my wiring and circuits good again. These medicines would stop the depression's black march forward; stop it dead in it tracks, give it the 'old heave-ho, out you go.' Then my brain would be happy and healthy and party as if there's no tomorrow. Lucky me, lucky me indeed.

My medical team insisted back in 2009, and still insist today, that I exercise my brain as much as possible. *Write* they told me, write, and do things to tax your brain cells. It's good therapy for depression. Take the medicines, work the brain, they said, and we'll kick this depression thing right off the planet. I dealt with specialist after specialist, all credible and highly regarded in their chosen field of medical expertise in the science of the brain. We changed medication, changed dosages, and still my brain remained confused, and messed up. My brain has been CAT scanned, MRI scanned, and there are so many drugs running through it, I should be declared illegal.

Today, it is the month of May of 2014, some five years later, as I pen these last words to this story. I sit in the pleasant gardens of a private hospital in Melbourne, Australia. Melbourne is heading into its winter period, as I'm going into a course of Electroconvulsive Therapy (ECT). This is a medical procedure done under general anaesthetic. The brain is then stimulated by a series of electrical pulses which cause it to have seizures, hopefully, to reactivate the bits that don't work anymore.

You see, the medications that were meant to repair my brain *haven't* worked properly. The *fuck-up fairy* still comes and visits me, and my *depression* still bubbles in my blood. I've baffled the medical experts in the workings of the brain. I'm now classed as *treatment resistant.*

As I sit, enjoying the sun, a cat wanders over and jumps on my lap. It's the hospital cat. Some hospitals have them hanging around in the garden areas to give its patients something to hold, to pat, to love. The cat doesn't know me from a bar of soap, yet it trusts me. It doesn't judge me. All the cat wants is some of my time, a scratch, a lap to sit on for a while, a friend. Such a pity the human race is not like this cat. Sadly, my illness, my depression, has cost me friends, family too. People who I once thought were good and wholesome, people who I once entertained in our house, decided that associating with people like me, people who have *depression* is not the *done* thing. In their eyes I'm not whole anymore; I have a mental illness. These people have judged me on the *stigma* my mental illness unfortunately attracts. Another reason my head needed to laugh.

So there you have it: the reasons I wrote this story.

Importantly, I did *not* write this story to belittle, insult, or to cast doubt on any religion or any person's religious beliefs or opinions. I fully support a person's right to practise religion, providing such practice does not negatively affect or harm other people. But for me, for many reasons – I choose *not* to believe. I've seen Hell, and there is *no* Devil. I've seen Heaven, and there is *no* God.

Finally, I hope you get a laugh or two from my book. I hope you find it a fun story. I wrote for the fun of writing and the therapeutic value to be gained from messing with words. My head needs it.

If you have one, may your God go with you!

Hayden Bradford
May 2014